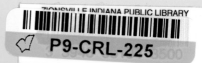

SUMMERS AT BLUE LAKE

Summers

AT

Blue Lake

A Novel by

Jill Althouse-Wood

ALGONQUIN BOOKS OF CHAPEL HILL   2007

Published by
ALGONQUIN BOOKS OF CHAPEL HILL
Post Office Box 2225
Chapel Hill, North Carolina 27515-2225

a division of
Workman Publishing
225 Varick Street
New York, New York 10014

Printed in the United States of America.
Published simultaneously in Canada by Thomas Allen & Son Limited.
Design by Anne Winslow.

This is a work of fiction. While, as in all fiction, the literary perceptions and insights are based on experience, all names, characters, places, and incidents either are products of the author's imagination or are used fictitiously.

Library of Congress Cataloging-in-Publication Data
Althouse-Wood, Jill, 1969 –
    Summers at Blue Lake / Jill Althouse-Wood.
        p. cm.
    ISBN-13: 978-1-56512-496-7
    1. Grandmothers — Fiction.   2. Inheritance and succession — Fiction.
    3. Diaries — Fiction.   4. Family secrets — Fiction.   I. Title.
    PS3601.L828S86 2007
    813'.6 — dc22   2006031678

10 9 8 7 6 5 4 3 2 1
First Edition

For Gundy and Schultz, who gifted me
with *"Once upon a time . . ."*

Acknowledgments

THIS NOVEL HAS BEEN a long journey for me, and many have shared in my path. It is my deepest privilege to thank them. I'd like to start in the beginning by thanking my parents, Marty and Dave Althouse, who gave me the gift of faith. No writer can begin a novel or endure the process without it. I'd also like to acknowledge my extended family—including my siblings (the J-crew), their families, and my in-laws. Special merit to Tammy Wood, who had no choice but to listen to major plot points on our long training runs. As for my friends, I'll be eternally grateful to my inner circle: the Paisleys (you know who you are), the Peterys, and the Steeds. These are the people who helped me lift my glass not only in the times of celebration, but in the murkier hours of rejection as well. Thanks to Monty Smith and Suzy Arrington for reading the earliest manuscripts and checking my college remembrances of metalsmithing against the actual practice. Angela Maloney was my connection in the Richmond area, and I thank her for her insights and help. I'd be remiss if I didn't mention Sue Engleman, who nurtured my children while I worked toward my goals.

I'd also like to pay homage to my mentors, including some exceptional teachers and female role models, without whom my education would not be complete: Joanne Shaak, Deanne Buffington, Sally Watkins, Faith Lange, Vera Kaminski, and Anne Graham. Continuing on into the gurus of the publishing process, I thank my agent Denise Marcil. She brought this book to fruition, with unwavering belief, through its many incarnations; few agents would have invested as much as she did to see a story brought to light. To my editor Chuck Adams and the staff at Algonquin, I offer gratitude for the chance they took on a new voice and for leading me through the art and science of bookmaking. Writer Sharon Naylor is both friend and mentor. She read my first short story and encouraged me in writing and in life on a daily basis.

Finally, I want to honor the people who share my life. No novelist lives for fiction alone. My family is my real (and best) story. My husband, Mark, a self-proclaimed geek, kept me in computer heaven. But it is his love, support, and tolerance that really powered me through this process. Jonah and Maren, my children, are my pride and inspiration. They are the reason I strive. It took being their mother to start me on my path to writing. Thank you, all.

SUMMERS AT BLUE LAKE

PART ONE

God of Mermaids

· 1 ·

MY GRANDMOTHERS WERE LESBIANS, a truth they neither exposed nor concealed. Every Sunday they took their place in the third pew, left of the aisle, at Lakeside Lutheran. Their white-gloved daughter sat between them, drawing Jesus in the margins of the bulletin while they nodded and fanned away their sins or their guilt (or whatever it was they came to church to exorcise). Their fellow parishioners embraced them in the cool shadow of the Sunday sermon, even loved them as one should love sisters in Christ, but not without question. During the steady marches that Lutherans often mistook for hymns, the board members took turns policing the third pew—if only to convince themselves that my grandmothers' bond was solely economic. And they were momentarily convinced that it was. *The daughter is an angel.* Or, *They are members of the social committee.* But at the service's end, my grandmas would lean into their final *amens* with more tilt toward each other than to the altar. Then, even their friends accepted the verdict: these women were the daughters of Eve.

The congregants weren't proud of their judgments. Quite the opposite. They were as uncomfortable with them as they were with the stiff collars and shoes that pinched their flesh on the Sabbath. For my mother and her mothers, Sunday was a day of grace. People folded under the influence of the Gospel and chicken dinners until they were drunk on their own goodness.

Monday would come, and with it, a spiritual hangover. Once again, my grandmothers were acknowledged with a whisper, a nudge in the hardware store, a smile that lasted a second too long. There were other things, too—unspeakable other things that caused my mother to turn away from me when I asked her about her childhood. She described the happy times to the window or the wall or her magazine instead of to my upturned face.

Maybe she was right to not tell me, her only daughter. She had moved away from her childhood, geographically and emotionally. She and my dad had married—a move that had taken her away from the dimpled hills of Pennsylvania to a similar topography in Virginia. They bought a house in a subdivision with driveways notching the sidewalk at regular intervals, and mailboxes (with one surname only!) flagging each notch. I completed their lives two years later. We had a perfect little family, tainted only by my mother's inability to deliver any in a string of promised, but premature, brothers.

"You are blessing enough," my parents told me so often that it couldn't be true.

I was a child of the 1970s. My mother pulled my hair back into daisy barrettes for most of the decade, and I never lacked for anthems—mostly disco music at the roller rink. Attitudes had changed in the twenty-five years since Mom was a girl, at least on the outside. Feminism, along with civil rights, had strangled the press with its message of tolerance, but inside the bi-levels of Jefferson Heights, the slogans softened to a tap on the shoulder rather than a grip.

In our household, my father listened to my mother with more respect than most husbands, but he voted a straight Republican ticket, prayed the Pope's prayers, and watched sports while Mom cleaned the dinner dishes. Under this reign, the three of us watched the TV news of gay activity in San Francisco as if it, too, was an example of liberal extremism rather than a limb of our family tree.

The word was not forbidden in our house. I had heard it often and had practiced saying the beautiful syllables in my mirror. "Lez-bee-an." It sounded exotic like *sapphire* or *emerald,* only more purple like *amethyst,* jewels that were secret and dark and lovely in velvet boxes.

"Lezzz-be-ann." There was power in the *z* sound as it chiseled through my mouth. With only one child in the house, my parents seemed to forget the careful zones of adult conversation. My father squinted as he said the word in not so hushed tones to my mother. But the *z*'s didn't change his expression. He could order extra *cheese* or ask if Mom had used his *razor* without even a slight crinkle on his face. *Lesbian.* Though the resonance hypnotized me, and the power entranced me, the meaning evaded me.

For my fourth-grade family heritage report, I boasted that I was Scotch-Irish on my father's side, and on my mother's side we were Lesbian. I did not understand when Mrs. Faust sent me to the nurse's office to wait for my mother after school. Nurse Witmer and my mother tried to explain the meaning of what I had said by using several visual aids. After pamphlets of young girls with new breasts and one long filmstrip about special kisses and touches, I said, "I already know about sex. What does that have to do with us being Scotch-Irish?"

My mother nodded to Nurse Witmer, and together, they fumbled over blunt phrases they had hoped wouldn't be necessary. With those judicious definitions, my education was complete. Visits to my grandmothers became charged with my new knowledge, as if I had just been given the secret ingredient in the family recipe for barbecue sauce. I never had to entertain the baggage of Mom's childhood; I could see my grandmothers with the wonder they were due. When I was with them, I felt cemented into my heritage in a way that surpassed the fourth-grade curriculum.

My grandmothers also taught me lesser lessons along the way. In Nonna's kitchen, I learned how to make baklava. The oven taxed the already steep price of the summer heat, but we willingly paid the toll. Nonna mixed stories, as well as nuts, into her gooey filling. Between tastes, I stirred the honeyed syrup and listened to her history, which was, after all, my history, too.

"I received several wedding proposals after serving this to the sailors in Greece," she boasted.

Nonna's blue eyes twinkled in their Scandinavian naughtiness. She professed a Greek ancestry as well as a kaleidoscope past. Although I had my doubts about the Greek part, I knew that her true-life story had to include a dalliance with least one man in uniform. I pulled apart pieces of phyllo with my sticky fingers. Later, as we cut the pastries into their diamond shapes, I imagined brooding men with cups of dark, sweet coffee toasting a young Nonna.

"Anja, please have my babies."

"No, Anja, marry *me*."

And Nonna would turn and smile with the inky lips of a black-and-white film star. The men thought she was smiling at them, but she was looking beyond the sailors for the mermaids.

Grandma Lena was one such mermaid. She was a champion swimmer. During the hot afternoons of the 1970s gas crisis, she would shuffle me off to the lake near their house. The orange plastic straps of my flip-flops carved white ridges into my sunburned feet. For the half mile we walked, my attention was drawn downward on my blistering toes, but as soon as the water cut through my pain, I would look up to see Grandma Lena diving into Blue Lake.

She was a mer-goddess in her white swimmer's cap and skirted suit. Grandma Lena was not a woman of fashion. Her bathing suit had molded bra cups that had a tendency to indent. But she was a mer-goddess all the same. Though her strokes impressed me with their strength, it was her ability to recline on the water that amazed me. Grandma Lena could read a newspaper while doing a back float. She could even nap soundly while I swam in concentric circles around her sleeping, floating form. When she awoke, she would show me how to do a back flip and the breast-stroke, keeping at it until the lake glittered with the diamond possibility of a sunset.

And so Nonna the Greek and Grandma Lena (said in all one breath—like *ballerina*) became the mythos of my quiet child-hood. They transported me away from the horn-rimmed glasses of my father and the *Redbook* of my mother. When summer released me from my school desk, I turned to my grandmothers' house on Mulberry Street for the enigma that was also their magic.

· 2 ·

Summer 2000

PENNSYLVANIA HAS ARGUABLY the worst roads in the United States, and while this opinion is reinforced by surveys put out by Triple A and the Teamsters union, you won't hear any complaints from me. My two-year-old Toyota, a car that had not previously graced the state, arrived in Nonna's driveway after a journey of exactly ten hours (four of them in the Keystone State), delivering us by some autopilot refinement I never knew it had. Even before the engine stopped, Sam catapulted from the backseat to relieve himself on a once carefully pruned hedge. My first instinct was to scold him, but he had suppressed his urgent business for the entire last hour of the long trip. I made a cursory effort to avert my eyes to give him privacy, but I couldn't help myself. In the midst of the overgrown vines, flowering their magenta triumph, and roses, which refused to be outdone, my son looked like the national statue of Belgium: Manneken-Pis. Little boy pissing.

The trip itself had been long, made even longer by the needs of a young boy and a dog. How could I simultaneously accommodate bathroom breaks for both? Each needed my attention, and neither could be left alone. Luckily, some compassionate dog-loving strangers had helped me with my dilemma. They watched a tethered Jules while I shepherded Sam into the less-than-sanitary ladies' room at the turnpike rest stop. *Don't touch anything.* I had never before traveled alone with my son, much less with the dog, but this trip would not be the last. With no choice but a successful outcome, I flexed my mothering muscle in training for future strain. As with most exertion, this first foray tired me: my nerves were shot, and my insides writhed with the memory of something I had supersized (in the faulty expectation of sharing my food with Sam).

Jules barked from his crate in the rear, and I freed him to follow Sam's lead. The boy with the tawny hair and his golden retriever danced celebrations around their wet spots on the lawn. They circled the mailbox and conjured hopscotch on the flagstone path that led to the front porch.

"Come on, Mom," Sam called, but now I was the statue, frozen by the seventeen Junes that had come and gone since I had last spent the summer here. As I stood, the weeds curled around my exposed toes, and ladybugs ascended my legs. I half expected a bird to perch on the hand that I was using to shield my eyes from the sun.

The house looked the same and yet different, which was odd. I had stopped by the place a few weeks ago on the day of the funeral, but I hadn't gone inside. That memory was blurry now, shadowed with people and emotion. I hadn't had the time then to really consider this house, its contents, and the possibility I might actually spend another summer here. *What did I expect to see now?* Great sandstone slabs, quarried from the family farm, framed too-white windowsills. The steep roof, also, was shocking in its brightness. It was metal, silvered with paint, not patina. Last summer a troop of college painters had refreshed the exterior of the house and, no doubt, refreshed their parched throats with glasses of Nonna's rum-laced lemonades, which she served on the wide front porch. Nonna had maintained her home and Lena's gardens until the end. In her last years, she seemed to pick up speed and do the work of two. That was the gift and the curse of good health followed by a sudden brain embolism: at eighty-three, Anja Graybill had died young.

Here I stood, like a stone sentry, the last relative of a great woman. My mother, Nonna's daughter, had preceded her in death. Mom's passing in January had been a relief ten years in coming. It was the culmination of mounting grief I experienced since she found the first lump in her breast ten years ago. Hers was a singular death made up of smaller losses along the way: one breast, then the other, then the glands, the hair, the skin, the bones. Dad and I wondered that we had anything but Mom's heart to bury. I questioned, at the time, if Nonna's body would be able to withstand the grief for her only child. She had been strong at Mom's funeral, but I suspect that most of that show of strength was for me. Who was left now?

Grandma Lena had kin: one estranged sister and one semi-estranged nephew. At Lena's funeral ten years ago, his only representation had been a wreath of roses and a condolence card signed by Travis and Liz. Though I had known Travis in childhood, his marriage or pairing (one can't assume) had been news to me. The gesture of roses seemed so impersonal at the time of his aunt's death that I felt it was unlikely Travis would materialize when Nonna died. When I couldn't find a listing for him on the Internet, I shrugged away any attempts to inform him of Nonna's passing. This legacy was mine alone.

So accompanied by Sam and the dog, I had embarked on this journey with the intent of cleaning out the house on Mulberry Street. Dad had offered to come with me, but I told him no—he was sweet to offer. After the ten-hour drive, we had arrived at the past home of all my summer longings. And now that I was here, I had to ask myself, what was it? My escape? My duty? My birthright? My future?

I ached to run to the porch and fling open the door. But I knew that behind the front door was a combination black hole/funhouse that might suck me into a dimension where time laughed. Behind that door, ponytail holders and wedding rings, vinyl records and CDs would all collide. *I am Bobbi Ellington, was Barbara Jean Foley, am BJ and Mom, was Honey and Darling and back again.*

I had every right to be fearful; however, the haunting came not in facing who I was, but who I would become. Never again would I cull the identities that had carried me this far in life. Even in my muddled state of mind, I understood. The names of the past began to pulse in me like an earache. I wanted the comfort of this old, ancestral house, and I wanted the ghosts to nurse me.

I drew on my recollections and churned them into sensory expectations. This house beckoned me, and I knew what I would find. First, I would breathe in the scent of Cachet lotion and English Lavender soap. Then the lost smells of chopped olives and lemon chicken would accost me. They wouldn't really be there—except in memory: Nonna stopped cooking elaborate meals after Grandma Lena had died, preferring instead to alternate dining out with the early-bird crowd and eating her doggie-bag leftovers. But I would swear I could smell her cooking, and my stomach would growl in anticipation of a fine meal. The house would still possess the hints of long-ago cigarette smoke. The soft gray scent would be there, holding tightly to the fabric of the heavy drapes, the memories of fabulous parties clustered deep in the folds.

I longed to touch those drapes and the old, bottom-thick glass of the windows. I wanted to collapse into the hard springs of the davenport and eat cold SpaghettiOs with an orange plastic spoon. I wanted to glide on the porch swing while skimming a used paperback. I wanted to rediscover the oils that my great-grandfather painted during the cubist movement in Paris. (A contemporary of Braque, Sid Stevens had yet to come into vogue with anybody but me, his great-granddaughter. Even Nonna had wanted to take down those "horrid, boxy landscapes.")

And I hoped that fulfilling these expectations would be enough for me. I tried not to think about the things I would never again have inside that house. The evening phone calls back to my mother in Virginia. Nonna's lamb pie. Grandma Lena's fingers braiding my hair. A body built for a bikini top and cutoffs. And my life the way it was before Bryce said, "I'm not sure if I ever really loved you."

The past mattered so little now, or too much; I didn't know which. With the armor of two wash baskets filled with clean bedding and towels, I followed Sam to the front porch. The floor-boards creaked an eerie welcome. Putting the baskets down, I fumbled in my pocket for the key that had been digging into my thigh since the moment we left home in Michigan. I found it, and the skeleton key slid over my sweaty fingertips into the keyhole. It turned effortlessly.

Sam looked inside and said, "It's not so bad."

"It's not so bad," I echoed, without conviction.

"Welcome back," the ghosts greeted.

And Jules, self-appointed guardian of the aggrieved, barked in defense of all of us.

· 3 ·

Summer 1983

THE SPATULA CAME DOWN hard on my wrist after I took the sticky fingers out of my mouth.

"Don't let anyone see you," Nonna said in something between a hiss and a whisper. "This cake is for hundreds of people, and here you are licking the icing. I'll have the board of health after me."

"Right," I said. Nonna never could maintain her anger around me. She couldn't do it when I was little, and she couldn't do it now that I was almost fourteen.

"A little bit of my spit is not going to wreck Sara and Tom's wedding, Nonna. I'll bet you five dollars, they'll cancel that fiasco before noon."

"Well, they'd better not. They haven't paid me for this cake yet."

"Well, I'm not even sure Tom is finished paying for his divorce yet, not to mention the child support he owes," I muttered.

Nonna clicked her tongue at me in disapproval. "You have been listening to Joyce again. You must take what that woman says with a grain of salt."

Nonna stepped back to look at her creation. The seven layers were spread out over her kitchen bar. She squinted, and then ever so lightly smoothed an edge with her spatula. I wanted to tell her she shouldn't use the spatula she had just used to smack me, but I became mesmerized by what we had created. The cake was beautiful. I wanted to tell her so, but I was brooding.

My mother was finishing her master's thesis, and Dad was busy working; consequently I had to spend the entire summer, instead of the usual two weeks, with my grandmas. Ordinarily it would not have been such a terrible sentence, but my summer absence from home meant I had to surrender my eighth-grade boyfriend, Jimmy, to the pouncing Sue Lipkowski. "Lips," as all the kids called her, was actually better known for a physical feature somewhat south of the face. She had been the earliest bloomer in our class and had not been shy about her development. As was her modus operandi, Sue clamored after the older boys. How lucky was I that she broke her code this summer? So I did what was natural and blamed Nonna for my predicament.

Though they tried, my grandmothers could not seem to transform my pout. They offered everything from taking me to see the movie *Flashdance* to heavy bribery (a new bike), and although I really didn't care that much about Jimmy Fuhrman, I began to see sullenness as an art form.

After their first round of enticements seemed to have failed, Grandma Lena suggested that we call Travis, the son of her much younger half sister. He was currently doing some work around the yard, but what Grandma Lena had in mind was a bit more social.

"It'll be nice to have your cousin around."

"Travis is not really my cousin," I objected. Lena was not related by blood; Nonna was my biological grandmother.

Lena looked taken aback. "Well, he's family at any rate," she said quietly.

I tried to bargain with Nonna when we were alone with the cake. I could already picture a coerced outing. Travis would be jabbering about ham radio frequencies while we made our way to a museum show of insects native to the Susquehanna River Valley.

"We have nothing in common, Nonna. Travis is so dense," I argued.

"Barbara Jean, that's enough name-calling. Travis McKenzie isn't dense. He's a sensitive, quiet boy. If you took some time to get to know him, I think you would be surprised."

"I know enough about him already," I said. And it was true.

I had grown up with Travis McKenzie my whole life. If he were like most big brothers or cousins, he would have teased me mercilessly and pulled pranks, but that was not him. He always had his nose in some thick book or was active in some equally autonomous behavior. Last summer during my visit, he spent the whole time sitting on Nonna's porch making his own fishing lures. At first I tried to draw him into conversation or an occasional game of tag, but to no avail. He looked at me as if I was more of a pest than the critters he was simulating in his art of making bait. I guess I didn't blame him. I mean, he lived alone with his mother, Aunt Margot, who, though far from dull, could be counted on to do only so much. Even with that allowance, there was no denying it: Travis McKenzie was about as much fun to be around as a detention monitor.

However, I knew it was senseless to object to Nonna and Grandma Lena's attempts to bolster camaraderie between us. The fight wasn't even fair—two grandmas against one me. My only hope was that Travis would say no to an invitation to spend time with his spinster aunt, her same-sex lover, and their granddaughter. Travis was fifteen. Even he couldn't be stupid enough to walk into that trap.

Nonna was just adding the last icing rose to the top of the cake when we heard someone yell "Jesus Christ almighty!" from the powder room off to the left of the kitchen.

"Either Janelle is having trouble with her wedding dress in there, or we've just had a divine visitation," Nonna said without a flinch.

During the week, my grandmothers' house was a bohemian carnival—hard to ignore even if one was pouting. Monday through Thursday, Nonna and Grandma Lena lived a carefree existence that included weekly pinochle parties, barbecues on the back patio, and poetry readings on the porch. Sometimes, brides would stop by during the week to be photographed for the newspaper or to pick out a design for the wedding cake. Most times, they ended up joining the party, not leaving until their heads overflowed with stanzas of sonnets that would slur if they tried to give them a voice. Nonna's rum drinks saw to that.

Janelle Swanson had not had any rum drinks—being that it was only nine o'clock in the morning—but she had had two Greek coffees. Grandma Lena came running in from the rose garden where she was preparing for a photo shoot under the arbor.

"What's going on?" she asked.

I just shrugged and sneaked another fingerful of icing.

Grandma Lena knocked on the door.

"Are you okay?"

Janelle emerged from the powder room with a twisted expression on her face.

"I just can't get it to close. I don't know what happened. It fit fine at my last fitting."

Janelle was wearing a replica of Princess Diana's wedding dress, for what was intended to be a replica of the entire royal wedding, down to the horse drawn carriage and tiara. She even planned for the event to coincide with Charles and Diana's second wedding anniversary. I wanted to gag. It was safe to say that while most girls my age fantasized about the princely event, I had the tendency to see weddings through my grandmothers' eyes—as nothing but work, a royal pain in the ass.

Grandma Lena swung Janelle around, and I could see the gaping expanse of her skin framed by each side of the buckling zipper. There was no way she would get that zipper closed. Grandma Lena wouldn't even be able to bridge the gap with some of the huge double clips she usually put into service for emergencies such as this.

"Janelle, honey, did you just start oral contraceptives?"

Janelle slumped over.

"The Pill, hon, did you start taking the Pill?"

By the way her back was quaking, I could tell that Janelle was sobbing.

"Yes," came the tiny voice, "about four months ago. I was going to wait until right before the wedding, but we couldn't wait, if you know what I mean."

"Well," Grandma Lena said with a frown, "you're not the first bride to put on a little weight with the Pill. Let's see what we can do."

By "we," she meant me. Grandma Lena took me off cake duty to become the photographer's apprentice. Lena positioned me in a crouching pose behind Janelle's full skirt. I then had to reach my arms up and hold her dress together so it wouldn't flap forward for the pictures.

Within minutes, my arms started to ache.

"Remind me never to go on the birth control pill," I said after the tenth click of the camera and the fourth change of position.

"Oh yeah?" Grandma Lena said. "What are you going to do?"

"The rhythm method," I said in repetition of my Catholic upbringing.

"Oh, Lord," Grandma Lena said with a laugh. "Well, be prepared to wear a maternity wedding dress."

"I'm not going to have sex before I get married," I said, and changed position again to ease the shooting pain in my left arm. As I did so, I could feel Janelle's giggle.

"Sure, laugh at me for having values, but I'm the one holding Princess Diana's dress closed so nobody gets a peep at the royal bum." I was being insensitive, but I didn't care.

Grandma Lena's voice came from around the great folds of cloth. "I apologize for her, Janelle. Our Barbara Jean is experiencing her first heartache. You'll have to forgive her."

I didn't want Her Highness to forgive me. I just wanted everybody to leave me out of it.

"Okay, Barbara Jean, you can rest a minute, I need to reload my film. How about we move over to the Peace Roses beside the clematis."

I helped Janelle with her train, and we picked up and moved about ten feet to the right.

"So did he dump you or did you dump him?" Janelle asked. I hated having small talk with the brides. As a group, they were pretty egocentric. *My big day. My dress. My bridesmaids. My shower. My fiancé.* But now I almost wished Janelle would talk about herself.

"What do you think?" I fanned Janelle's train out behind her the way Grandma Lena had taught me.

The winding sound had stopped, and Grandma Lena opened the back of her camera.

"He broke it off with you?" Janelle offered sympathetically. I had been talking about her dress, but somehow she thought we were still on the subject of my pitiful love life.

I played along. "Yes, and if you must know, it was because I'm not as promiscuous as some girls," I said. It wasn't true, but I emphasized the sins that had landed me this undignified assignment in the first place.

"Barbara Jean, that is enough." I heard Grandma Lena's sharp voice. "Get back into position."

"I'm tired, Grandma Lena."

She just looked at me and held her camera in ready position.

"You already took plenty of full-length pictures. Do some head shots now," I said and marched off to help Nonna clean the kitchen before the big card party.

PERHAPS THE PIVOTAL CHARACTER to my summer transformation, from sulking to semicontent, was Vera Wagner. That summer, Vera fled Pennsylvania for Montana, on a mission to save her newborn grandson from that "dimwitted, debutante hybrid" that had married her son the year before. Grandma Lena had appointed me to replace Vera as her pinochle partner at the weekly get-togethers.

"I never know what to bid," I objected.

"Nonsense. You could play pinochle before you could read. Besides, Vera and I always had a system."

Which meant they cheated. All the women did, but as long as we didn't call it cheating and never actually said the words aces or spades, nobody complained. Before Vera's eyesight declined, the signals were gestures. Last summer, Grandma Lena had switched her indications to a few throaty chirps.

As it happened, my eyesight was very good. So good, that I didn't need Grandma Lena's system; I had one of my own. When Mrs. Bomberger had four red aces and one black one, five little A's danced around on her bifocals. Seeing them, I passed emphatically, then cleared my throat so Grandma Lena would do the same.

Nonna suspected my device. When we played against her and her partner, Gladys Metz, they would put away their reading glasses and reach for the pack of cards with the jumbo numbers. We hardly ever beat Nonna and Gladys, which inspired some rather irksome qualities in Grandma Lena.

The ladies initiated me into the club the very first Tuesday of my summer vacation, after the fiasco in the garden with Janelle

Swanson. It wasn't much in the way of ceremonies. Nonna re-introduced me to women I had known since I was born, and they embraced me with kisses that smelled of cheap cosmetics and old coffee.

"Enough of that smooching, gals. Barbara Jean, you can sit down now. We have a tournament to play." Nonna clapped her hands in anticipation of the competition.

I would not exactly use the phrases "fed to the wolves" or "trial by fire," but I jumped right into some seriously aggressive play. With my cheat-sheet on standard bids, I learned quickly to cover my confusion and to fake whatever I didn't know. I discovered which women were playing as a social grace (and wouldn't notice a misappropriated trick) and which women had keen eyes (and would expose the aforementioned foul). Nonna belonged to the latter group.

Sometime during the third round of card playing—after all the good gossip had been exchanged and before lunch—we heard the sound of the lawn mower.

"I told that boy not to cut the grass on a Tuesday." Grandma Lena, particularly churlish after losing the second round to Nonna, thumped her knuckles on the table to indicate her pass on the bid.

Seated next to the picture window, I could observe Travis on the John Deere riding mower. Even sitting down on the tractor, he seemed taller to me than the last time I saw him. His hair, a little longer now, curled in lawless, dark waves around his neck. His shirtless figure revealed tanned, though underdeveloped, pectoral muscles, but my gaze followed the purled and bronzed knobs of his shoulders as he steered the tractor toward the front of the house.

"Barbara Jean? Barbara Jean! You won the bid. Are you going to name trump?"

I glanced at my cards and the red haze before me.

"Hearts, I mean diamonds."

"Which is it? Heart or diamonds?" Mrs. Peale asked.

I glanced at Grandma Lena who was pulling on her earring.

"Definitely diamonds," I said, placing the king and queen of diamonds on the table to collect my four-point meld.

I looked up to see that Travis was nearing the window. He saw me, and for a second, he looked perplexed, as if he didn't know who I was. Then, just as recognition came, we heard a crash, and Greystoke, the smallest cat of the three, jumped from his sunny window ledge.

"What was that?"

Grandma Lena ran to the window, followed by the more agile guests. I didn't move because I already had the queen's box for this event. Queen of diamonds and jack of spades. Or was it the queen of spades and jack of diamonds? I could never remember which two cards made up pinochle. Either way, this jack was in trouble.

In his moment of distraction, Travis had wedged the John Deere under the porch. Wedged it good, too. Reverse gear was doing nothing to rectify the problem. The gentle bucking of the tractor loosened the trellis from the porch, and an ancient vine of prickly roses soon descended onto Travis's naked torso.

"Son of a bitch. God damn it!" he howled loud enough for all the ladies to hear through the open window.

"Oh dear," said Mrs. Bomberger.

Each woman shuffled amusement and concern in her head like a new deck of playing cards. All except for Grandma Lena, who saw the scene as a terrorist act, a suicide bombing of her gentle roses. She hurried to police the scene, but Nonna pulled her back from her charge.

"Lena, I think our guests could use some refreshments, don't you agree? I'll take care of Travis."

"My roses—"

"That vine was more thorn and bark than rose."

But Grandma Lena wanted to hear no more. She was still sulking from the last hand in which we did not make our bid, thereby losing to Nonna. My two grandmas stomped away in opposite directions. One to the realm of mushroom mini-quiches and social decorum; the other to the flowered curtain call of a John Deere, jack-of-diamonds, rodeo clown. And for the first time all summer, I smiled. This could be fun after all.

· 4 ·

2000

IT RAINED FOR THREE DAYS after we arrived at Mulberry Street. Like a runner's cleats on aluminum bleachers, the rain tapped the metal roof of the sleeping porch. The sound drove me into heavy dreams that I could not remember upon waking. Each morning, I awoke with my mind muddier than it had been the day before. *Where was I exactly? Why was I here? What was my name? How old was I?* But Jules would bark, and from the folds of his own questions, Sam would appear with crusty eyes and the comforting smell of baby bad breath.

He crawled into the brass bed and snuggled beside me. His nightshirt, one of Bryce's old concert T-shirts, lifted to reveal the abacus that was Sam's spine. I pulled the shirt down, counting the bony beads as I covered them, and in doing so, I reconnected with the physical world, the world full of numbers and bones, bones and names. After I counted the bones, I spoke the name, *Sam,* holding the *m* in my mouth like the taste of a Life Saver I was trying to commit to memory. And he did the same with

Mom. We nestled in the sheets, sucking on spearmint, on butter rum, until the flavors disappeared and Jules barked again—our cue to begin our day.

Three days of rain were not unwelcome. I used the mornings to convert Grandma Lena's darkroom into something that resembled the jewelry studio I had dismantled in Michigan. Almost unnoticed was the shift from the sour smell of fixer to the metallic taste of silver dust. Nonna had donated most of Lena's photography equipment to the college years ago. The vacated space was an excellent match for my purposes—even better, in some respect, than the studio I had pieced together in Michigan. The rear lean-to of the Mulberry Street house had ventilation hoods, large flat worktables, and the possibility of daylight.

When I first pulled off the brittle black blinds, I was dazed to see the pervasive nickel color of the horizon. If the gray scale was any indication, I was ascending in my efforts. I had no intention for the studio on Mulberry Street to be a permanent installation, though perhaps I was lying to myself. What was permanence anyway? I had a few commissions to finish this summer, but September, like the neutral country of Switzerland, was noncommittal and far away.

In homage to my indecision, I left some of my jeweler's tools in cardboard boxes. Basic tools, like my torch and soldering pad, sat under the hood ready for fire. I had been nervous about transporting a tank of acetylene gas on my long trip (made ever more volatile by my rattled state of mind), but I had managed to transport and unpack it safely, without incident. With my equipment arranged, I was ready to test the flames and the ventilation hoods to make sure they worked. The room had an immaculate feel that told me it was not truly a working space. Looking around at the empty studio, I could not find a scrap of metal to use in my experiment. I sighed. My scrap metal container was deeply buried underneath my lathe in the largest cardboard box, and that was still somewhere in the garage. Regardless, I wanted to at least light my torch and make sure the connections were satisfactory. Just as I turned on the gas for the torch, I noticed my wedding rings still twirling on my left hand. *Bingo!* I felt the laugh spring from deep in my throat.

Oh yes, there had been another woman, perhaps more than one. But the discovery of one had been enough to send tremors through my skin, my organs, and even my teeth. The timing was horrible. I heard news of Nonna's death three nights after Bryce's forced admission. My tremors progressed into vomitous seizures that quaked until dawn. Dr. Radcliffe gave me a couple of options, and I chose the one I could hold in my hand and swallow with water.

Those hours were dark with the revelations and fuzzy with my medication. I asked Bryce to advise the mortician. Both men tried their best to neutralize the solemn emotions with their navy pinstriped suits. They did a good job. At the viewing, nobody could determine which man was the husband and which was the funeral director. I kept my wedding rings in place for the parade of card club members, neighbors, and former brides who shook my hands and kissed my drugged cheek. My failed marriage could liven up next month's card club. Card club. Deck of cards. House of cards . . . falling.

What did Bryce tell his girlfriend for those three weeks? She never called the house, but even unnamed, she still seeped into our home. A handout from a realtor. A strange towel in the laundry. But mostly she made her presence known in Bryce's refusal to respond when I attempted to provoke him, which was often. We made our way home from the funeral, back to Michigan, where I counted the days. One, two, three—taking a breath. Four, five—listening to my own heartbeat. Six, seven, eight, nine—watching the clouds for rain. Finally on the tenth day— folding my summer clothes next to Sam's in the big suitcase.

I packed the car as Sam watched from the east-facing bay window.

"I need to go. Just for a few weeks. I have to empty the house on Mulberry Street. We'll sort things out when I get home. End of August at the latest." I spoke bullets instead of sentences and phrases.

"You don't need to do this. I'll get a place."

"I'm taking Sam and the dog. Don't do any legal stuff. Wait until I get back. Promise?"

"Bobbi"—he never called me BJ—"look, I'll give you a fair settlement. You can keep the house. We can work out custody."

"Promise me you won't do anything!"

"I . . . okay. End of August."

The rings were still on my hand. I pulled at them. Fingers that only weeks go had flesh enough to keep the rings in place now surrendered them easily. Bryce had given me the diamond on the day he finished law school. The ring had a round stone with a wirelike band. Nothing special. Though I was ecstatic over my prospects, my inner artist had cringed and had set about to make a wedding band that would ignite the diamond on my hand. I had done it, too, with a beautiful ring of overlapping gold leaves like a laurel crown. My clients continued to request that ring, often enough that the ongoing orders kept me from the despair of scanning the classifieds for a *real* job requiring an alarm clock, pantyhose, and a team mentality.

I shifted the band to my right hand. It had always been more a present to myself than a symbol of Bryce's fidelity. That was obvious. But what was this diamond ring? I clamped it to a small stand where, with precision, I aimed the hissing, blue flame of my torch. Soon the metal started to color in the heat. I took my pliers and wrenched back the prongs on the setting until, with a satisfying *clink-a-clink,* the diamond bounced off a clay crucible and onto the counter. As if to applaud, the rain stopped its whirring and echoed *clink-a-clink* on the roof of the lean-to. The sound of rain and falling diamonds.

Yes!

I opened the back door and stepped outside. The rain fell upon my hands and neck. Jules slid by. He wanted out, a desperate dash into the weather. I didn't move back into the shelter of the house. Even after Jules had dampened my thigh with his return, I remained outside. The weather summoned me into a trance, and I obeyed the call of the thunder, letting the rain bejewel me.

· 5 ·

1983

THOUGH I HAD MADE FRIENDS at the lake in previous summers, I was never eager to renew these friendships. It was too much work to figure out how the local cliques had rearranged themselves over the course of a school year. The girls would eventually come to me if I ignored them long enough. The beach was sparsely populated, and I attributed the lull to an unusually cool and rainy spring. Because of the lake's chilly reception, potential beachgoers questioned whether the baton had officially been passed from spring to summer. I did not care about the relay of the seasons. I wasn't at the beach for the purpose of water sports; I just wanted a quiet place to read. I spread out my beach towel on the pebbled sand and opened a book from Nonna's cache of Harlequin Romances.

"I don't read them for the sex," she had confessed to me. "I read them to be young again."

As a kid, I had read good quality literature: Newbery Medal winners, children's classics, and Little House books. But at thirteen I was in a literary wasteland. Nothing seemed to span the gap between juvenile fiction and adult literature. V. C. Andrews gave me mild hope, but I had already read her latest scandalous book in a series about a brother and sister's forbidden love. Grandma Lena snorted at Nonna's stash of romances, but I was glad to have something to read. No matter the subject, books were educational. "Better than television," I told Grandma Lena.

At first I could not understand why the nineteen-year-old secretaries fell in love with their contemptuous, thirty-eight-year-old bosses. What was appealing about being stern and pompous and conceited? But within reading a few volumes, I not only accepted the backward principles of attraction, I absorbed them.

"Hi, BJ," the voice above me loomed anonymously in the bright sun. I assumed the voice was calling someone else until I heard it again.

"BJ, I'm talking to you."

I turned a squinted eye in the direction of the voice.

"BJ?" I asked.

"For Barbara Jean, silly."

Karen Sewicky threw her towel down next to mine. She had been one of the girls in the group into which I was assimilated during last summer's visit. I couldn't say that we had been great friends, but I had given her my address before I left for home, and she had mailed me a few short letters on terminally cute and heavily stickered stationery. Karen plopped down beside me with an expectant smile. Her presence was not a welcome interruption. Blaze Cunningham was about to undo the top button of Angelica's gauzy silk blouse. *He was the sexy tennis pro. She was his stepfather's niece in need of a solid backhand shot.*

"Mom told me that Travis had an accident at your place. I wish I had been there. My God! He is so cute. Too bad I'm not old enough to join the card club."

"Yeah, too bad." I flipped to the next page where more breathlessness awaited me.

If Karen was hoping to jumpstart her love life by talking to me, she could do it after Blaze's hands sought Angelica's creamy spheres of pleasure. And aspiring to the card club? It was laughable. I did not make it known that I was already a reluctant member.

"Ooh. You're burning." Karen took some Hawaiian Tropic SPF 4 out of her bag and handed it to me. The bottle was sticky, sand encrusted, and it smelled strongly of coconut.

"I'll wait until after I go for a swim," I said, ignoring her gesture and continuing to read.

Karen cast her eyes downward with rejection. I caught her reaction out of the corner of my eye. Just what every teenager needs—more emotional manipulation. It was obvious she was not going to leave me alone to enjoy a good sex scene.

"Come on. Let's get in," I said, disguising my disgust.

She perked up. "Great!"

When I stood I got the full view of Karen in her summer attire. She was gawky, all legs, in a pink striped cotton bathing suit with a ruffle around her hips. Featured in teen magazines, this style was popular with many girls my age, and they all looked equally stupid. My suit was solid black. Compared to me, Karen looked like a baby doll. I walked two steps ahead of her so nobody would mistake me for her babysitter.

Though the lake was cold this early in the season, a few people were already swimming or floating on inflatable rafts. Karen hemmed the edge of the water. Her big toe dipped in and out like a needle on slippery gray satin. I plunged in with a small yelp. I had been so caught up in my book that I had forgotten to flip onto my back. The water clarified the differences in my sun exposure. On my front, the lake water was refreshingly chilly, but on my red side, it was so cold it burned the back of my legs like a whipping. Once my hair was wet, I started to feel better.

Karen remained tentative, standing on the shore. She looked small and alone. Karen was used to being at the center of a large gathering of girls, but I surmised that her friends must belong to the group headed for Camp Susquehanna in the Poconos. I had overheard card club mavens discussing, with both delight and trepidation, the mass exodus of their daughters for the month of June. Karen had it rough. She might have pined away in her bedroom awaiting stories of poison ivy and cute counselors, but her parents wouldn't allow it. They were forever shooing her away from the house where Clarence Sewicky III, esquire, had his law office. Karen's mom, Clarence's junior by about ten years, was his secretary. She took Tuesday mornings off to come to card club and Thursday mornings off to get a manicure.

Karen's mom wasn't on my list of top mothers, but I had a fascination with her. Unlike my own mother, who was as artless as she was considerate, Karen's mom always seemed to be perfecting her polish and using bad news as currency. Certainly, Joyce Sewicky was a valued member of the card club because she gave away hints, without jeopardizing attorney/client privilege, about which marriages appeared to be in trouble and who would file for bankruptcy. She never told us anything that would not be public record sooner or later, but we felt duly informed. Always, as a reminder of the delicacy of the situation, she would press one perfectly manicured finger to her lips and whisper, "Ssh."

Now, for the first time, I wondered how Joyce had met Clarence. Was he her surly, older boss who suggested, no, ordered her to wear her hair down during dictation? Had they cleared off his desk in an act of passion? Clarence was not a handsome man, so the thought spiraled down to the realm of the icky, like the idea of old people or fat people or your own parents having sex. Would I have to confess these thoughts to Father Thomas when I got back home in August? Two months seemed too long to go without cleansing one's soul of sin.

I dove under water and held my breath as long as I could to clear my brain of the disturbing images. *Hail Mary, full of grace! The Lord is with Thee. Blessed art Thou amongst women . . .*

When I emerged from my watery confessional, Karen was still standing at the water's edge, but she was no longer alone. Travis was standing beside her.

Even from a distance I could make out the scene in detail. Travis had long abrasions on his upper body from his run-in with our roses, but I didn't focus on him. Instead I watched in dismay as Karen's hips leaned into their conversation. The bathing suit ruffle that had looked so immature now fluttered coyly against her upper thigh. Karen laughed, and then laced her arms across her chest as she moved pebbles around the sand with her toe. I couldn't believe that I had actually felt sorry for her.

Instantaneously the image of Jimmy Fuhrman popped into my mind. I longed to be back home in Virginia with Jimmy—the two of us taxiing around the swimming pool with Sue Lipkowski glaring at me from the snack bar.

How I wished that Mary, full of grace, had more power than simply interceding with God on behalf of my tawdry musings. Why couldn't she be more like Glinda the Good Witch from *The Wizard of Oz*? *There's no place like home.*

I shivered, but there was no way I was getting out of the water and back to my book with the two of them standing there ignoring the whole world—and worse, ignoring me.

Nonna was shelling peas and watching *General Hospital* when I returned to Mulberry Street.

"Margot and Travis are coming to dinner. You just missed Lena. She went out to get some steaks."

On the TV screen, Luke Spencer was embracing his sister, a prostitute turned nurse. "Don't worry, Barbara Jean. I will be fine. I'll call you when this is all over," he said. Luke was the only one to call her Barbara Jean. Everybody else on *General Hospital* called her Bobbie.

I had never heard of anybody else who had my same name—

anybody who was alive, at least. I was named after Dad's sister who had died at age seven in a car accident. The first Barbara Jean was a cute, blond-haired girl. In the last picture before her death, Barbara Jean sported a smile with many voids, as if her baby teeth had preceded her in death.

"Her adult teeth just never did come in," my dad would say before putting the picture back in the drawer.

The Barbara Jean on TV was a dark-haired temptress and, in a word, voluptuous. The directors kept her out from behind the nurses' station as much as possible.

"How about if you call me Bobbie?" I asked Nonna. I was drinking a Coke out of a can.

"Save it for your stage name. *Bobbie Foley*. Hmm." She paused and looked up at an imaginary marquee. "Then again, it doesn't sound so good."

"Karen Sewicky called me BJ today. What do you think about that?"

"BJ Foley. Hmmm." No marquee this time, just the TV.

"Do you like it?"

Nonna looked away from her stories. "What is all this fuss about your name?"

How could I explain to Nonna that this *brink of womanhood* stuff really sucked? I was tired of having passionate feelings without an object of desire, and tired of having a bra without breasts. What were these tentative protrusions I was growing, anyway, these demi-boobs? I was stuck halfway between the gapped grin of my child aunt, Barbara Jean, and the lush womanhood of Bobbie, the nurse. Maybe it was as simple as changing my name. *Abracadabra, Barbara, Bobbie, BJ*. If I could name my next incarnation, I could live it.

"I'm just tired of Barbara Jean. So when Margot and Travis get here, would you please call me BJ?"

Nonna resumed her shelling. "Okay."

I left the room to change out of my wet bathing suit. Once I was in the hallway, I pulled the front of my suit away to view my chest. It had looked bigger in the mirror that morning. Against my cold wet suit, my breasts had shrunk away to mere nubs. *UGH.* I snapped my suit back into place.

"Nonna!"

"Yes?"

"Please tell Grandma Lena to call me BJ."

I waited for an answer.

"Okay, Nonna?"

"Okay, *BJ.*"

· 6 ·

2000

I HAD WANTED TO SHOW Sam the summers of my youth, but though the house on Mulberry Street supplied the architecture, it was missing the spirit. How could we live within its sandstone walls for three days and still feel so empty? I tried everything. One afternoon, I barricaded Sam in the kitchen with me. Together we recreated Nonna's lemon chicken from a recipe card my mother had passed down to me. (Nonna never wrote down recipes for her own use.) The kitchen began to take on the familiar aromas, and I thought we were finally reviving the aura. But after I finally took the bird with its accompanying citrus cloud out of the oven, Sam turned to me and asked, "When we are done eating, can we go home?"

He spent his mornings in front of the television feeding videos of the *Star Wars* trilogy into Nonna's ancient beast of a VCR. Every time Sam put another movie into the mouth of the thing, I said a little prayer that the VCR would not digest the tape. They were all I had to entertain Sam on rainy mornings while I cleared out Nonna's belongings.

Finally, on the third day of rainy boredom, I strapped Sam into the car and circled the nearby towns looking for anything with kid appeal. Chuck E. Cheese's, glowing orange from its seat across from the strip mall, beckoned us. Not only could Sam expend his pent-up energy in the game room, but I could also grab a gallon of milk from the grocery store at the end of the strip. The additional errand made the outing seem less of a bribe on my part and more of a compromise.

Inside the restaurant, an attendant stamped our hands with some ultraviolet numeral that was supposed to bind me to my child. It didn't work. As soon as he was in the door, Sam tore away from my grasp and raced toward the skee ball.

"What about over here in the ball pit?" I called after him.

"Mo-om, I'm almost six," he said, nearly beyond my range of hearing.

I wandered over to the food counter where two high school girls were trying to correct a mistake with the previous order. After the cash register started beeping, they called their manager, a college girl, over to help them. As is the way of most managers, she took care of the problem with a plastic smile and the twist of a little gold key. When it was my turn at the front of the line, I realized that I had been so absorbed in the drama that I had not given any thought to what I wanted to order. Embarrassed, I chose the first pizza combo and discovered later that it was large enough to feed a family of four. Sam came running over for his plastic cup full of tokens, and after trying a round of Hungry Hungry Hippos for myself, I went to wait for our food.

I sat near the toddler area, which up until this year had been the place where Sam had spent most of his time. I missed his presence here and found myself getting teary thinking about my growing boy. I blinked and scanned the room. The ball pit, all pink and yellow and blue, surprised me with its color. I had thought the world would be rain-gray forever. The swirl of pointillist colors had a hypnotizing effect on me. I only realized I was staring when a young mother took her baby girl out of the ball pit whispering, "Time to go somewhere else, sweetie."

I shook my head to change my focus. *Snap out of it.* I smiled, a little more detached this time, as another little girl rushed by me. Beyond her, I took notice of a man sitting alone in a booth across from a table of discarded party hats and plates of half-eaten cake. Had he been there earlier? He seemed to be watching me, and I turned away quickly. *Could this man be a child predator?* The local TV news always warned parents that freaks of society haunted parks and school yards, preying on children.

I spun around, anxious to locate Sam. He waved and held up a fistful of prize tickets from a fishing game he had conquered. He really was too young to be playing by himself, but I was drained of all energy. When boys and girls are kidnapped, the tearful mothers always say, "I only turned away for a second." They never told the truth—how motherhood numbed you sometimes; how you spent days in a sleepy fog and nights in a state of alert; or how in your deepest self, you couldn't even picture yourself grown up, much less somebody's mother. And the worst truth of all—so secret it is unutterable: how the thief wouldn't even need to steal the child, who, on the days of constant pulling, you would give away to the first person who asked. (Unless the first person who asked was your soon-to-be ex-husband. Then you would take the second.)

At the next table over, Chuck E. Cheese was singing "Happy Birthday" to a two-year-old. The little girl started to cry. Her father took several pictures of the giant mouse without the crying girl—a deception worthy of the family photo album.

That father's ruse reminded me of Grandma Lena's tactics. She often took deceitful photographs at weddings. I recalled the Stiller/Dietrich wedding in particular. It was one of the first times I had assisted Grandma Lena at her job. Everything had gone smoothly until the limo pulled up to the church. At that point, the bride stopped speaking to the groom because he tipped the limousine driver, whose tip had already been included in the car rental. But the pictures had to go on. Grandma Lena had tried everything to make the bride smile naturally and lovingly at her new husband. In the end, she had snapped a shot of the two of them in the back of the limousine, after which the bride got out and rode with her parents to the reception. And yet Stiller and Dietrich, married ever after, managed to parent two kids and celebrate anniversaries in complete ignorance of their misery.

Sam was having too much fun to stop playing when the pizza arrived, but with the child predator making occasional eye contact, I reined Sam in for a slice of pepperoni. He was full of his usual chatter and had little interest in helping me put a dent in the family pizza combo. I chewed and swallowed two slices robotically, not tasting them. Pepperoni could have been Play-Doh for all the attention I paid it. Sam had taken three scant bites. The whole outing seemed a failure. Before I could consume any more careless calories, I declared that our meal was over. The man in the corner still had not moved, nor had he eaten. He seemed to be waiting, and I, transformed into Mother Bear, was not interested in the *whys* or *for whats;* my imagination could supply those details.

"Come on, Sam. We are leaving." I slid the hefty remains of our pizza into a cardboard box.

"But I didn't get to cash in my tickets for a prize," Sam said.

"We'll come again. You have to save up for the good prizes anyway."

"I want the gumball machine."

"You don't even chew gum."

"I can fill it with M&M's."

"Okay," I said.

What choice did I have? I was a mother on the edge of divorce. I knew I would not deny Sam anything, even if I had to battle fatigue, a child molester, and a giant singing rodent to give it to him.

· 7 ·

1983

GRANDMA LENA PREPARED THE GRILL. As a general rule she was not allowed to cook in Nonna's kitchen, not because she couldn't cook, but because Nonna had a system, and Grandma Lena seldom stuck to the rules. For example, Nonna liked to store all her bakeware in one place, but Lena saw more logic in putting all the glassware together, regardless of purpose. Thus, casserole dish and loaf pan went into the same cabinet, which infuriated Nonna on baking days.

As a result of her banishment from the kitchen, Grandma Lena claimed the grill as part of her command of the garden. She was as good a cook as Nonna. She would grill peppers alongside steaks. Or if she barbecued chicken, she would garnish it with grilled pineapples or kebobs of pearl onions and mushrooms. For that evening, when Travis and Margot would join us, the menu was simple: steak and potato salad. The meat hissed and spewed its aroma so that all of the Mulberry Street neighbors poked their heads out of the windows and wondered jealously if they still had some rib eyes in the back of their freezers. As I waved to Mr. Kovack next door, I was glad to claim ownership of the aroma of grilled meat.

Margot drank a virgin daiquiri (alcohol didn't mix with her meds) and directed Grandma Lena as she cooked.

"I think they are done on this side."

"I'm grilling here. Why don't you have a seat?"

"No, I'll stand. I have been sitting all day in Dad's hospital room."

Margot was Grandma Lena's half sister, but she was more like a daughter. She was only a couple of months older than my mother. Although they never lived together and weren't related by blood, Mom and Margot acted like sisters in a way that Lena and Margot never did. In fact, Mom was maid of honor at Margot's ill-fated wedding. They didn't see much of each other after Mom moved to Richmond. On the few occasions I saw Margot, I liked to address her as Great-aunt Margot. I had used the title earlier, when she and Travis arrived for the barbecue.

"Stop, you make me sound ancient and decrepit."

Margot was not close to being old. She seemed a decade younger than my own mother. Margot's vitality made the age gap between her and Lena even more pronounced. I studied them, looking for an undeniable connection. They had similarities—an athletic slimness, a tilt of the head when deep in thought—but it did not seem enough to prove a relation.

Margot stopped and smacked an imaginary bug on her thigh and curled her thumb as if she had caught something. She had waited long enough for Grandma Lena to inquire after her ailing father. "The nurses said it won't be much longer now. He doesn't make much sense these days. On Sunday, he thought Travis was his father, and he kept screaming at him to get away. I have no idea what that was all about." Margot took a long sip from her glass and reached for her cigarettes.

"Travis, honey, will you get me my lighter?"

I had been listening to the conversation while setting the table. Grandma Lena came over and grabbed the vinyl place mats out of my hand.

"Barbara Jean, this table needs to be wiped off first," she said tersely. She had already forgotten that I had asked to be called BJ.

Normally, she wasn't this prickly, but Margot had set her off by talking about her father. Grandma Lena had never liked her stepfather, the Reverend Ernie Platz. Now he was dying of complications from a stroke, of which doctors had no medical evidence. Margot did not press her older sister to go see him, even though he had been the only father Lena had ever known. I had never met the man.

"You wouldn't want to," Nonna had told me, but I didn't quite believe her. Travis had always spoken fondly of his grandfather. They had gone fishing together, and he had shown Travis how to wire his own radio. I wondered if Travis was sad about his grandpa. He hadn't seemed distracted by grief that afternoon when he was flirting with Karen.

I never had a grandpa. Well, I suppose I did at one time. Dad's father had died before I was born, and his mother died soon afterward. The only grandparents I had ever known were my grandmas. As I circled the glass table with wet paper towels, I wondered about my other grandfather—the one nobody ever talked about—Mom's real dad. He was a war hero. Nonna had his silver star upstairs in her music box along with a small photo of him in uniform, but that was it. The box played "Edelweiss" from the movie *Sound of Music*.

I had seen *The Sound of Music* several times, and my grandpa looked less like the romantic lead, Christopher Plummer, and more like the young telegram boy. I couldn't think of Grandpa as being a war hero when, to me, he was the traitorous Rolf. The two ideas twined themselves in my thoughts until I had given my grandfather an absurd complexity considering he was little more than a picture to me.

"Steaks are ready," Grandma Lena called from the brick patio.

Travis, the slap-on-the-back growing boy, was first in line to get his sirloin. Margot sucked down the last of her cigarette. Nonna hastily shuttled the potato salad and steamed peas to the table. I sat on the aluminum chair to wait for my turn. This was my extended family, not Auntie Em or Frauline Maria. Just two grandmothers who loved each other more than was prudent and a cousin with his mother, my grandaunt, who weren't really related to me at all.

· 8 ·

2000

AFTER THREE DAYS of summer rain, the plants tangled each other in plush new growth. Dead lilacs bowed as roses and hostas and ferns introduced the world to June. The greens were so brilliant they burned a fluorescent path in the slanted shaft of morning sun. Even the abandoned vegetable garden, which should have been a wasteland, was spilling over with a few stubborn strains of last year's arugula, butterhead, and cress—lettuces that should not have been perennials here in Pennsylvania's Zone 6. And as I thought about it, maybe they weren't. Maybe Nonna had planted them before she died. Either way, I anticipated a bittersweet harvest.

Although I had hired a neighboring teen to take care of the lawn during the summer, I forced myself outside to pull weeds and tend the flower beds. As the queen of inner sanctums, I had never quite caught the landscaping bug. Bryce had taken care of the lawn when he wasn't at the office or on the golf course. But today, I didn't mind sinking my knees to the rain-soaked earth and wrestling with stubborn weeds. In all truth, I was glad for the diversion.

Sam and Jules bounded out of the house at first morning light. Sam had found an old canvas tent in the attic, and I had followed through on my promise to set it up for him. Luckily Sam was used to playing alone. He had a great imagination and an attention span to see his adventures through until naptime. Now and then, he would sail past me and turn my bent form into a part of his story line.

"Imperial troopers ahead—activate the force field."

He would zoom out of sight again to the tattered canvas spaceport. He loved the original *Star Wars* trilogy so much that I often thought he must be a carryover from the boys of my generation. It was as if he were one of the brothers I was supposed to have instead of the son that he was. Whatever his preference, it was a relief to see him having so much fun and expending his pent-up energy.

Last night, after Sam and I had returned from Chuck E. Cheese's, the message light shone its red alert on the answering machine. It was Bryce, of course. Erroneously thinking he might actually care that we had made it safely to Pennsylvania, I had called him the night we arrived at Nonna's house.

"We made it here in one piece. Call us when you get a chance." Then I added, "Sam wants to talk to you," hoping that would get his attention.

It had taken him three days to respond. True, I hadn't called him on his cell phone, but I thought he would at least have the courtesy to check the machine at home.

Eventually Bryce had called back, not with a message for a son who was hungry for attention from his father, but with a point on legal matters—and this before we had a chance to sit down together and talk to Sam about the possible dissolution of our family.

"Uh, Bobbi, it's, uh, Bryce. I have looked into a few things. We could have this all wrapped up by Christmas, if that's the route we decide to take. Call me and we can go over my notes. Don't worry, I haven't gone to a judge for any of this. I have just taken the liberty of drawing up a few documents. Call me. Oh, hi Sam, buddy. Are you practicing your putting? Bye."

Sam blinked back at the answering machine—a poor substitute for a father. He was quiet. Then he said, "Daddy should know I didn't bring my golf clubs. They are in the back of his car."

"I know, sweetheart. Daddy has a lot on his mind right now."

"Are you guys getting a divorce?"

I stepped back, stung by Sam's frankness. He was a smart kid; I had expected him to pick up on the current climate, but I didn't even know that he had ever heard the word.

"Do you know what *divorce* is?"

"It's bad, but Daddy gets money from it. Is Daddy going to take all of our money?"

Our money. One of the reasons that I was able to continue as a studio craftsperson was that Bryce had carried me financially when I was between commissions. It had seemed like an equitable arrangement considering that I shuttled Sam back and forth to preschool. Sam had never been put into day care. Three times a week, a sitter came to the house while I was in the studio. And once a week, the two of us went to playgroup. But what would happen now? Would I be forced to get a nine-to-five job?

I thought quickly and answered Sam. It was far from the well-worded explanation I had been mentally composing for the last few weeks. "Daddy will not take our money. I'm not sure if we are getting a divorce, but Sam, nothing will change the way we love you, okay?"

Sam looked unconvinced, and I took a strange pride in his skepticism.

"Look, Sam. As soon as Mommy knows what is going on, I will tell you. You're my guy, but right now Mommy isn't even sure what is going on. Let's just take it one day at a time and enjoy our adventure this summer, okay?"

It was a cop-out, and I knew it, but *Damn, Bryce,* I wanted him with me when we explained everything to Sam. He owed me that much.

After Sam fell asleep that night, I thumbed through Nonna's address book, my finger resting on the number I found. *Sewicky.* Karen had joined her father's law office a few years ago. Her dad was looking to retire. When Karen approached me at Nonna's viewing, I recognized her immediately but was unprepared for the age that had crept onto her face. Lines and softness, a couple of gray hairs. I had automatically touched my cheek to question the play of time on my own face.

Karen, though matured, had sparkled in her condolences. She was newly married to a man she introduced only as Shelly. In full calculation mode, Nonna had asked Karen to take care of her final will so that I would have a friend, geographically near to the estate, who could lead me through the process.

I pounded out the dirt from a clump of dandelion. The will was not on my mind when I dialed Karen's number last night. In reality, I was calling on her more as a friend than as an attorney, which gave her license to be straightforward with me. And though, previous to the funeral, I had not spoken to Karen in years, we renewed our acquaintance and assumed an easy sisterhood. Karen had listened attentively about Bryce and had interjected "that bastard" when it was appropriate, which was often.

But even today as I ripped at weeds that danced with images of my husband's smug face, I knew the failure was not Bryce's alone. I had never worked at the marriage. I hated Bryce's law buddies and his golf cronies. They were pompous and condescending. I had never tried to see beyond their bravado, but instead chastised them and compared them to my crowd of artist/activist friends. My friends had ideals that transcended bank accounts and country club memberships. They fought for freedoms and rallied, armed only with slogans and chants.

"There is a reason they throw protestors in jail," Bryce argued.

"Yeah, so you can get a payday," I replied.

"It's so easy to renounce a paycheck when you are living so comfortably off of mine."

The contrast in our personal values seemed adorable at first. Yin and Yang. We balanced each other, especially at public functions. We were that golden couple who volleyed off each other's lines as if we were performing a comedy sketch. Our rebuttals were light and humorous and improvisational. But then Sam came, and the differences that were so fresh a couple of years prior turned into stale shouts and rehearsed accusations. Slogans: *Lay off! It's not going to hurt him.* Chants: *Fine, go! See if I care.*

I began to spend more time in my studio when Bryce was home, which was seldom. I used the excuse that I had to take care of Sam when he wasn't around, and therefore my work was suffering. (It wasn't.) Bryce justified his absences with the fact that he was trying to make partner before thirty, a goal he easily accomplished. As a couple, we ceased to exist. We shared an address, but lived as two planets in different orbits around the same sun (son). I went to gallery openings, including my first solo exhibition, alone. To awaken my husband to his own behavior, I stood him up the night the senior partners and their wives were taking us out to yacht night at the club. Sam had caught a slight cold, but I had not bothered to call Bryce to tell him I would not be there.

And sex. The great indicator. We used sex as a way to disappoint each other and to keep score in our little game. *Tit for tat,* to use a bad pun. Denying each other sexual gratification was rejection in its most blatant form. I wasn't so much surprised that Bryce had an affair as I was surprised he had been secretive about it. Then again, maybe his discretion was more for the benefit of his professional image than for me. I didn't tell Karen everything. Why make myself culpable? Lawyers didn't want to know the truth anyway.

And that's exactly how we ended our friendly chat—in lawyer mode. Karen had promised to call Bryce the next morning and get him to fax his notes to her. "You have got to try to keep this in Michigan if at all possible. It will be easier for you, but I can advise you until you get a chance to talk to someone there." I was glad I had called my old friend. Karen had proved to be sympathetic. Before Shelly, she had been married for eighteen months—to someone she described as "a real shit." *From shit to Shelly.* Hoeing the ground, I laughed aloud at my private little joke.

"Something funny?" A voice startled me, and I recoiled.

I looked up to see *him,* the child stalker, hovering above me.

I dropped the hoe and then fumbled unsuccessfully as I tried to reclaim my grip on the only weapon I had. *Sam? Where the hell was my son?* I swung around scanning the empty yard and growing more agitated with each passing second. Without thinking, I raked my dirty, gloved hand through my hair.

"My God, Sam. What have you done with him?"

"Who?" the stranger asked as Sam came zooming by with an Imperial X-wing fighter.

"Oh, God, I'm sorry," I apologized. "It's just my son, see and . . ." My words trailed off to bury themselves in a heap of my humiliation.

Thinking a handshake might be in order, I removed my garden gloves. Even though they had been covered, my fingers had half moons of dirt under each nail. The dark side of the moon. I hid my hands behind my back.

The man shifted his weight. "I thought that was you at the restaurant last night, but I wasn't sure."

"We know each other?" I squinted to see his face in spite of the strong back lighting.

"Travis? Travis McKenzie." He laughed then, knowing he had my attention.

I repositioned myself out of the sun. "Oh, my God." In the shade of the large rhododendron, I finally got a good look at the man before me.

In my defense, he looked nothing like the lanky youth who used to mow this very lawn. He had a small clipped beard. His hair was cut close to the scalp in the places where he had any hair at all. But he was sexy bald; his stance was secure, and his smile held me in devilment as he waited for me to finish my appraisal of him. In the same look, I found that he was measuring the changes in me. I took a step closer, and in the radiating amber of his eyes, I finally glimpsed the boy I had known.

"I'm sorry, Travis. Wow. It *is* you."

"Yes."

"I won't tell you what I thought when I saw you yesterday."

He laughed again. "That bad? I thought you looked a little spooked."

"You're here. Wow! I have been really trying to find you to tell you about Nonna, and here you are."

"Yes, here I am."

Had I *really* tried to find him? I looked down at my filthy hands and hastily spun around hoping for a towel or old shirt to wipe them. Seeing none, I glanced up and saw a wry grin once again come over Travis's face. *Great! I amuse him.* I stumbled backward over my hoe and only increased my discomfort and subsequently his pleasure.

"I'm sorry I am such a mess."

"No, you're not. You look great. As beautiful as always."

I sputtered some indecipherable sound, hoping to convey a general denial. "Let me go inside to rinse off, and then we can catch up. Would you like some iced tea?" I asked. Nonna's trademark hospitality—I had almost forgotten.

"Sure."

"Lemon?"

"Please."

I scurried away like I had that night at the restaurant, but this time I let Sam continue with his fun. Travis would not endanger my son, though I didn't know if the same could be said for me. Travis's devastating impact on me had been well documented— "Dear Diary," not to mention my early sketchbooks.

I should be immune to him. I should be immune to all men.

Inside the house, I washed the dirt from my hands and arms, letting the cool water wash all over me. *Calm down.* What was this feeling inside me? Was it merely surprise at seeing Travis here after these years? I distractedly dried my hands on the linen towel I used exclusively for the dishes and removed the heavy cut-glass pitcher from the refrigerator. Hurriedly I carried the tea to the counter and steadied myself. *Tell me this isn't happening.* Through the lace curtains in the open window I could see Travis petting Jules and talking with my son.

Sam was a dry riverbed in his need for attention. If I was honest I would have admitted to being a bit parched myself, but like most mothers I had learned to push my needs into small thirsty pockets of denial. Pockets, like the kind old actresses tout in those TV ads for superabsorbent paper towels. Sam didn't have the same affliction. He showed Travis his *Star Wars* action figures with one unendorsed space alien thrown in for effect. Then he grabbed Travis's hand and led him into the tent.

As Sam disappeared from my view, I gasped knowing that tears were on their way. I wasn't sure why my emotions came flowing out just then, but I could guess. After four days of living with ghosts of my grandmothers, ghosts of my girlhood, ghosts of my marriage, the reality of my past had confronted me—in the form of a real person who could verify that I had lived well during those hot and hasty days of my youth. Travis McKenzie was my alibi for a summer when nothing made sense, yet it happened in sequence, as fate scripted. Maybe I would never be able to reconcile that summer with the facts I had growing up, but a big piece of that puzzle was currently sitting under an old canopy with my son, waiting for me to bring him a glass of iced tea.

· 9 ·

1983

"Stop it! Ow!" I cried as Grandma Lena pulled another lock of my hair.

"Hold still."

I sat on a garden bench. Beside me, my *Seventeen* magazine was opened to page eighty-three, "The New Braids." Grandma Lena passed her right hand over her left hand in an attempt to turn my thin tresses into the full fishtail braid. It was no use. As soon as she pulled a slippery strand into the finished rope, another strand freed itself to float around my head like an aberrant thought.

"Go into my emergency wedding kit and grab the Aqua Net," Grandma Lena said.

"I can't use hairspray. I'm going swimming. The braid has to be tight on its own."

"Why do you want to get your hair all fancy if all you are going to do is go in the water?"

"I just want it to look cool."

The model on page eighty-three didn't seem to have a problem keeping her braid in place as she bounced a beach ball in the spray of the ocean. Her Bonne Bell lip gloss was shiny and her tan was even. A piece of pink cellophane accented the bottom of her braid.

"Good luck, sweetie," Grandma Lena said as she pulled harder.

I bit my lip to suppress the howl, but it didn't work. My scalp was on fire.

"Ow, you are hurting me!"

Mr. Kovack looked up from his garden with an evil grin. Grandma Lena waved at him with a comb.

"The hydrangeas look marvelous, George," she said, then whispered to me, "The coot. I caught him in our mailbox yesterday looking for a missing phone bill, or so he said."

I suppressed a laugh. My grandmas and George Kovack had a history of disputes since the day he moved in four years ago. Usually, my grandmothers got the best of him.

"You are just going to make him madder," I said, handing Grandma Lena the elastic band.

Last August, Mr. Kovack had called the police because my grandmas were making too much noise. When Officer Steffy arrived, he found six women and two men engaged in a poetry reading on the porch. One thing about Officer Steffy, he loved to recite Keats's "Ode on a Grecian Urn" even more than he loved to recite the Miranda warning. He left my grandmothers' house only briefly to return the squad car, give his report, and punch out. He came back later with his wife, and they stayed until Keats could no longer be heard over the roar of a hundred mating crickets and the distant lament of a cat in heat.

In early fall, it was Nonna's turn to contact the authorities after Mr. Kovack shot an arrow into Greystoke's hind leg. Apparently he was angry because Nonna and Grandma Lena's three cats were defecating in his prized flower beds. The huge fine that followed the police visit did not help to diminish the animosity. Although some of the neighbors didn't agree with their lifestyle, most of them sided with my grandmas—even the ones who complained about cat poop in their own yards.

Those neighbors were the families who had bought their property from Nonna when she sold off plots of the family farm. They were with her when she christened Mulberry Street in a block party like no others. And when they needed someone to water their plants or collect their mail while they went on vacation, they called my grandmas. But Mr. Kovack didn't care. He interrupted his vigil only to mutter the words *vile* and *dyke* into his rhododendrons. Even then, Grandma Lena couldn't keep from goading him.

Grandma Lena snapped the last loop of the elastic band over my finished fishtail.

"There," she said triumphantly. "It's as good as it's going to get."

I reached my hand up to touch the slippery plait.

"Does it look like the picture?" I asked.

"Who are you trying to impress, young lady?"

All my intended sophistication suddenly seemed as childish as play cosmetics or dress-up clothes.

"Can't a person try to look her best without a having motive? I'm just trying to express the inner me," I said. It was not the best exit line, but I took my remaining dignity with me toward the house and left Grandma Lena to harumpf over the rest of my magazine.

From the hydrangeas came a snicker.

"Back at ya, George."

· 10 ·

2000

I WISHED I COULD have filled Nonna's fruit tray with something besides tea and glasses, but I had yet to go to the grocery store—even for the milk I was supposed to get the previous night. And I had no lemons. Why had I even offered them to Travis? Shopping was near golfing at the bottom of my list of possible pastimes. Most often, my attention span petered out before the back nine or around aisle eleven. Either way, it was about an hour into the exercise when my focus would soften, and I would miss an easy putt or need to double back to aisle five for the salsa. Neither deficiency had helped me score any points with my husband.

Travis took no notice of the missing lemons. He drank the iced tea slowly, perhaps out of kindness. I fumbled with my own glass, using it as a prop as I decided what to say next. My mind was generating questions even faster than it had when I had mistaken Travis for a child molester. Part of me wished he had stayed in that persona. I felt pretty sure I could protect my son from a predator, but what about me? Maybe Travis was the one in need of protection.

"So, what are you doing here?" I wanted to be direct, but the question was lacking in civility.

"I live here."

"Live here where?"

"About five miles away. I'm renting. It's a dump, but it's fully furnished."

"How long have you been here? You weren't at Nonna's funeral." I felt my voice getting tight. I sounded like I was attacking him, but Travis remained unfazed.

"I only just found out that she died. I don't read the papers much. May is one of the busiest times for me with Mother's Day and spring planting. I'm sorry I missed the funeral." Travis leaned back into his chair. "Anja was a sweet woman. Damn fine cook. To this day, I dream about her pastries."

I was satisfied by his answer, but I didn't reply. In the pause, I gauged our silence for signs of discomfort, but I found none. Travis fit into this garden, even though time had passed and the vegetation shadowed more of the yard than it had seventeen years ago. I leaned back in my chair and closed my eyes, partly to relax and partly to understand the moment.

"Didn't Karen tell you I was coming today?" Travis asked.

"No, and I just talked to her last night, too." I popped one eye open at him. "I wonder why she didn't say anything. Last thing she told me about you was that you were in New Jersey."

"Yeah, well, I left there about nine months ago after my ex-wife bought me out of our landscaping business. I'm working at Konkle's Greenhouse until I can get some clientele in this area."

Two eyes open now. I hadn't missed the *ex-wife* reference, but I was biding time, organizing my thoughts. "You are in landscaping? I find that hard to believe. You didn't like working on this lawn."

"That was a long time ago, BJ. I worked ten lawns that summer, I'll have you know, not just this one. And I was an English teacher for a couple of years, but I liked my summer work better, so I made that my full-time job."

"So your ex-wife," I said coolly. "That would be Liz?"

"Yes. Elizabeth."

I wanted to ask him more about her, about them. I stopped myself because suddenly I realized I wasn't prepared to speculate about the state of my own marriage. To Travis's credit, he didn't ask.

"And you've been in touch with Karen?" I asked. *Safe questions now, BJ. Stay focused.*

"She was in the greenhouse last week. They buzzed me because some woman wanted to know about crepe myrtle trees. I came to the front of the store, and there was Karen with her husband."

"You met Shelly?"

"He introduced himself as Ross, but I didn't catch if it was his first name or last name."

"She told me his name was Shelly."

"Maybe it's Ross Shelly," Travis said.

"Or Shelly Ross."

We laughed. I couldn't help myself. In spite of my longing to establish the pace of this interview, I let go, uncoiled the kite string that carried the sound of our laughter to the trees.

"What's so funny?" Sam poked his head out of the tent. His hair was rumpled from play, and his eyes were glistening in a way they hadn't for weeks. He came running over to me, and I wrapped my arms around him.

"Do you have kids? You must—to eat at a place like Chuck E. Cheese," I said. Sam crawled onto my lap. He was getting too big for the habit, but he was as curious as I was to see if Travis had kids, hopefully a boy his age.

"No, I don't have any kids. I was getting a trailer hitch put on my truck at the U-Haul place across the street. I just needed a place to wait out of the rain."

Now Travis was speaking Sam's language. At the word *truck*, his curiosity blossomed.

"Travis, what do you haul with your truck?" Sam asked. The *r*'s came out like *w*'s. *Twavis. Twuck*. His nursery school teacher had told us not to worry, his *r*'s would come in time.

"I haul my landscaping equipment: tractors, edgers. And my boat."

"Mom, he has a boat!"

"Ask your mom if you can go to the lake sometime. I only go on Sundays because, in this area, people don't like me to work on their yards on a Sunday. Plus the greenhouse is owned by Mennonites who don't keep Sunday business hours."

"Can we, Mom, please? This Sunday, please."

I looked from Sam to Travis. The affirmations that escaped my lips echoed in my thoughts as I got ready for bed that night. *Yes, Sam. Yes, Travis, we'd love to go. Yes, we can be ready early.* I pulled on my tank top and pajama shorts. The air was close. Already sweating, I turned on the window fan. My grandmothers never installed central air; it wasn't a priority. They had only a small window unit in the kitchen to keep Nonna's cake icings from melting. I had forgotten how hot the nights could get in these bedrooms. Even though the stone walls were thick and cool and helped somewhat in the lower part of the house, they couldn't keep the rising heat from reaching our bedchambers. This was the first night I had needed relief from the heat, the damp muck of the air after all that rain. I washed my face, not bothering to dry it. I wet my hair, too, and the back of my neck. Anything to soothe myself. But inside, I knew it wasn't the heat that was vexing me. More troubling was my encounter with Travis and the promise of more encounters.

We had made the decision: we were taking his boat to Blue Lake on Sunday. It was the same lake that swallowed every wish I had ever made while skipping rocks. The very lake that held all my confessions, my girl prayers to Mary, full of grace! The lake where Travis had first kissed me on my fourteenth birthday. *Mer-y, full of grace!* A kiss wet with the water, my prayers, and his mouth. *Mermaid, full of grace!* The first kiss and the last kiss. It wasn't supposed to be good-bye or even happy birthday, just *Thank you, God (of mermaids), Amen.*

· 11 ·

1983

GRANDMA LENA REQUIRED MY HELP with two weddings in one day. With the high season upon us, it was not uncommon for my grandmothers to be involved in as many as five weddings in one weekend. Nonna referred to the end of June as the first harvest. We started our work at ten o'clock on the last Saturday morning in June. The bride was fat and pink with eyes that blinked through heavy eye makeup. Her big white dress, ornamented with thousands of crystal beads, sparkled so brilliantly in the sunlight, I thought our efforts were doomed. Like photographing a snowstorm. I underestimated Grandma Lena's talents. She artfully arranged the peach bridesmaids in a cluster around the bride. The frightened, thin groom perspired heavily as he waited for his turn to pose. I smiled at him, but he didn't smile back.

"Don't worry," I said. "This is the worst part."

"Not by a long shot," he replied under his breath, as Nonna called him to get his picture taken.

After that, I said very little but handed out tissues and a few bobby pins.

The next wedding, one that also featured Nonna's cake, was more subdued—only one attendant apiece. We zipped through the pictures in no time at all. There was no long train for me to artfully arrange, and I had few names to call as Lena progressed to each new group shot.

"She was married twice before," I overheard the soloist explaining to the organist.

As a form of self-flagellation (what other reason could there be besides penance?), the bride had chosen to wear a beige suit. The wedding party didn't require anything from Lena's emergency kit, but at the reception, I gave the maid of honor a wintergreen candy anyway. It matched the roses in her bouquet and would do nothing but improve her breath after her repeated assaults on the crudités platter with ranch dip. Twice in the same day, I did the Hokey Pokey.

It had been a long day, and I was tired, but happy about the pay I received for my work. When we got home, Nonna was standing, hand on her hips, in the middle of the kitchen.

"That phone has been ringing since you left. That girl hasn't stopped calling here all day."

"Who?" I asked as if I didn't already know.

"Joyce Sewicky's girl. If she talks as much as her mother . . ." Nonna's voice trailed off and then surged again. "Well, you just better call her back, that's what."

I reached for the phone, but before I picked up the receiver, it rang.

"Hi, Karen."

"How did you know? Never mind. I have got to talk to you. Meet me at Kampmeier's in ten minutes."

I hung up the phone and shrugged at Nonna.

"Calling all afternoon for that?"

"She wants me to meet her at Kampmeier's," I said. Suddenly I did not feel quite so tired.

Nonna shook her head and handed me a five-dollar bill along with directives to be home before dark.

Kampmeier's had the best hot fudge sundaes in the world, or so their billboard claimed. They also had a ten-hole miniature golf course. I was hoping we were going for golfing and not because of the sundaes. The two wedding dinners, both with stuffed chicken breast and wedding cake, weighted my stomach as I pedaled my new bike to meet Karen.

"Please no ice cream. Please no ice cream," I moaned with the hum of my bicycle wheels.

As it turned out, we neither golfed nor ate ice cream. The place was overflowing with tourists in town for the annual Blue Lake Craft Show.

"Let's ride out to the Zechman's bridge," Karen said. It was a demand, not a suggestion.

Zechman's bridge was more of a balance beam than a thoroughfare. It was wide enough for only pedestrians or a single bike to pass. We parked our bikes and sat underneath on the cement supports.

"Okay," Karen began. "I want to ask Travis to come to the Red, White, and Blue Lake celebration with me."

"So."

"What do you think?" My approval was preordained. She didn't wait for my answer. "I have four tickets. My dad's on the committee. You can ask someone, too. We'll go on a double date. My parents won't let me do it if I don't double. Oh my God, he is so adorable. I will just die if he says no."

"I don't know anybody to ask." I really didn't.

"I thought of that. You can go with Ray, my brother's friend."

"Mushmouth Ray?" I had met him several times over at Karen's house, and I could never understand a word the guy said. He had a mouth full of orthodontic devices that spilled out onto his head and neck.

"He's quasi-cute, and he said he'd come with us."

"You just think he said he'd come with us."

Karen ignored my flippant remark. "It's all set. I just need one favor."

"What?"

"I need you to talk to Travis for me. Ask him to come with me."

"Why don't you ask him?"

"I can't let him think I am too interested. Please. For me? Make it sound like you need him to balance out our group."

To refuse was not an option. I had been chosen for the role of Karen Sewicky's best friend, but I had to defend the honor. That summer she made two requests of me, to be her emissary with Travis and to sneak her into Macy Killian's wedding and pig roast.

Macy Killian was a local celebrity. She had been Miss Pennsylvania 1980, and currently, though she read the weather on Z Rocks FM, she was applying for (and would most likely land) a similar assignment in the more conspicuous world of television. Her real name was Marcia, but she had changed it to Macy when she started doing pageants.

That request was still days away, but I had my present assignment. Karen made me double swear that I would ask Travis within twenty-four hours.

"I'll call you as soon as we get back from our church picnic around two o'clock," she said.

I didn't call to her attention that it was five hours shy of my twenty-four hour allotment.

· 12 ·

2000

BLUE LAKE RECEIVED ITS appellation as a result of miscommunication. There was nothing blue about it—not even a slight tint of azure or cerulean or any of those paint box hues. If you were naming the lake for its color, then perhaps you would have chosen Drab Lake or Lake Pewter, and then only if you were being kind. The original name was Brubaker Lake because Jacob Brubaker's farm butted up to the south side of the water. But in the 1920s, a surveyor with a bad right ear heard the name as Blue Acre Lake—a silly mix-up since the lake spanned almost five hundred acres. When the county map came out in 1923, the large body of water in Juniper Township was simply labeled Blue Lake.

And, as the name had evolved, so did the memory that I held of the lake. I remembered it as being bigger, more picturesque, and less noisy. A teenager zoomed by on a Jet Ski. *Who were all these people?*

For Sam it was all new and unspoiled by expectation. He was

enjoying his first experience on a boat. I took pictures of him wearing his orange life vest and green swimming trunks that came down past his knees. Together he and Travis steered the craft. I sat in the back, eating the wind as it blasted my face. Nothing about this place called to my senses, and that surprised me.

I closed my eyes and imagined I was under the surface of the water. I could see myself grown, thinner perhaps, but not in teenage proportions. My hair was waving like the surf, and air bubbles, those tiny gems, rose up from my mouth. Under the mirrored plane of the lake, I could dart around ancient fossils of fish and slide away from all time, simultaneously hiding and playing the seeker.

This lake was the place I had always conjured if I could not get to sleep, if my day kept rewinding and playing again. I'd shut off the redundant worries, mentally dive into the lake, and imagine hearing the sound of my exhalation as it bubbled underwater. It never failed to soothe me. But here I was gliding along the lake's surface, and it was not the place I thought it should be. For one thing, this lake brought anxiety instead of calm. It was more secret than solution. Bad memories surfaced after a decade's deceit. The real Blue Lake, not the one of my dreams, was subtle and mocking, with one memory in particular.

Nonna had been livid the evening of my fourteenth birthday when I had returned from these very waters with a small hickey on my neck.

"I'm old enough to kiss a boy."

"Not on my watch you aren't."

Unbeknownst to me, my mother had been waiting in the living room. She had been there for two hours. It had been a surprise. *Well, hello there, young lady.*

And Travis had just disappeared into the decades. I had watched the hickey fade from my neck as the people around me dissolved their relationships. Mothers, daughters, sisters, aunt.

With the moon and the bruise on my neck, the family I knew had waned.

But this was the present. The motor slowed. I opened my eyes. Travis stopped the boat so we could swim and get some lunch. Before the motor was silenced, Sam was already in the water. His vest allowed him to paddle around as if he could really tread water.

"Mom, watch me!" Sam thrashed himself around in a circle.

"Stay near the boat, Sam."

Travis handed me a life vest, but I refused it. I felt shy without knowing why, and I turned my back to remove my T-shirt.

"BJ, I never did tell you why I came over to the house the other day." Travis said.

I turned around. He had removed his shirt also and was standing before me in his navy swimming trunks. Travis was taller than Bryce, and more fit. Not noticeably so, but I could see a natural toil in Travis's arms that my husband had to buy from a gym. I hated myself for comparing the two men. These days, anybody standing next to Bryce would win favor, and I wanted Travis to earn his passage back into my realm, not gain it by default.

"Oh, I guess I just thought you were there to say hello." I adjusted the strap of my bathing suit, wishing I could also reposition my cleavage without being obvious.

"That, too. But the real reason is that when I was talking to Karen the other day at the greenhouse, she said that Anja had made a bequest to me in her will."

"She mentioned to me that there were a few small ones, but we didn't get specific. What did Nonna leave you, the John Deere?"

"Hardly." He laughed. "No, she left me the paintings."

"Paintings?"

"Her father's landscapes."

There it was. On the same day that I lost my place of calm, my lake oasis, I lost the family heirlooms that I most identified with my past and my destiny. I alone loved those paintings, and Nonna knew it. They were the reason that I went to art school. *I studied painting and metalsmithing, for Christ's sake. Why would Nonna give them all to Travis?* As far as I knew, Nonna and Lena had not spoken to nor heard from Travis in years, nor his mother Margot for that matter.

I didn't reply to Travis. Instead, I looked into the sheen of the water for my reflection. Nothing about the face I saw looked familiar. This mer-self contorted and laughed as my dry body remained sober. I dove into the image hoping to break her spell. But my anger accompanied me, like hot metal, forged and ready to be annealed. Or was it healed? I let all the air out of my lungs and sank down as far as I could. Into deep Blue. I had been wrong yet again. There was no God in this lake.

· 13 ·

1983

JUNE DAYS STRETCH FOREVER, but my ambition did not. When I did not see Travis all morning, I let the time slip casually by. After the busy day I had helping Grandma Lena, I was not eager to accomplish anything but my own agenda. Not that there was anything remotely important on my to-do list. I slept in until eleven and then spent the last sliver of morning writing long overdue letters to my friends at home. Toward midafternoon, my loitering turned into fear when I realized that my deadline was near. I needed to find Travis so I could honor my promise to Karen. I discovered him in a trickle of smoke behind my grandmothers' barn.

"Jesus, Barbara Jean, give a guy some warning." He was stubbing out a freshly lit cigarette in the wet grass. He had thought I was Lena.

"It's BJ," I said.

"What?"

"I am not going by Barbara Jean anymore. It's BJ."

"Sure. Whatever." He lit another cigarette. I picked up the discarded one on the ground—Virginia Slims, lifted from Margot's purse.

"You've come a long way, baby."

"Shut up," he said and handed me the lit cigarette.

I was not old enough to know that there was a choice associated with the offer. Of my working vocabulary, "gross me out" and "gag me" seemed inappropriate. I took the cigarette with my left hand and pressed it to my lips for a quick inhale. Don't cough. Don't cough. But it was pointless. I could no more repress the ensuing hacking than I could stop the grass from growing.

"Bar . . . er . . . BJ, are you okay?" Travis asked. He bent over to see my face.

I dropped the cigarette while I was trying to catch my breath. It rolled into a muddy spot near the spigot.

"That was my last one."

I glared at him.

"Tough shit," I said, still coughing.

"So why did you come out here anyway?" Travis asked. He was annoyed and didn't wait for my reply. "Are you going to help me with the garden? Lena wants me to hoe the rows."

The garden was huge, and the weeds were growing higher than the potatoes and bush beans that they separated.

"What's my take?" I knew he was getting paid.

"You already robbed me of two cigarettes."

"Big deal," I said.

"I'm not giving you any money. I'm saving to buy a car."

"Look, I need a favor . . ." I began.

"Oh," he said, looking suddenly amused. "This should be interesting."

He wasn't kidding. That favor cost me several more hours of unfettered summer—this time unpaid. I was angry that I had agreed to the labor when it should have been Karen, pulling weeds in my place. But some unnamed purpose drew me to the task. Beside me, Travis worked steadily in his pared down attire. His shirt lay crumpled next to our growing pile of weeds. Below the tanned orbs of his shoulders were white triangles of skin that seemed even whiter against the dark hair of his armpits. It was the lightest part of his body in my view. And I refused to think about the still whiter parts I couldn't see. I couldn't help but notice it when I lifted my neck. Little beads of sweat accumulated there on Travis's ivory patch of skin until they dripped down his side or onto the earth we were tilling. In the same physical region, I was having my own problem as my bra strap kept peeking out from my *Flashdance* slashed T-shirt. But Travis wasn't paying attention to me unless it was to bark more orders at my bent form. What did Karen see in him anyway?

The garden stretched before us. The tomato plants were starting to swell with new green fruits. I watched as Travis pinched back the plants at the fork in the boughs. Then he tied the new growth to the trellises that supported each plant. Had Lena taught him those tricks? When he looked up, I returned my focus to my own job. My tasks were more primal, hoeing the rows and cutting spiny weeds away from the soil's grip. Grunt work.

Sometime around five o'clock, Travis released me from my servitude.

"Come on, let's go," he said suddenly.

"Where?" I asked, though I was running after him without much care about his response. As soon as we turned the corner I had my unspoken answer—the lake. At that hour, most of the local beachgoers had gone home, and the weekend guests were already the subjects of the weekend traffic reports. The sun was volleying low-angled rays from the lake to our squinting eyes. We raced across the beach to a long wooden dock, from which we dove into the water fully clothed, as in a soft-drink commercial—shoes, shorts, and all.

"Oh, my pockets." Travis pulled out his nylon wallet with its sodden five-dollar bills and a half a pack of raspberry Bubble Yum.

"I am with you for three hours and I've ruined my cigarettes, my gum, and my money," he said.

"Your money isn't ruined, and neither is the gum." I reached out, grabbed the pack, unwrapped a piece of gum, and put it in my mouth.

"Yuck," Travis said.

I blew a big bubble right in his face.

Could it be? Could she really have feelings for Blaze Cunningham, the man who insulted her at every step, who abhorred her very presence? Angelina touched her lips, newly bruised with his angry kisses, and she knew it was true. She loved Blaze with every fiber of her being.

I had been waiting for love to be like it was in a Harlequin novel. I did not notice this other thing that had crept up on me. This unnamed longing to be in another person's presence even if it was just a friendly game of tag or a splash in the lake. When, years later, an arrogant future lawyer crashed into my life, I would count that experience as real, a love with substance, a romance with plot and the appropriate cast of characters. The feelings I had for Travis at age thirteen and three quarters did not even constitute a crush.

When I got home a half hour before dinnertime, Nonna had a stack of messages for me, all from Karen.

"When you call that girl back, tell her I can take a message. She doesn't need to keep calling," Nonna said.

I didn't even need to ask who "that girl" was this time. I knew.

"I'll tell her." I kissed Nonna's cheek. "I'm going out for a little."

"You just got back." But she waved her hands in the air, signaling her resignation.

"Just put some dinner back for me. I'll eat it later."

With the lake still in my hair and clothes, I rode my bike to Karen's house. I dashed up the stairs and opened the door to her bedroom. I was out of breath. Karen was sitting on her bed, painting her toenails when I arrived. Next to her sat a new Cabbage Patch doll, the latest bit of compensation Karen's parents had paid instead of their attention. It was an inanimate reminder of their love, complete with a pacifier and a birth certificate bearing the name Evan Randall. Karen looked from me to the phone on the bedside table and back to me.

"Well? Is he coming to the Fourth of July celebration?" she asked. Evan Randall, pacifier in his molded grip, smiled inarticulately from his pillow perch.

"Travis will be there," I said, fairly singing my answer.

· 14 ·

2000

Karen handed me the opened bottle and I waited a moment, just letting the cool, wet comfort of the glass exorcise the demon heat of summer from my skin. I was cranky from a day of working hard and accomplishing little. It seemed the only real achievement of the day had been to expand my growing list of things I still needed to do. Out of desperation for the absurd measure of the work at hand, I finished my list with, "Write a best-selling novel and find a cure for cancer." I would laugh about my limitations if I didn't feel so overwhelmed.

I tipped the brown bottle in my hand and watched the pale bubbles as they rose to meet my mouth. The sweetness shocked my senses with the hundred memories of this very taste. I nodded, as I savored the root beer, knowing that it had succeeded in giving me what nothing else had this summer—namely a moment of pure joy. For so many weeks I had begun each day with only two imperatives, to distract myself with work until bedtime and to put on a brave face for my son. I actually braced myself against these obligations at every sunrise. But now, standing on my lawn with friends, I had confirmation that I would not merely survive, but that I also had the ability to experience pleasure, even something as fleeting as a swallow of pop. I looked around, but everyone was blind to my epiphany. The moment passed, but I had noticed it.

Karen handed me another dripping bottle to pass to her husband. Shelly turned out to be a beefy man, somewhat defensive of his feminine sounding first name. When I asked if he'd rather be called by his surname, Ross, he had shrugged. "Ever since the show *Friends* came on the air, I've taken some ribbing about that name, too." I didn't know what he was like as a kid, but Shelly Ross, the man, looked like he could defend himself.

Sam and one of the new neighbor boys he had befriended came running at the sound of bottle tops popping. They had been promised root beer floats. Karen scooped vanilla ice cream into two frosty mugs. The root beer hissed as it hit the ice cream.

"I think I did this backwards," Karen said, mopping up the overflow.

"This is such a treat." I handed her some more napkins.

Karen nodded. "You aren't kidding. You should have seen the first batch Shelly tried to make." She licked her fingers. "It exploded all over the garage and my new red Audi. Do you know what soda does to a paint job?"

"I'm still paying for it." Shelly leaned over and kissed his wife. "Excuse us, BJ."

"Not a problem. Just pretend I'm not here." And I wasn't there. The problem wasn't confined to standing on the outside of a particular embrace. I was on the outside of all embraces. Sometimes I felt as though I were hovering over this plane of existence, waiting to float away in thought.

Only Sam kept me planted—while I read stories to him or tucked him into bed at night or watched him at play. He alone had the power to bring me back to the physical. Things would get better. My joy would increase as I became aware of it in the traces of my day. Was it Buddhism that placed such heavy emphasis on the power of the moment, the now? I would have made a poor Buddhist if I weren't already such a poor Catholic. Fellowship of friends—my only congregation. Communion with root beer—my only sacrament. But it was as much religion as I could tolerate at present.

Karen and Shelly stopped their display of affection, and Shelly looked up at the house.

"Good exterior. Paint is still good. It shouldn't be hard to sell. Do you mind if I look around inside?"

"Be my guest. Do you need a tour guide?"

"No, stay here with Karen. I'll be quick."

Karen waited until he was out of earshot until she spoke. "He's the top man at his agency. He'll be able to get it off your hands if that's really what you want."

I looked away at the two boys and Jules playing in the yard. I didn't know what I wanted. I had been here for two weeks, and I had barely cleared out any of the living areas. I had not even attempted to open any doors to the closets and the attic. My movements were slow and deliberate in this house, as if the memory of my grandmothers depended on it.

For today's exercise in futility, I had spent an entire eight hours going through a filing cabinet of wedding photos. They were a parade of brides, unabashedly easy to date in their frocks: the seventies gowns with their unfettered lines, the pillbox hats of the sixties, and the beaded decadence of the eighties. I could easily have chucked the whole piece of furniture out with the garbage, but I couldn't bear the thought of discarding all those memories. I was glad I didn't, because I came across an interesting find, more interesting even than the photos themselves. No, the real discovery had been in the organization of the photos.

Grandma Lena arranged her files alphabetically according to the groom's last name, but when I got to Z, I noticed that the files started all over again at A. I examined the second set of records more closely.

To my amusement, I discovered that Grandma Lena kept a separate file for those pairs who eventually divorced. And in the back, she even had a file marked "pending" for those couples in the heat of litigation. Those poor schleps: Grandma Lena had died almost ten years ago, leaving them to hang in marital purgatory. I wondered where in their lives they were now. Was reconciliation even possible these days, ever successful? Surely I could move them to the divorced file.

Grandma Lena did not have a wedding file on me; she had died a month before Bryce and I eloped. That same summer my mother had found the first lump in her breast. Looking back, I wonder if I should have sensed the omens of my mother and my adopted grandmother, but at the time, I didn't know that bad luck came in threes. And I certainly didn't know that Lena had a file of divorcees almost as thick as her file of married brides.

Lightning bugs started their phosphorescent mating rituals on the back lawn. It was the hour when the more cautious motorists turned on their headlights, and the cool of the earth rebounded hard into the graying air. Other, peskier insects joined the parade, and I lit a citronella candle in sad defense.

Sam came running up to us. "Do you have a jar for us to put our bugs in?" he asked.

"I think I have one by the sink. Watch the kids a second, Karen, I'll run in and get it and see if I have any more candles."

I stepped inside the house from the back door. My eyes took a second to adjust to the harsh artificial light, and I bumped into Shelly making notes in the kitchen.

"Oh, sorry," I said making my way to the sink.

The jar was sitting there, but it still had the smears of mayonnaise clinging to its side. I turned on the faucet and proceeded to rinse out the jar. I didn't realize I was humming until Shelly asked me a question.

"Maybe you can tell me. When was the electrical work last updated? Do you know off the top of your head?"

"Nonna had some work done after Lena died. Maybe 1992." I struggled to arrange the events and dates in my head. "Yes, it was definitely that year. We had just moved to Michigan, and I had come back out here to help her clear out the garden."

Shelly scribbled more notes.

"Was the plumbing done around the same time?"

"No, I think that was a few years earlier. I'll have to get back to you on that."

When I returned to the porch, I saw Sam directing his friend in the dark.

"It's right over there. Go get it."

Sam, afraid of flying insects, wasn't the one who wanted to catch the bugs. I should have guessed—but the neighbor boy wasn't complaining as he zigzagged to the next glowing target.

Karen motioned for me to join her on the porch swing. We sat under the blue wooden canopy of the porch and downed the remaining swigs of root beer. It should have been relaxing, but the air between us was taut with something undefined. I had known that Karen wanted to get me alone all evening. The beverage dispensing was just a ruse for whatever it was she had on her mind.

"Spit it out. You have something to say," I said, breaking the silence.

"How did you know I wanted . . . never mind. Look, you're right. I have something to tell you." She paused to arrange her words, but decided to pare her thoughts, stripping them naked of her usual sentimentality. "Bryce really wants out of the marriage. You should go to Michigan and sign." Karen didn't mince words. "I don't give that advice very often, but he is offering you one sweet deal."

"What if I decide to stay here? What about custody?"

"It would be trickier, of course, but I think Bryce is open for negotiations."

"Hmmm."

"Negotiation was never a big part of our marriage." *Especially in the last year.*

I could see that Karen was ready to take this conversation to the next level, but I turned away. I didn't feel like discussing my marriage tonight, with all the other questions on my mind. My courage came and went. I wanted to query Karen, but I didn't want the answers.

"What is it?" It was Karen's turn to ask. "Now *you* have that look on your face."

"It's nothing," I said.

"Tell me."

"It's not about the divorce."

"What then?"

"It's about Nonna."

Karen waited. A lightning bug landed on the railing and blinked. I thought back to the conversation I had with Travis on the boat. Travis had known I was upset, but he didn't try to soothe me or refuse the paintings. Maybe he was using them as leverage, but for what?

"Karen, you were there. What made Nonna bequeath her father's paintings to Travis?"

"Did Travis come to see you?" Karen asked.

"Yes. He hasn't taken the paintings yet. He wants to buy a house in the fall, so he's asked me to hold them for him. Did Nonna say anything to you?"

"She amended her will only recently. You might have grounds to contest the will, but she was pretty adamant when she came into my office that day." Karen paused, remembering. "She told me that she had just spoken to you earlier on the phone. I assumed she had discussed the changes with you and that you were okay with them."

"When was that exactly?" I didn't recall our ever discussing the paintings.

"I don't know. I'll have to go back and check my notes. I think it was early fall."

"About the time that Travis had come back into town." I spoke my thoughts aloud.

"I don't think she had contact with him, but she may have known."

"But why did she change her will?" I asked.

"I gathered that it was because of something you had told her in your phone conversation."

What had Nonna and I talked about last autumn? I could tell Nonna almost anything, though all of our recent conversations revolved around Sam.

With a creaky swing of the front screen door, Shelly made his presence known on the porch. "Are you girls having a heart-to-heart? I can come back later."

"No," I assured him, "come join us. What have you got for me?"

"Not much, yet, I'm afraid. I'll have to compare similar properties before I can finish my appraisal."

He tucked his notes into his back pocket and squeezed into the empty spot on the swing. The chain groaned under his weight, but none of us bothered to move. The night with its fireflies and fizzy root beer was too buoyant for body weight to be an issue.

Karen and Shelly left soon after they drained their bottles. They both promised to be in touch with various quotes, forms, and estimates. I had the nearly impossible task of ensnaring my son when it was bedtime. Sam would have sooner touched ten winged creatures than gone to bed. He fought my orders until his friend's mother appeared on a lighted porch two doors down and called, "Hayden, time to come home and take a bath."

"Hayden. That's what his name is," I said under my breath. Only terrible mothers did not know the names of their sons' playmates.

Capturing sleep proved to be much easier than capturing bugs for Sam. He was exhausted after a long day playing in the fresh air. My activities of the day had also been mentally and physically draining, but sleep evaded me. I wrestled with sheets as I tried to pin down my thoughts. My mind kept circling around the phone call I had with Nonna last fall. *What had we said to one another?* I tried to remember the sound of my grandmother's voice, but my brain faltered over the memory.

Around midnight, in that hazy realm near sleep, I had a realization that made me jump out of bed and run barefoot to the kitchen. I tiptoed over to the phone and hit the button marked *Announcement*. Nonna's gravelly voice greeted me immediately.

"The lady of the house isn't in, right at the moment, but if you leave a message, and I can figure out how to retrieve it, I will call you back."

I suppressed an audible cry, but the silent tears flowed nonetheless. *Her voice. Her words.* It had been Nonna's joke to call herself the lady of the house after Lena's death. While Lena was alive, neither of them could be the sole titleholder. Now that title belonged to me. I was the lady of the house—a house that was haunted by the voices I knew once and loved. I slid down the wall to sit on the cool linoleum of the kitchen floor. I missed Nonna and our connection. My friends could never understand my closeness to my grandmother. Other people had grandmothers they loved, but it wasn't the same. The generations didn't dilute our relationship like they had between my mom and me. Nonna and I were sister souls, able to communicate with a look. Perhaps that was the key to our last conversation. Maybe it was never what I said to her, but the inferences that Nonna made. She knew me too well.

"Nonna, I need some help with this one. You're going to have to guide me through all of this." My thin voice echoed in the dark kitchen.

Contemplatively, I looked up. In the hazy moonlight, distorted even more by my tears, the painting on the far wall took on a luminescence. It did not look cubist at all. Had I ever really studied this particular piece? The fragmented light of my tears gave the painting an impressionistic feel. I wiped my eyes to see clearly, but that painting retained its influence, more Monet than Braque. But something was amiss. The gentle hills and water didn't look European; they looked familiar and familial.

I had looked at the painting perhaps a thousand times, but never the way I saw it now. The water in the picture was blue, unabashedly so. Not like any blue found in nature, more like the blue of a promise. The painted sky was dark, save a hint of a light source. The stately hills divided the sky and water like a chaperone separating two lovers. But the division was incomplete; the blue of the water dotted the sky, and the water reflected the purpled night. Not even the hills could come between them.

I stood up and walked over. As if led by instinct, I easily took the picture down from the wall. Behind it, the kitchen wallpaper brightened in a square of print, unbleached by years of sunlight. I took the painting to the window and turned it over. Enough light passed from the moon that I was able to read the inscription. "Brubaker Lake, 1909. Marry me, Ada. All my love, Sid."

I touched the inky loops knowing I was guided to find these words. My fingers traced the *o* in the word love. Round and round, like a ring. Exactly like a ring.

· 15 ·

1983

THE DAY BEFORE A WEDDING always held a heightened sense of drama. On those occasions, I awoke to the delicate aroma of cake and the anticipation of a sinful breakfast confection. My favorite cake was red velvet, but it was a mixed blessing because I would have to listen to Nonna cursing in Greek as she tried to get the pale icings to cover the dark red color. She resorted to a crumb layer for those—an extra step that hid the traces of dark cake. The easiest cakes to frost were the yellow and lemon ones. White cakes were too dry and crumbly to ice smoothly. Usually Nonna could steer her brides to select the less demanding options if she enticed them with a lemon curd or chocolate mousse filling.

On July third, she had no such luck. The bride was the daughter of the mayor. In addition to ordering the darkest chocolate cake, the MOB (mother of bride) had made several other demands that would invoke all of Nonna's skill and artistry. The wedding and reception were to take place in the top floor of the old bank building. It had a view of the lake and the fireworks. Mrs. Edson wanted the cake to simulate the lake with the happy couple watching fireworks, a.k.a. sparklers, from a white chocolate candy bridge—all of this in the heat of July.

When I peered into the kitchen and saw cutouts of brown cake spread all over the breakfast bar and table, I thought twice before disturbing Nonna. Instead I sneaked out the front door and circled the house to find Grandma Lena who was already at work in her dewy gardens.

"Barbara Jean. You're still in your nightgown."

"So?"

"So, a young lady of your age and maturity should learn to be more modest."

Modesty wouldn't get me breakfast. I reached over and picked some blueberries from Grandma Lena's pail. She slapped my hand, which sent several berries to trail crimson juice down the front of my white cotton nightgown like a bloody handprint.

Grandma Lena touched my nightgown lightly where I had stained it. "Boiling water will take care of that. But don't touch my berries. Those are all I have, and Anja promised me a pie as soon as she is finished with that cake in there."

"You're not going to get a pie." I reached for another berry. "Nonna is calling for Zeus to ride again."

"Good morning, ladies." Mr. Kovack hailed us much too cheerily from the other side of the bushes.

"Good morning, George."

I hid behind the hedge, but he had already seen me. Grandma Lena nudged me.

"Good morning, Mr. Kovack."

He disappeared into the house with his paper, and I scurried, too. Modesty was suddenly in vogue.

· 16 ·

2000

"GOD, JUST GIVE ME a break from this life," I prayed aloud.

June had ended, and July had begun with friction and its usual companion, the heat. I had spent only one other July, a disastrous one, at the house on Mulberry Street. I tried not to let the memory darken my expectation.

Even if I had abandoned past evidence of gloom, the day had brought new cause for dread. The July sun had shown its face for a mere five hours when I found myself cursing at the towers of boxes in the living room.

What had I expected when I called Bryce? *Sure, honey, go right ahead and enroll Sam in the Pennsylvania school system. I don't mind if I rarely get to see my son. Call me in twelve years, and I'll come down for his graduation.*

I hadn't even been sure about making our move permanent. I wanted to cover all the bases—just in case. But now, I had shown all of my cards. Bryce, though, was holding trump, and it wasn't hearts. He would agree to my custody terms, if I came to

Michigan to sign papers, his papers, as soon as possible. And he wanted Sam for the rest of the summer.

"You can make this as ugly as you want to make it, Bobbi. Or we can be nice. The choice is yours."

Doing things his way. *Stupid! Why didn't I listen to Karen?* By calling Bryce today, I might have jeopardized any chance I had of the big monthly checks he had dangled before me only two weeks ago. It hurt my pride, but I was a realist. Without alimony from Bryce, I would have to seek employment outside of my art to make ends meet. And then I might not have time to do my metalwork. Bryce had hinted today that he even had the power to take away my last name in this battle. Was this the end for Bobbi Ellington Designs?

"You're the one who left, Bobbi. We lawyers call that desertion."

"I'm settling my grandmother's estate. Besides—even I've heard of no-fault divorce laws."

"I'm just saying, don't make me use my weapons. It wouldn't be a fair fight."

Lawyering aside, I was seasoned when it came to feuding with Bryce. We had begun our relationship with an argument. At the time, I had thought that sparring with words was a passionate pursuit, but what does any twenty-year-old know? Bang. Bryce had backed his red Miata into my college clunker. I was livid at the time, remembering the recent garage bill that sucked up the last two paychecks from my job at the dreaded twenty-four-hour copy center. Even then, I hadn't entirely covered the bill. I had emerged from the old Dodge in a heated cloud of patchouli. To this day, I remember what each of us was wearing. I had on my black denim mini and silver bangles halfway up both arms. Bryce wore the uniform of every recent college grad, a leather bomber jacket and khakis. His aviator glasses hid his flashing eyes when he proceeded to curse me for the accident as though it were my fault.

"Damn woman. Can't you get your boat out of the way?"

"You arrogant son of a bitch. What's the matter? Doesn't Daddy know you are driving his car? For the love of—"

"Don't go conjuring the goddess on me now, babe. I can spot a frustrated feminist a mile away."

"Hah! Not true! You just backed into one, you bastard."

At that, he had laughed. Not a nervous laugh of someone involved in fender bender, but a snicker.

"It's not that funny." I was still angry, but Bryce kept right on laughing until he could see in my face that I was having difficulty finding the humor.

"Look, I'm sorry. I shouldn't laugh," Bryce said when he caught his breath. "How about if we sort this all out over dinner. My treat. How about it, goddess?" he drawled.

I bowed to his naked charm. "The name is BJ, or if you are nice, you can call me Bobbi."

"Bobbi? You really do wish you were a man."

"Good try. What is your name? And are you insured?"

"Bryce Ellington and yes."

"Bryce." I spoke his name for the first time. "Well, it rhymes with *nice*."

Did I fall for the man or the dialog? His words had the all the rhythms I had come to expect in foreplay. I had read the script hundreds of time as a teenager. Conflict was the parent of true love.

Now it was the child. I could very easily trivialize my eleven-year relationship with Bryce. It might even help me cope with its loss.

The good times, Bryce's sensitivity, the family events weren't erased, but transformed. Sam was the embodiment of all of our small celebrations. In these first hours of an uncertain July, I took as many opportunities as I could to hug Sam, tussle his hair, draw him to me, smell the scent of grass and fruit punch mixing on his person. For soon, this goodness personified would be surrendered so I could move on with my life. I wasn't even sure it was a fair trade. I had never before spent one night apart from my son, and the first would equal forty. Forty days and forty nights.

The phone rang a second time, and I warily answered it. I should have been more heartened when I heard Travis's voice calling to invite us to the lake to see the fireworks.

"Do you realize that in all the years of visiting my grand-mothers, I never did get to go to the Red, White, and Blue Lake celebration," I mused aloud to Travis.

"Does that mean you'll go?"

"Sure."

But I wasn't sure in the least. Was I courting an old curse, or was this a new beginning? With only three weeks left until I had to deliver Sam back to Bryce, I wanted the time to be memo-rable. Sam would love watching the fireworks over the lake from Travis's boat, but I was still skeptical.

"We were supposed to watch the fireworks together once be-fore, weren't we?" Travis asked.

"We did watch them together."

"Yeah, I guess we did."

· 17 ·

1983

Nonna spent all morning baking enough cakes to sculpt Mount Rushmore. Grandma Lena and I contrived a quick trip to the lake to get out of Nonna's way. I wanted to get back soon to help her decorate, but the swim felt good. A local band was practicing on a nearby pier. It was the big headliner for the next day's festivities. I didn't recognize any of their songs except for a cover of "Celebration" by Kool and the Gang. All along the beach, flagpoles supported patriotic streamers. Closer to the concession stand, workmen assembled striped tents to house the sale of additional novelties.

What started as a quick dip for me turned into a floating nap for Lena. I let her catch a few winks because I knew she needed to relax before tomorrow's big day of work. It was two o'clock before we started to walk back home. We had only to turn the corner of Mulberry Street when we saw it, the blue and white police cruiser.

"Anja!" A worried expression crossed Grandma Lena's face, and we quickened our gait as much as possible.

I ran ahead and rushed through the front door, which surprised the people inside. Lena stepped in behind me. Officer Frank Pettyjohn and Carole Muscavitch sat in the living room with Nonna. She had removed her apron. I had never met Officer Pettyjohn before that day, but I knew Mrs. Muscavitch. Her mother, Mrs. Bomberger, was a founding member of the card club. They all rose to their feet when we entered.

"Lena, you know Ted and Carole. This is Barbara Jean, my granddaughter. She prefers to be called BJ these days."

"I am sorry about this, Lena," Carole said. She was familiar with this house and the living room. Carole had been a June bride in 1979. Three-tier lemon cake. Some black and white photographs as well as color, with additional shots taken in the garden. She and her mother, Mrs. Bomberger, had gushed over those pictures, Carole smiling in every one. But today Carole wore no such expression. She was here as a social worker, not client or welcome guest.

"What is this all about?" Lena looked from Nonna to Carole.

"We've had a complaint," Officer Pettyjohn started.

"Oh, for the love of heaven," Grandma Lena said.

Nonna nodded. We could guess what was coming.

"What is George up to now?"

Carole Muscavitch spoke up. "I'm afraid our source is claiming that he has twice witnessed sexual abuse of a minor in your care."

The room fell silent. Nobody knew whether to laugh or scream.

"I'm the minor?" I asked.

"Yes," Officer Pettyjohn answered.

"But it's a mistake. I'm not being abused," I said.

Carole Muscavitch stepped forward and touched my shoulder lightly. She had the same red hair as her mother, only Carole's was pulled off her face in a tight ponytail.

"We take these complaints very seriously. We have to. Our policy is to move the minor to a neutral location to interview her. Her parents or guardians can be nearby, but not in the same room." She looked at Nonna when she spoke.

"This is a load of bull," Nonna said. "Have some lemonade, take her into the garden, and get this over with."

"We have to take her off site. I'm sorry, Mrs. Graybill. I don't want to take up any more of your Sunday than I have to. You can follow in your car if you wish."

"Am I going to the police station for questioning?" Episodes of *Hill Street Blues* flashed through my mind.

"No, we can use my office," Carole said. "I am sorry about this, really I am. I can see we don't have an incident here, but if I don't follow procedure, Mr. Ko— er, our source can make more threats and get my supervisor out here. I want to make sure this matter gets closed without further inquiry."

Grandma Lena remained quiet. Her rage was masked in a terrible calm, a resignation almost. I ran to her and gave her a hug and kiss.

"Don't worry. I won't tell them how you almost drowned me when I was eight," I joked.

She didn't smile. I hugged her again and went to change out of my bathing suit.

As I was climbing the stairs, I heard Carole tell Grandma Lena, "Think of the greater good. Children need this voice. This time, BJ will show us a loving family. My job isn't always like this."

Grandma Lena conceded with a small, "You're so right," before excusing herself to get dressed.

· 18 ·

2000

"You're dead! I'm not dead. But you are. Bang!"

"Sam, what are you doing?" I wheeled around to face my son.

"Playing army man like you told me."

Sam huddled in a corner of the hot attic with his green figures spread all over an old trunk. He had divided up the army men and lined them in formation, ready for battle. I abandoned my job of sorting some old camping equipment to inspect the scene and look for clues. Since the separation, I had been searching for the signs that the divorce was going to mess up my kid. Each day I braced myself for acts of aggression that never came.

Now I had proof, or did I? How was he supposed to play with his army men? They couldn't go on endless reconnaissance missions.

I folded a musty tarp. Most of this stuff had to be thrown away. A few of the items, old mess kits and lanterns, might sell well at the auction. I added them to the pile for the barn. Phillip's Auction House was coming soon to remove the items for sale.

I felt very fortunate that Nonna had the foresight to clean most of the attic out herself. The annual Mulberry Street yard sale had helped. I had to contend only with a small reserve: a heap of old camping equipment, a foldaway bed, tennis rackets, ice skates in various sizes, tax records since 1985, a lamp, an old trunk, a faded rug, and two working fans.

I put the fans to the test immediately. Their crosscurrent made cleaning the attic a slightly unbearable task instead of a fiendish one, but I didn't have the luxury of waiting for cooler weather. The owner of the auction house, Phillip himself, was coming in two weeks to haul away the growing piles of unwanted belongings. However easy it had been to get sentimental over the items, the sheer bulk of it all put an end to the romance. I became rather indiscriminate about what I was willing to part with.

This was one of the last places I had to clear. I had never come up here as a child: the attic wasn't forbidden, just uninviting. My grandmas had more exciting things to play with in their closets. Collections of hats from all periods, glittering costume jewelry, and movie magazines from the 1940s. Those were the things that would be worth money today, but they had been the first to be sacrificed to the Saturday morning yard sale queens. The early-bird collectors had scooped them up. They came with their quibbles and change purses an hour before the sale opened, and they left with their trophies.

I propped the window open for ventilation. From the small breach, I could look out over the entire rear of the property: the barn, the gardens, and the gnarled apple tree. It was a beautiful view, and one I had never seen before. Looking into the yard, I could almost imagine myself, at various ages, playing out the scenes of my life. Six years old: picking apples from the ground as Grandma Lena picked them from the branches. Ten years old: playing flashlight tag with the neighbor children in autumn's early dusk. And nearly fourteen years old: watching fireworks with Travis from the roof of the barn. All of these events were happening simultaneously, yet independently of one another. I suppressed a wave. I wanted to signal all my former selves. I wanted to shout at them, "I'm all right! I turned out okay." But I didn't. I wasn't sure it was the truth anyway. Those BJs and Barbara Jeans were busy with their own circumstances. What was so important about those deep days of childhood? I felt the need to remember—really remember.

"Knock, knock," Sam said, returning me from my vision.

I turned to give him my full attention. "Who's there?"

"Soldier."

"Soldier who?"

"Sold your ox. Sold your mare. Sold your grandma's underwear."

"Where did you hear that?"

"Hayden. He tells funny 'knock, knock' jokes."

"Yes, very funny," I said. My voice was as dry as the hot attic air.

"Are you soon done up here? I'm thirsty."

"Yes. We can stop for today." I wiped the hair off my face and mentally noted where I should begin again after the holiday.

"Um, Mom."

"Yes, bud?"

"One of my army men accidentally got into the trunk."

"Accidentally, huh?"

The hole where the lock had been was just the size for an army man looking to go AWOL. I tried to simply lift the top of the trunk, but it was wedged. Then I grabbed a hammer that had been stored with the tent stakes, and with a prying motion I was able to raise the lid. Light as it was, I had thought the trunk was empty, but Sam jumped when I opened it.

"Yikes! A skeleton."

"Sam, settle down." I looked, too, and at the first glance of the trunk's contents, even I had a start. The trunk contained an old wedding dress. It did look human or mummylike in a benign sort of way, and I could see where Sam made the association. Blue tissue paper filled out the bodice of the dress to help it keep its form and prevent discoloration. The paper must have worked; the satin fabric shone a luster of milk or bone, not a true white, but not yellowed.

With one hand on the hollow of my chest, I reached down with the other to touch the dress. It did not feel brittle with age, but supple and eternal. I was almost afraid to break the spell it had on time. Gingerly, I pulled the dress from its slumber. The skirt's folds fell in puddles in my lap. The satin caught coolly on my slightly stubbled thighs. The dress smelled fragrant, unlike the open mustiness of the attic. I breathed in the faint scent of lavender.

"It's got to be a million years old or something." Sam's eyes brightly reflected the dress. Twin ghosts danced on his gray irises.

I fingered the cuff and the four fabric covered buttons. They were knuckles, these buttons, four white knuckles.

"It can't be Nonna's. She eloped," I considered out loud.

"Look. My army man!" Along with his toy, Sam pulled out a piece of paper.

I grabbed at the paper. It was a typed receipt from Veronica's Boutique, dated January 1942. I studied it carefully.

This didn't make sense. Nonna eloped days after the attack on Pearl Harbor in 1941. Did she have a second, formal ceremony later? Where were the pictures? I turned the receipt over.

In small script, at the top, was scrawled the name *Lefever.*

· 19 ·

1983

"WHAT IS YOUR RELATIONSHIP with Lena Lefever?" Carole Muscavitch asked.

"She is my fictive grandmother."

"Your what?"

"*Fictive.* That's what you call someone who is a close family friend but not really related to you." I had learned that definition in my fourth-grade family heritage unit. The two words I had absorbed from that lesson had been *fictive* and *lesbian.* I was determined not to use the latter word in front of Carole.

"And you are staying with Anja Graybill and Lena Lefever for the summer."

"Yes. I live near Richmond, Virginia, with my parents Judy and Richard Foley, but I am here until August fifteenth."

Carole struggled to write down the information in the spaces provided. I slurped the remainder of my milkshake.

I had enjoyed my first ride in a police cruiser. My only request was something to eat. I was past hungry and was halfway to irritable when Officer Pettyjohn pulled into the drive-through at McDonald's. I didn't even care if I had made it look like my grandmothers were starving me.

"Do they have those new Chicken McNuggets here in Pennsylvania?"

"No," answered Officer Pettyjohn. He seemed well acquainted with the menu.

"We have them in Virginia. I like the sweet and sour sauce."

"Can you pick something else?" Carole asked. She was sitting up front with Officer Pettyjohn; I was in the cage for felons in the backseat.

"I'll have a cheeseburger, small fries, and a chocolate shake," I said.

Officer Pettyjohn sheepishly added a Big Mac and a Coke to my order. He looked questioningly at Carole who shook her head. I turned to look out the back window. My grandmothers had parked their car. I was sure this detour had them rattled. Nonna caught sight of me. I waved and gave them the thumbs-up.

McDonald's didn't charge us for the meal. The manager came to the window and smiled contractually at Officer Pettyjohn. From the backseat, I gave the drive-through attendant my best criminal glare as if I was going to hunt her down and behead her children as soon as I escaped the juvenile detention center.

Carole's office was a block away from the police station in one of the long row of brick homes. A wooden plaque beside the door said JUNIPER TOWNSHIP SOCIAL SERVICES in straight black letters. Being the weekend, Carole had to unlock the place and turn on some of the lights. The waiting room was standard-issue paneling adorned with paintings of wooded scenes. Nonna and Lena folded their rumps into two of the molded chairs. The polyester of their pants and the plastic of the chairs embraced like old friends, graduates of the same nonbiodegradable academy. An ancient cabinet TV with rabbit ears sat in one corner. Nonna tuned into a movie classic from the thirties—something with Grace Kelly. Grandma Lena groused, but the saga soon captured her attention.

"Take your time, BJ. I haven't seen this one." Nonna gave me a wink. It was a lie; there wasn't a movie she hadn't seen. She was putting on a show for Grandma Lena's sake. This was no big deal. Nonna acted like I was going upstairs for a piano lesson.

Carole Muscavitch's office was not what I expected. Pieces of primitive art lined her bookshelves and windowsill. Carved figurines of hunched women with long, nodding breasts guarded her important papers while wooden dolls in loincloths stood as centurions on either end of her professional journals. Tribal masks flanked Carole's college diploma.

"Were you in Africa or somewhere?" I asked.

"Yes. I was in the Peace Corps. That's where I met my husband."

Mrs. Bomberger had bragged that her son-in-law was a state lobbyist for environmental causes. She had called the two of them "the last two hippies on the face of the earth." They were building a solar-powered house in Ranklersville.

"Okay now." Carole had finally caught up in her paperwork. "Anja Graybill is your maternal grandmother."

"Right."

"What words would you use to characterize your relationship with Miss Lefever."

"Grandma Lena? She is my grandma."

Carole gestured for more.

"She's my mentor, my swim instructor, and my pinochle partner." I added the last part as a reference to Carole's mother.

"Do you have regular periods?" Carole asked casually. *Whoa! I didn't see that one coming.* The statue with dangling breasts kept her strange vigil.

"Yes." I pulled my shoulders back—a show of my own breasts, in case she questioned my answer.

"How long have you had them?"

"My periods?" *Or my breasts?*

"Yes." She meant my periods.

"For about a year," I lied. Seven months, really. The statue knew I was stretching the truth.

"Do you ever discuss your period with your Grandma Lena?"

"Only when I run out of maxi pads."

"Are you having your period now?"

"No!" I jumped up, but I sat back down, slowly. "Do I need to talk about this?"

"I'm sorry if this is making you uncomfortable. I'll move on." Carole studied her notes. "Can you describe the event that took place in your grandmother's backyard this morning?"

"I was outside talking to Grandma Lena. She was picking blueberries, and I was eating them."

"What were you wearing?"

I rolled my eyes. "My nightgown. I hadn't gotten dressed yet."

"Why were you outside in your nightgown?"

"I told you. I didn't get dressed yet."

"Weren't you worried about your neighbors seeing you?" For somebody with half naked figurines all over, Carole's line of questioning was bordering on sanctimonious.

"I hadn't thought about it. I just wanted to say hello to Grandma Lena and eat some blueberries."

"Did Lena touch you while you were in your nightgown."

"I spilled blueberries and got blueberry juice on myself. She checked out the stain. She might have touched the nightgown, but not me."

"So that was a blueberry stain on your nightgown, not blood?"

"That is correct."

"Did Lena touch you in any other way."

"No."

"Has she ever touched you in an inappropriate way?"

"Does changing my diaper as a baby count?"

Carole was not amused.

"No, she has never touched me like that. We hug and kiss, but nothing funny."

"We also got a report that Mr. Kovack heard you yelling to Lena in the yard last week. Do you remember the incident?"

"Grandma Lena was braiding my hair." I made each syllable into a staccato punch.

"That's it?"

"Yes."

"He claims you were yelling loudly."

"It hurt." I crossed my arms in front of me.

"Did you ask Lena to braid your hair?"

"Yes. *Seventeen* magazine, page eighty-three, 'The New Braids.' Number two: the fishtail. You can check it out for yourself."

The phone rang. Carole excused herself and went over to her desk. I slid closer to the open file folder on the couch. "Stop it. Get your hands off of me, you perv." The statement jumped out at me from the typed page. Somebody needed to hurt that small man, Mr. Kovack. Me. I pictured a wayward explosive finding his house on the Fourth of July. If only I'd had the foresight to import the contraband to Pennsylvania when I came in June. You couldn't buy any of the really good stuff here.

Carole hung up the phone. I took a sudden interest in the handwoven shawl that was draped artfully over the back of the couch. The folder remained open.

"Sorry about that. That was my boss. He has another case he wants me to see before the holiday." She crossed to pick up her notes. "I think I have enough here to exonerate Miss Lefever of any molestation charges."

Too late. Mr. Kovack got what he wanted just as if he himself had locked my grandmothers in the town stockade.

"Your grandmothers can drive you home."

It was after four by the time we left Carole's office. Nobody wanted to talk much. Grandma Lena turned on the radio, and we listened to the lament of a country song, which felt tame compared to our personal injustice.

We could not guess how the day could possibly get worse, but it did. In her haste to follow the police car, Nonna had neglected to close the kitchen door. All three cats found their way to the kitchen to dart among the cooling cake pieces, occasionally fighting over them. By the time we walked through the back door, Greystoke, Chaz, and Octavia slithered guiltily around a confetti of dark cake crumbs. The only cake left in its original location held the dainty impressions of paw prints.

Nonna was close to tears. Grandma Lena and I rushed to comfort her.

"Let's forget this mess," Grandma Lena said. "Barbara Jean and I will clean it up tonight. Tomorrow you can start fresh, and we will both help you. The reception doesn't start until eight o'clock."

"Yeah, Nonna. We can do it."

"We've all had a long day. How about we forget all of this for now and go to Red Lobster."

Nonna dried her eyes and laughed. "I love you girls." She kissed me on the forehead and Grandma Lena on the lips. The kiss was more solid than passionate, but I still looked away.

That night, we traded our group hug in for plastic lobster bibs. We traded in our neighborhood animosity for claw crackers and metal picks. We probed those poor lobsters and luxuriated in the taste of displaced aggression. As we dined, I watched my grandmothers. They did not talk about what had happened. The lines of their faces showed me that they had traversed that kind of hardship before. And I saw what it did to them: it toughened them in places and softened them in others. Their cheeks unfolded like old roses, although their jaws remained planed with the diamond angles of a trellis. Great crescents of skin hung from the back of their arms, but their shoulders refused to tilt into the posture of defeat. Bigotry had summoned gravity to their flesh, but my grandmothers had good bones.

Grandma Lena was slightly thinner than Nonna, yet they matched, like couples should who had been together for a long time. Mates. Their relationship was not sanctioned, overlooked by some of their friends, perhaps, but not publicly condoned. And yet all of this adversity had soldered them together with a seam stronger than the parts it was binding.

I wanted a love like that, but I didn't think I could endure what it took to forge such a union. It was a quality I would see one day in my parents' marriage, but only after doctors and diseases supplied the blows. *Easy love*—maybe there was no such thing. It was an oxymoron like *bittersweet* or *jumbo shrimp*.

· 20 ·

2000

SIX MINUTES. That was exactly the amount of time it took for the sun to slip entirely from view once its bottom edge grazed the zenith of hill behind the lake. The anticipation of fireworks, a celebration that requires darkness, seemed to stretch the sun's descent tenfold. Six minutes became an hour. I draped my sweatshirt over Sam who was sleeping on the front seat of Travis's boat. His nap was the inevitable result of many hours of water sports and sunshine. Sam not only frolicked on an inner tube, but he also helped Travis steer the boat as I made a fool of myself on water skis, my first ever attempt at such a folly.

Now with Sam asleep, the absence of his chatter hollowed out the evening, even though the noise of the nearby party seemed inescapable. This emptiness echoed the feeling I had after I took Jules to the vet to be kenneled for the night. How lonely the house seemed without his vigilant barking, but I had no choice. He had to be tranquilized every Fourth of July after his first, a nearly epileptic encounter.

In contrast to Sam's inertia, I experienced dusk in the form of jittery anticipation. And now I felt the need to be sedated. Being alone with Travis didn't make me nervous so much as it filled me with awareness. And awareness was not something I wanted to feel while the nouns *death* and *divorce* were seeking present tense verbs. I reached for some of the prohibited wine that I had disguised in a thermos.

"Want some?" I offered Travis a plastic cup.

"No, I'm driving," he answered. He was so relaxed out here on the lake. The anesthetizing effect of alcohol would have been wasted on him. For the first time I realized why he had chosen the boat over the business in the divorce settlement, and I wished that I, too, had a token, some souvenir of solace to take away from my marriage.

But all I had was a thermos of cheap wine. I was tempted to chug my cabernet to get to the awaited buzz, but I was already exposed. I had told Travis more than I should have in the early afternoon, while Sam was busy playing in the gravelly sand. I couldn't help it; of all the men I had known (not an extensive survey, by any means), Travis had always projected a vulnerability, a poignancy that reeled me in more than a swagger ever could. Call it my personal kryptonite, or even better, call it my phenobarbital, because my truths had overflowed in its presence.

"I can tell you the first night Bryce cheated on me, though I wouldn't admit it to myself at the time. He had gone to a party without me. It was some sort of business function. And when he came home—it wasn't like I smelled perfume on him—he was just different somehow. He started to blame me for all kinds of things, including letting him go to the party alone. Like it was my fault he had strayed."

"That sounds familiar."

"Did Elizabeth cheat on you?"

"No, she blamed me for things."

"What things?"

"Oh, not the real issues. She found fault with my work, my ideas for the business. It seemed to center more around my inadequacies as a business partner than as a husband, but it was really the husband part she had issues with."

"Was it difficult being in business with your wife? I've heard people say it can be too much togetherness."

"No. Togetherness just accelerates the inevitable. In the beginning, it was great. Liz had been traveling too much with her sales job. I hardly got to see her. So one summer she announced she was going to quit, and she did. She just started showing up at my job sites. I did landscaping in the summer, even when I was teaching." Travis paused as if he were caught in the web of the memory.

"Anyway, she'd bring these elaborate picnic lunches, but I couldn't just stop what I was doing, so she'd pick up a spade or some clippers and work right alongside of me. I think some of the best times in our marriage were when we were working together side by side. We'd dream and make plans. We fed off of each other's enthusiasm. That's why the decision to quit teaching and go into landscaping full-time was so easy to make."

That conversation had ended there without an awkward pause. I considered what Travis had said. I couldn't imagine Bryce and myself ever working together at the same job. At times it seemed we hardly inhabited in the same house. I had crumpled the wax paper that had held my sandwich. Travis had interpreted the signal for what it was: my reluctance to delve deeper into this topic. We finished our lunch, gathered the sand toys, and launched the boat. The energy of our confessions circled us the remainder of the afternoon. Even now, on the cusp of fireworks, that energy was expanding.

"How is Margot doing?" I asked, sipping my wine.

"Believe it or not, she's getting married. Maybe third time's the charm."

"Really? I missed a marriage in there somewhere."

"You didn't miss much. I hardly knew number two, but Ken's a nice guy, a few years younger than she is. She moved to North Carolina to be with him. He's a professor down there."

"Where?"

"Murfreesboro. Are you familiar with it?"

"Chowan College, sure, it's not too far from Richmond. I had a high school friend who went there. Too bad Mom's not still alive, they could have . . ." I could feel my voice splintering. For a second there was an expectant void, then the sound of a fire-cracker cut through the calm, and a chill ascended my spine.

Words unspoken—questions, never posed—hung in the air with the achy, gray smell of gunpowder. It wasn't that my mother was dead, but the other—the bigger silence. Longer. And all at once, I let it go to join the smells of festivity, the ripple of white water, and the dreams of a small sleeping child.

"Travis. I need to ask this. I don't want you to think I'm stupid, but I really don't know. What happened with Lena and your mom?" And the question I didn't ask, *Why didn't I ever hear from you again?*

Travis eyed the setting sun. He seemed jealous of its easy departure. "God, I don't know. I thought you might be able to tell me. There was some kind of fight over Granddad's funeral. I know that."

The splash of water and kids having one last swim sounded into the twilight. As noises, they fused and emptied the air like silence. Travis looked at me. He knew what I was really asking him.

"BJ, I wanted to call you." He stroked his beard, and then turned away. "Mom had forbidden me to talk to you after she had her fight with Lena, and it tore me up. I can't tell you. I mean, normally a kid of sixteen doesn't listen to his mom, but you should've seen her. I was so worried about her." He paused.

"Hell, you know her history. I didn't want her to try anything. I felt so protective of her after Granddad was gone. We were all each other had after that. Even now I worry. I shouldn't. She has her own life, but all along I've felt like I was the parent and she was the child."

"The fight between her and Grandma Lena didn't have to do with me, with us? Did it?"

"No. It was about Granddad. Something Lena said about him, or maybe that she wouldn't go to the funeral. Something that Mom couldn't forgive. You and I were just the victims of it all."

All of the tacit questions that separated us now had commonality. Neither of us knew what transpired between Lena and Margot, but we shared the ignorance.

"What would Margot say now, about you running into me? About us spending time together? Have you told her?" I asked.

"I told her. She changes the subject when I mention other women. I think she is still holding onto the convoluted hope that Liz and I will get back together and give her grandchildren."

"Ah! The scourge of being an only child. I felt it, too, but I obliged my mother." I looked at my sleeping son. The gold eked its way back into his hair after it had dried. He was so peaceful.

"Oh, I wanted to oblige my mother. Nothing would have made me happier, but it wasn't a possibility. I have a ridiculously low sperm count."

"Oh, Travis, I'm sorry. I shouldn't have said — "

"It's okay. I have come to terms with it a long time ago. I just never told Mom. She shouldn't give up her dream. Besides it's not like I don't have any swimmers. They're just a proud and select few." Travis straightened his posture as if to restore something that was bent inside of him. I wasn't uncomfortable around him after his admission. Quite the opposite. I felt folded into his confidence.

I smiled. "That's the thing I am the proudest of. That Mom got to be with me and Bryce when Sam was born. She was in the room with us. I am so glad I made her a grandma before she died."

It wasn't the time to cry, but the wine and the breeze opened me to my easy tears. I didn't try to hide them. If Travis continued to hang out with us, he'd see the waterworks before too long. Across the lake, the sun had finally set, though its light still left a queer tint in the sky above the hills. I looked at the water for comfort. It was blue, the unnatural hue found only in a paint box. Not flag blue or blueberry blue. It was Sid Stevens blue. Blue Lake blue.

The first of the fireworks erupted over the northwest shore. Travis began to nudge Sam awake in the front seat. The loud sounds had done the job for him. Sam sat straight up with a "Wow." I dried my eyes, determining not to make this Fourth of July as tearful as the last one I had spent with Travis, all those years ago.

Travis winked at me; Sam sat on his lap. It was perhaps the third time Sam had witnessed fireworks in his short life. Each time the rockets spat into the air—red, green, gold—they illuminated the wonder on his young face. Red wonder. Green wonder. Gold wonder. The lake, swallowing its blue, reflected this new spectrum. A triple showcase: in the sky, on the water, on Sam's face.

I faced away from the display, watching the fireworks only as they bounced off my son. Travis smiled at me and at the well-being of the child on his lap. Cheers resounded from a nearby boat.

The slow awakening. I began to feel a delicate tug at my loins, almost imperceptible at first. The sensation was so distant I hardly recognized the symptom of my own longings. The floating boat nodded us: my son, a man from my past, and me. My thighs shivered in return, and I could not deny what I felt. Sexual awareness I thought had expired, now steadied and bloomed. A faint pulse inside. I wanted to wrap my arms (and legs) around Travis and conquer death. I had begun the month of July by praying for some relief from my life, but now I pleaded with the universe for a resurrection.

· 21 ·

1983

FOR MY PENANCE I had to give Karen my favorite bottle of platinum nail polish, help her spy on Travis the next time he did yardwork, and get her into Macy Killian's upcoming nuptials.

"I can't believe I had to go to the Blue Lake celebration alone with Ray. It was like I was one step away from dating my brother. It was so gross. I think he wanted to kiss me. He even took off his headgear while we were watching fireworks."

I let her prattle on before I reminded her that it was a deathwatch and a police action that had kept Travis and me from the event. What I didn't tell her was that after I had helped Nonna with the cake and Grandma Lena with the photographs, I had gone home and watched the fireworks from the roof of our barn. And even more damning was the fact that I had done it with Travis.

"BJ, we have got to buy new outfits for Macy's wedding. What do you wear to a pig roast? I know. We could ride our bikes to Aaron's to go shopping. Mom said they are having summer clearance."

"Summer clearance? It's only July fifth." But I knew I would have to do anything Karen said, at least until she forgot the way I ditched her to help out my grandmas.

That afternoon, with the eighty dollars I had earned as an apprentice, I pedaled with Karen to Aaron's. To call the clientele snobbish would have left no room to label the women who worked there. With one contemptuous eyebrow raised, the saleswoman asked us if we were lost. Karen brushed her aside and headed for the juniors department.

"I hope Kendall is here. She is the one who waited on us when Mom and I came here shopping for bathing suits last month."

Kendall was there, but Doris got to us first. She showed us to the rack of summer dresses that were marked 25 percent off. I gulped as I fingered the four twenty-dollar bills in my pocket. Nothing on the hangers was going to leave me any change. I would have to skimp on school clothes, but I couldn't quite bring myself to tell that to Karen. Her mother had a running account at this store.

Karen selected a linen jacket in a sophisticated salmon color with matching pin-striped pants. Doris accessorized the outfit with a matching necklace of sculpted wooden beads.

"These are the latest pieces by Cairo, a jewelry designer from New York. We can't seem to keep her work in our store."

Doris need not have wasted her sales rhetoric on Karen.

"Cool."

I decided on a pair of drop earrings that were on sale and approached the cash register with my weak claim that nothing fit me very well. I wasn't ashamed of the clothing I already had to wear, but I was embarrassed and a bit jealous of Karen's access to funds.

I was dying to tell Karen about Monday night. I didn't, and I had to be satisfied knowing that her envy would eclipse mine if she knew all that had transpired.

My grandmothers had stayed to enjoy the wedding reception. They had earned some fun after the day they had. I was so tired after baking and assembling and smiling, that I begged them to allow me to walk home while it was still light outside.

The sky was dark by the time I got to the front door, but the streetlights illuminated the sidewalks for the final two blocks. I began to hear the rumblings of the celebration by the lake, though the apple tree was blocking the view from the porch. When the sky lit up from the first explosion, I noticed the ladder beside the open barn door. Was somebody there?

I should have been more afraid, considering the animosity in the neighborhood, but I wasn't.

"Who's up there?" I called.

"Go away, BJ." It was Travis, but his voice was funny—hollow almost.

I didn't listen to him. Instead I climbed the ladder without my usual fear of heights. Travis sat huddled on the lower roof above the garage doors. He was crying. I didn't know what to do; I was already at the top of the ladder. To climb down would have seemed insensitive.

"I'm sorry, Travis. Is it your granddad? Did he . . ."

"No. He's still alive. I just wanted to get away from everybody. This seemed like a good place."

I crawled over to join him. I was still wearing my dress from the wedding. My nylons, which had seen their last party, were wadded up in my pocket, and my shoes hung by their heels on the top ladder rung. I didn't say anything for the longest time. Travis tried to hold his tears back, but he succeeded only in a few dry convulsions. When I put my arms around him, he sank into my lap.

The first of the fireworks lit up the sky. We could see only the highest, most spectacular explosions. I waited for the rests between displays.

"How is he?" I smoothed his hair with my fingertips. The dark curls rebounded.

"They called Mom and me to the hospital at two a.m. His breathing and heart rate were all screwed up. They thought it was the end." His voice was ragged. Travis sniffed, and the phlegm gurgled in his throat. "We got there, and he was sleeping. Then this morning, he woke up, and he talked to me like he hasn't talked to me in months. We had an actual conversation."

"Did he know who you were?"

The fireworks lit up the night again and muffled Travis's answer. I could feel the "Yes, he knew" as I stroked his temple. When I was in Virginia, I had kissed Jimmy at the last school dance, but somehow this felt more intimate.

More fireworks erupted. I didn't know what else to say. Travis's breathing quieted, and I assumed he was watching the sky from between the folds in my skirt. I watched them, too, and wondered if across town the newlyweds were looking out the window atop the bank building. I could picture Nonna and Lena standing side by side, not touching, but wanting to. The newlyweds would kiss and cut the cake. The cake was our hardship, not theirs.

But we shared the same fireworks. Travis and I watched without speaking until the sky resembled ashes and diamonds on velvet. The wind blew exactly right, and I could smell the fire, the water, and the earth all at once. Travis sat up. My skirt had a damp divot where his head had rested.

"Are you okay? We can talk about it some more if you want," I said.

"I'm done talking. Sick of it. God, BJ, I am a terrible grandson. I wish he would just die already. I didn't want to talk to him about the Phillies' chances this year or what I'm going to do when I graduate."

"But it might have been the last time you'll get to speak with him."

"Don't you see?" Travis looked straight into my eyes, just inches away. In the reflected light, his eyes were gold and brown, sad and fervent. "It's like he was still here all these months just locked away where I couldn't reach him."

A car drove by with the radio blaring. The bass shook the barn. The windows rattled. More cars began the exit parade along Mulberry Street. A jeep, full of fraternity boys, stalled in front of the barn. One of the guys yelled, "Look at this action!"

His friend joined in, "Keep it up, brother!" They got the engine started and pulled away. Their echo of their laughter and the exhaust fumes lingered to taunt us as they raced down the block.

Travis and I sat on the roof, continuing to watch the parade of beachgoers as they headed home. We didn't talk more about his granddad, though I tried my best to distract him with a game of Punchbuggy. We were supposed to punch each other when we saw a Volkswagen Beetle, but Travis's heart wasn't in the game, so we descended the ladder. I had tied my skirt between my legs. Travis had to coach me down because I was scared of the height we had climbed. At the bottom, he was silent—neither accepting nor refusing my offer of some lemonade.

I watched from the porch as he walked toward his home ten blocks away. Even though his figure got smaller with distance, he didn't leave me. What Travis had emoted that night was so real to me that I dressed myself in it, too. A lavender silk scarf. I tied it tight around my throat and then let it flutter against my collarbone.

No, I could not tell Karen Sewicky about my night on the roof with Travis. She wouldn't understand. How to keep Mushmouth Ray from kissing her was as serious a crisis as Karen could handle during summer vacation—that and what to wear to Macy Killian's wedding. When she harped on the state of my wardrobe, I could not tell her that I was clothed in my friend's fresh grief.

· 22 ·

2000

WHEN I SLID INTO the booth at the pub, my drinks were awaiting me, a shot of tequila and a Corona with a twist.

"This isn't root beer," I said to Karen who was already seated across from me.

"I've got news," Karen replied grimly.

I looked from the shot glass to the bottle. "Are we celebrating or drowning our sorrows."

"It depends how you look at it."

I held up the shot glass. "Okay, hit me."

"Guy Christopher, the lawyer I put you in touch with in Michigan?"

"Yes?"

"He ran into Bryce over the holiday."

"And?"

"Bryce was with his girlfriend."

"Okay."

"His very pregnant girlfriend."

I carefully lowered my shot glass to the table and waited for a thought to pop into my head. Something to clue me into my feelings. I was drawing a complete blank. Then slowly my consciousness returned to me. I felt a flash of anger, just enough to feel human, but it was clothed unexpectedly in pity.

"BJ, are you okay?" Karen searched my face for a sign that I understood the implications of what she was telling me.

"I feel sorry for him," I whispered.

"BJ?"

I looked at Karen. "I feel sorry for her, too. Who wants to have a baby under those conditions? But Bryce? He's stupid if he thinks he can escape one family and find what he's searching for in another. I actually feel sorry for the bastard."

"You should feel sorry for him. He's agreed to sign the original settlement agreement. You will have full custody of Sam. You alternate Christmas and Thanksgiving, and Bryce gets Sam for spring break and six weeks during the summer."

I grabbed a menu and pretended to be considering my lunch options. Knowing that I'd order my standby, a BLT, gave me the space to think. My emotions were not as simple as anger, as condescending as pity. I needed to sort through years of interaction with this man and make it fit with all the questions I had in my mind. And not the least of these interactions was sex. As much as I would have liked to unhinge myself from any desire for my husband, it was still there, beating like a faraway drum sending me a signal. But what was the message? Two nights ago, I dreamed that Bryce was making love to me in an empty courtroom. The dream left me breathless and mortified. If that didn't confuse me enough, the following night I had a dream that I murdered Bryce by locking him in a trunk and throwing it in the lake.

I drank my tequila and felt it burn all the way down to my empty stomach. *Let the mind haze begin.*

"The chicken salad is good here. It has almonds in it," Karen said. She obviously didn't need a menu, either to order or to camouflage her emotions.

"Oh, and the waitress told me that the soup was gazpacho."

"Hmm."

I pretended to be interested in Karen's words, but they could not draw my mind away from thoughts of Bryce and his pregnant girlfriend. The tequila was working, blurring my thoughts. I remembered telling Bryce that I was pregnant. We had taken a dinner cruise for the anniversary of our first date. Lake Michigan in the spring—it was cold. I had worn my red dress and a new pair of slingbacks with a silver buckle. A band was playing that song "The Lady in Red," and I felt as if I were momentarily queened. Queasy and queened. My grand coronation was interrupted when I dashed to vomit over the side of the boat. I made it to the railing, but I twisted my ankle in the attempt.

That night, Bryce had carried me into our house and bed. He kissed me with more tenderness than I had ever experienced before. He kissed my ankle and my belly and my breasts and spots along the way. We made love. Afterward we lay knotted in each other, holding on to that moment before we had to share our joy with everyone else.

We joked about names. Bryce liked the name Daniel, but his niece's name was Danielle. "We could still do it. It would really piss off Andrea and drive Mom nuts at the same time. We could kill two birds with one stone."

I took one look at his naughty grin, and I swear that I saw a vision of my future son. Then the moment was interrupted. I sprang naked from the bed and heaved into the trash can across the room. Bryce held a towel to my clammy face and wrapped my sweating body in a blanket so I wouldn't get chilled. I didn't get sick again for the rest of my pregnancy.

I wondered now if Bryce's girlfriend had gotten sick. How had she told him she was pregnant? When? That night he tore down those walls and confessed everything? Had she done it then?

I felt a breeze on my arms. The air conditioning vent was directly above our table. I looked down at my sleeveless red shirt and rubbed my arms. Here I was again, dressed in red and feeling queasy. More comparisons, my mind kept racing and making the leap, asking the questions. I wondered if Bryce made an association every time his mistress reached a milestone in her pregnancy. *Did he go with her to her doctor's appointments? Had he heard his new child's heartbeat? Did he drop his hands low on her belly to feel the baby hiccup?*

Bryce had moments of sensitivity. He could not have forgotten. That family dinner at his mother's house when I first felt the flutter of a kick. Bryce had determined on that day that the baby would be a son. *Did he ever tell her, the other woman? Did he relive his past life out loud so she would know who he had been these last years?* Maybe he was silent, letting her think this new voyage into parenthood was singular in its magnitude.

The thoughts and questions didn't parade by in ceremony. They swirled in an instant and were gone, a vortex which left me numb.

"BJ?"

"Huh?"

"Your order?"

The waitress stood smiling above me.

"A BLT, no, make that a tuna melt. That's all."

The waitress reached across the table for our menus, and I could see clear down her shirt. Karen must have caught the awkward expression on my face because she laughed. I looked around at all the businessmen having lunches and wondered if this is how it happens, the other woman. Is it as innocent as that? Catching a whiff of perfume and seeing the rise of a breast.

Karen returned to the matter at hand. "I got some more information for you, if you're ready, though I don't know if it's going to cheer you up at all."

"Okay."

"Remember when you asked about Anja changing her will to

include Travis? She did that on September twenty-seventh. She said she talked to you on the twenty-sixth. I even wrote it in my notes."

September twenty-sixth. The date didn't ring a bell. I resolved to go home and flip through my sketchbooks. Sometimes I made journal notations in them. If not, maybe I had written something in my day planner.

"Are you considering contesting the will?" Karen asked.

"No. Nonna had a reason to give Travis the paintings. I'll make sure he gets them." I blushed slightly, and then made a distracted attempt to raise the bottle of beer to my lips.

"BJ, is there something you aren't telling me?" Karen paused to watch the color rise to my cheeks. "There is! Come on, girl-friend. What happened with you and Travis out there on the boat?"

"I am afraid I don't give that kind of information away after only two drinks."

"Bartender," Karen called out.

"Don't waste your money; nothing happened. We talked." I could see the disappointment sweep across Karen's face. She patted my hand.

"Talking is good," I said.

"Fucking is better," Karen rejoined.

"Karen!"

"Well, it is. You need a good rebound fling. It might as well be Travis."

I blushed again, more completely, telling Karen with my color that I had already had that same thought about the same prize. Who could blame me? It wasn't often a girl could banish a husband and fulfill her teenage fantasy with one naked transaction.

"Thanks. I am good for now," I lied. "But ask me about Travis again after all the papers are signed, and my kid is back here in Pennsylvania with tales of his new baby sister."

"Speaking of the kid, where is he?"

"Didn't I tell you? My dad drove up from Richmond. He got in last night. It's been great to have him around, especially for Sam."

"Have you told him about the divorce?"

"Very little. I did some research at the library about how to talk to kids, but I'm waiting until Bryce and I are together."

"Not Sam, your dad."

"Oh, Dad. Well, I think he suspects, but we are having such a nice time. I don't know if I want to do it this week."

Karen rolled her eyes. "My advice? Do it soon. The baby will be here in September. It will make a heck of a family picture for your Christmas cards."

"On second thought, Karen, go ahead and order me that drink."

· 23 ·

1983

"DID YOU HEAR about Vera Wagner?"

"No."

"She's moving to Montana permanently."

"No! What about her job?"

"She's going to be her grandson's nanny when his mother goes back to work. And get this—they are building her an apartment off the back of their house."

Card club was twice as animated as usual. After the news of Vera Wagner, my grandmothers recounted their rendezvous with the law to which our guests responded by growling in the direction of Mr. Kovack's house. Later, when he came outside to garden, the women clucked rudely at his bent form, which was visible from our picture window. Predictably the conversation moved on to the Edson-Hollinger wedding and the Hollinger-Kauffman divorce. My grandmothers had been front row center for both spectacles. Mrs. Katie Kauffman (née Hollinger) was sister of the groom at the Independence Day wedding. She was using Clarence Sewicky to represent her in the divorce, thus treating all of us to a double perspective on the split.

However, in the heat of the second game of cards, even the society news became vapid. Grandma Lena and I had finished our game against Mrs. Bomberger and Mrs. Millhouse when I started to eavesdrop on Nonna at her table. We were going to play against her team next, and I wanted an edge. For Grandma Lena's sake I hoped to keep our winning streak alive.

"Anja, this baklava is simply the best I've tasted. I'll have to hire you to make some for the anniversary party Clarence and I are having next month." Joyce Sewicky was gushing. She was futilely trying to distract Nonna from counting trump cards.

"No problem, sweetie." *Here it comes.* "You know, truth be told, several Greek men proposed to me after sampling my baking. If memory serves me right, two came from the baklava alone," Nonna said.

I had heard this claim a hundred times. Outside the window, Mr. Kovack stood up and readjusted his shorts over his backside. That place—*where the sun don't shine*—had started to see daylight. Mr. Kovack appeared sweaty and fatigued, and his face stuck out like a pimento against the olive green of his shrubbery.

"Nonna," I said. "How would you like to put your baklava to the test?"

"What, dear?" Nonna placed her final card on the table.

"Your baklava. If it is as good as you say it is, bringing men to their knees and all, I have another proposal to add to your list."

"That's game," Joyce Sewicky announced. "Anja and Gladys, you beat us again."

Nonna turned, acknowledged victory, then she looked at me. "Okay, Miss BJ, what is this all about?"

"It's a bet, over our card game."

By now Grandma Lena was becoming quite interested. The

stakes were always high when my grandmothers opposed each other. Nonna and Gladys shifted around to sit at our card table.

I spoke so all the women present could hear me. "The loser of our game has to take that plate of baklava over to Mr. Kovack as a peace offering and invite him to our poetry reading tomorrow night."

"Oh, for the love of heaven. He wronged us. I'm not going to waste my bak—"

"If you don't think your baking can sway a man's heart . . ." I baited her.

Thirteen women, amusement on their faces, waited anxiously for Nonna and Grandma Lena to agree to the challenge.

"Oh, it's up to Anja. It's her baklava," Lena said.

"All right, but we are still reading Anne Sexton and Sylvia Plath tomorrow evening. We are not changing our agenda for that man."

"You're pretty sure of the power of your baking." Gladys Metz winked at me as she shuffled the cards.

"Deal, woman. We have to teach this youngster a lesson."

It took five hands, but Lena and I, the underdogs, pulled off the incredible—a win by thirty points. Grandma Lena played with the focus and strategy of a chess master. It did not hurt her strategy that I had aces around in one hand, and she had a run in another. Nonna was not happy. We had not bettered their score all summer. I did not gloat, but I did place the stack of teetering desserts next to Nonna.

"Oh, go on." Nonna pushed me aside and walked nobly out the side door to the property line. Fifteen pairs of eyes followed the course of her stride. We were not subtle about it either. Mr. Kovack rose from his gardening and waved weakly to us. A piece of sweaty hair escaped his scalp to measure the direction of the breeze. Through the open window, we listened.

"George, the girls and I had this extra plate of baklava. We wanted you to have it. You have been working so hard out here. We thought it would make a nice treat." I caught a flirtatiousness in Nonna's voice that I had never heard before. I began to suspect that her brazen delivery, not her baked goods, had solicited the marriage proposals.

"It's my special recipe. Go ahead. Try one." A serpent was loose in the garden—or at least Eve.

"Uh, thank you, Anja. That's very kind." Mr. Kovack nervously removed his gardening gloves and accepted the gift. He lifted a sweet to his mouth with an air of caution, but immediately a syrupy smile crossed his lips.

"My grandmother was Greek. I haven't had baklava like this in years."

"Enjoy, George. Bring the plate back when you are done."

Nonna started back toward the house, but stopped. "Oh, we are having our July Poetry on the Porch event tomorrow night. You are welcome to join us. Anne Sexton and Sylvia Plath. You'll come won't you, George?"

Mr. Kovack looked from the plate to Nonna. His mouth was full. "I, uh, will."

"We'll see you about seven-thirty."

I whooped from the window as the crowd dispersed. Grandma Lena continued to stare out the window. "That old bird never ceases to amaze me."

"Mr. Kovack?"

"No, honey, your Nonna."

· 24 ·

2000

As soon as I pulled my car in front of the barn, I knew I was in trouble. Dad and Sam were presiding over a pile of lumber that had not been present when I had left that morning. *What is that heap doing in my backyard?*

"Dad?"

He spun around. "Barbara Jean. We were just getting started. Want to help us? That's not really a question. I am going to need your help." My father kissed me on the cheek. His scent of limes and the ocean was a combination of his aftershave lotion and his sunblock.

I looked from my son to my father. "Do I have a choice? What is this?"

"Grandpa is building me a playhouse with a sliding board and swings."

I moaned. Sam was transported from the bored child I had seen a week ago, but it was no excuse for my father to presume to build him a magical playland without my permission. I felt the old rage ignite within me. I was ten years old again, and Dad was asserting dominion over the household by changing the TV channel from the cartoon I was watching to the Redskins game.

"Dad, I need to speak to you. Alone, please. Let's go into the kitchen. Sam, stay in the yard where I can see you, and don't handle any of that wood."

The hinge of the kitchen screen door shrieked with our entrance.

"Barbara Jean. I know what you are going to say—"

"You don't know anything, Dad. Why would you build a swing set here? It's like you think Sam and I are moving to Pennsylvania."

"Aren't you? You and Bryce have split up, admit it. I want to hear it from you."

"Dad. It's none of your concern. But if it were true, it doesn't automatically mean I want to live here. I have a business in Michigan, my clientele. Even if I am staying here, you don't have the right to recreate Disney World in my backyard."

"Disney World is an overstatement, don't you think?" Richard Foley, the father, crossed his arms in front of him. "Barbara Jean, you are going to have to face up to the fact that you no longer have sole control over Sam's life, so lighten up with me. He's going home to Bryce in a few weeks. This is what you can expect. Bryce is going to show him a good time in a place that Sam used to call home." His voice softened. "I've seen the kindergarten registration papers. I know you are sending him to school here. Now, doesn't it make sense to make this house into a place he wants to return to?"

"So this was all a big lesson for me in separation. Is that it?"

Dad opened the screen door. Another whine from the hinges.

"It's certainly not a lesson I wanted for you. When you are ready to talk, I brought some information from Father Carris on annulment procedures, though I am sure your local priest would be happy to assist you."

The door shut, but I continued to talk through the screen. "Dad, how did you know we were getting a divorce? And about Sam going back for the summer?"

"Bryce called me in Richmond."

I winced. "Is that why you came here?"

"Don't be angry at him. He did it out of concern. He is worried about you, and he wanted you to have some support."

I rolled my eyes (again—the inner ten-year-old). "Yeah, if you believe that . . ."

"He knew you wouldn't tell me yourself. And he was right."

I stared at my dad. I was prepared for any answer but that one. How could I argue with the truth?

This summer was supposed to teach me how to separate myself from my husband. I could handle Bryce's nonchalance but not his concern.

I watched Dad as he took inventory of his supplies. He was right. I was losing my son and my sovereignty over him. I should be realistic about it and talk to Bryce. But Bryce had not asserted himself as a parent in so long. What would change now? I could make the appropriate lists. Daily vitamins, eating vegetables before sweets, bed by eight, no video games on weekdays. In the end, they ensured nothing except my desire to regulate Bryce. And those days were over.

Sam was floating away from me. His summers in Michigan would shape him much in the same ways my summers in Pennsylvania had shaped me. Sam would have his own stories. And I would probably never hear the important tales, the ones of transformation. Just as I never told my parents the full story of my own hot-weather pursuits.

Some summers I had returned home to Virginia with a buzz, anxious to tell anybody about everything, but most years I would return quiet and introspective and changed. The last summer had been like that. Those weeks after Travis and Margot left their wake of family hostility, I turned to art as transference for all my abandoned emotion. I took an old sketchbook to the lake, and with my toes submerged in its shallow pools, I smudged out landscapes, heavily textured with my angst.

When I returned to Richmond, my mother took one look at the sketches and called the school guidance counselor. "I don't care if Typing I is part of the college track, I want my daughter enrolled in an art class next semester."

And so began the melancholy years of high school.

My father had been befuddled by the transformation. "Are you sure you want to give up basketball? You loved basketball. And chorus? What about that?" I had been adamant in my new solitary pleasures. Sculpting, painting, photography. Boyfriends came and went. Dad didn't like the haircut of one, the clothing of another.

"Is that boy wearing eyeshadow?"

He would always blame that last summer in Pennsylvania for the downward spiral of his little girl. Perhaps that was why it had been the last. "Barbara Jean, it's time you had a summer job."

The Dairy Queen, while monetarily rewarding, did not alter my course. During my senior year, my dad caught me trying to sneak away to D.C. to go clubbing. I was wearing only a black bra and an orange vinyl miniskirt. At the time, I was seventeen and had already been accepted to Tyler School of Art, part of Temple University, in Philadelphia.

While King Richard (my pet name for him in those years) had the discretion of withholding my college tuition, to do so would have jeopardized the last remaining dream he had for me. Instead of meting out punishment, he made me pledge to take at least one business course a year, and to reject any blue-haired boys if they proposed marriage. With a medal of St. Thérèse, he sent me, his only child, back to Pennsylvania with his prayers.

When I called two years later with news of my latest beau,

King Richard had a flash of hope. Bryce had so many of the outer qualifications of a good husband that my dad didn't even care about getting to know his heart. He couldn't see, as I saw it now, that I was settling for his vision of a family provider. But I didn't care. Bryce gave me something I hadn't had in years—the approval of my father.

Now the disappointment was back. I saw this sadness in my father's shoulders as he sawed the wood into manageable pieces. I knew he felt unnecessarily responsible for my predicament. Mom was no longer there to share the burden. By building this swing set, his first solo attempt at parenting, he was attempting to re-father me, teach me the truths about separating from one's offspring. Or maybe he was just trying to get closer, by planting part of himself in the earth where I was.

· 25 ·

1983

FROM THE SIDE WINDOW in my bedroom, we could see only the side yard and the corresponding chunk of the backyard. Karen situated herself to wait for Travis as he made each pass of the back lawn. She sat up when she heard the crescendo of the lawn mower. Travis was only in clear view for about ten seconds in each row, but Karen was convinced that during those ten seconds he would suddenly decide to remove his shirt. Such a move would be a subliminal message, she told me, but she didn't say what that message was.

Bored with her little game, I leaned back on my bed and pretended to read the new *Seventeen*. The meager July issue was always lame. I was waiting for the thick back-to-school fashion bible, the August issue, packed with more clothes than I could ever hope to buy. Karen was paging through *Tiger Beat* when Travis was not in view. Karen had turned fourteen last April, while I still had two weeks to go until my birthday. We were only three months apart in age, but she made it seem like all of adult development occurred in those three months. I didn't bother to point out to Karen that I had been menstruating half a year longer than she had. Chronological age still had dominion over physical signs of maturity.

Karen, and those her age, had what she termed *lustful desires,* which I would not understand until I turned fourteen. Only then would I comprehend the tremendous pull that Scott Baio and Rick Springfield had on her. She had wallpapered her whole room with pictures of those two, and she confessed that she kissed every one of those pictures before she went to sleep each night. When I was in her bedroom, I looked closely at the photos, checking for lip stains or dried saliva. I tried to feel tinges of *lustful desire,* but I could muster only mild disgust.

My bedroom on Mulberry Street had been my mother's bedroom when she was a girl. It had old flowered wallpaper and a matching bedspread that Nonna had made out of sheets. The lamp, topped with a ruffled shade, featured a pink ballerina base. Mom had never taken dancing lessons, but she had always wanted them.

The curtains hung long. Those summer sheers parted playfully if a lake breeze turned from its usual course. A wind like that was usually an indication of a summer storm. Sometimes I worried that a person out for a stroll would be able to see through the curtains while I was changing. I dressed in the dark most nights, and, as an added precaution, under the covers. Beneath the bed frame, I had squirreled away my romance novels and magazines. That was the only part that resembled my bedroom at home.

Karen didn't understand that this bedroom was not evidence of my true character. She babbled about redecorating possibilities.

"Put up some posters at least."

At home in Virginia, I had plenty of posters: purple posters of unicorns and sad clowns and a Monet calendar from the National Gallery. I also had a brass daybed that was piled high with pillows, a new stereo with cassette player, a mauve beanbag chair, and taffy yellow walls (with absolutely no spittle on them).

I never cared that Karen thought she was a step above me. She could think whatever she wanted. What did matter was that she still believed she was in love with Travis and the growing possibility that I, too, shared her emotion. I did try to articulate my feelings once when I was with her, but she said something like "Ew! Gross. He's your cousin." Against which my "Nuh-uh, Karen, not really" sounded weak—especially since I was also questioning how weird I was to harbor an attraction to Travis. I dropped the whole discussion but still found myself peering furtively out of my window when Travis drove by on the John Deere. I hoped he would keep his subliminal, shirtless messages to himself.

Travis was doing better these days. His grandpa had stabilized, and though the deathwatch was fixed, it was not vigilant. Margot asked not to be notified at every turn. She was resigned, for the sake of her son, to allow her father to die alone and confused. I did not bother Travis for details.

While we were waiting for Travis to cut the side lawn, Mr. Kovack appeared and started his own lawn mower, an ancient push cutter with a motor that sounded like an afterthought. The timbre of dueling engines reverberated through the neighborhood. I stood up and closed my windows partway and drew the curtains closed.

"Why did you do that?" Karen asked.

"Who wants to see Mr. Kovack. He's a pig anyway."

"I thought everything was cool. He came to your grandmas' poetry reading didn't he?"

"Yeah, he came. I wanted my grandmas to make peace with him, but it doesn't mean I like the guy. He's still slime," I said.

"Come on," Karen said. "You can kind of see the guy's point can't you? Living beside two queer women. They're your grandmas. You have to accept them. But even you have to admit, the Bible says that the stuff they do is a sin. It's just wrong."

"What did you say?" I asked, not knowing if I had heard her correctly.

"Don't get all defensive on me. I didn't write the Bible—God did or his disciples did it for him," she said flipping another page in her magazine.

"Huh?"

"Check it out. It's probably in that part about 'Man should leave his parents and cleave to a woman' or something like that. You should know—they read it at weddings. And I am sure there is another part where it says the really sinful parts. Everybody knows being gay is wrong."

I was hot. I had never contradicted anything Karen had said. I even shielded her when I thought that she could not handle certain truths. She knew nothing. She was probably just repeating something she heard her parents saying. Karen Sewicky was a pampered princess without any notion of how to develop theories and ideas for herself. I wanted to explain it all to her, how my grandmothers had a noble love for each other and this community, how Karen and her mother had been welcome guests in their home, and how I was a better person for growing up with their guidance. I thought Karen lacked the conscience necessary to hear these words, but in reality, I lacked the courage to say them. I did what I knew. I redirected my anger, turning her bigotry into something greater.

"Wrong? That's not what's wrong. *Wrong* is you thinking you have a chance with Travis. He told me he thinks of you as a spoiled brat bitch with too much free time and a daddy with just enough money to make him overlook your faults."

"W-when did he tell you all of this?" I could see the tears forming in Karen's eyes as she spoke.

"When he and I watched the fireworks together from the roof of the barn."

"You didn't. You said—" Karen made all the connections in her mind, and the story finally fit. Her mouth opened in horror. It was the last insult of the day.

Karen stormed out of my room and ran down the stairs past Nonna who was preparing dinner. I didn't try to chase her or return her forgotten magazine. I was hurt and angry, and I turned to the picture of John Stamos staring up at me.

"What are you looking at?" I snarled.

Downstairs Nonna continued her dinner preparations. Her special lemon chicken was already baking as she folded a rolled pastry into the pie tin. Her hands knew the cadence. Nonna then turned her attention to the berries in the sink. She sifted through the filled bowl, picking out the bad fruit, adding a little sugar, flour, and lemon rind to the rest. She let out a small sigh as she poured the berries into the unbaked crust. The scene with the girls was not new to her, though she had not experienced this particular drama for twenty-five years.

I came down the stairs as casually as I could. I snatched a berry from the pie. She gently slapped my hand away. Outside a lawn mower stopped its humming, and the quiet startled me. I wanted to kiss Nonna's cheek, but that would be an admission of my guilt. Like my mother before me, I was hoping to shield Nonna from the unpleasantness, but also like my mother, I failed.

Nonna knew the nature of people. Even without the prejudices, she had witnessed enough war to know that humanity had an ugly countenance. But this face wasn't the whole of human temperament. She held on to other knowledge and other truths, among them: friendships between teenaged girls are surprising—both in their fragility and their strength. They are more elastic, more forgiving than most brotherhoods. But I had yet to learn that lesson. When Karen walked out of my room that day, she took all the air with her. I had done something terrible, something that, had she done it to me, would have been as irreparable as a busted balloon. I didn't understand my worth as a friend, and I underestimated Karen's.

· 26 ·

2000

WITH DAD VISITING, the three of us spent Sunday in church rather than at the lake where Sam wanted to be. Sam wore a frown that exposed me in front of my father. His expression was a billboard that proclaimed how lax we'd become in our church attendance. As an adult, I was entitled to shape my own religious experience, and by default, that of my son's. My father would see it differently, however. My lapse in church attendance was something much bigger in my father's eyes. He would come to his own conclusions, mainly that I, a Catholic—gone solo—had not asked God to help me fend off the temptations in my marriage. And if Bryce and I divorced, which was more inevitable every day that passed, my dad would never accept the outcome as a fact of life, but instead he would view it as negligence on my part.

Sam was crestfallen about this deviance from our schedule.

"Can't Grandpa go to church by himself?"

Travis reassured Sam. "I am not taking the boat out anyway. I need to make some adjustments on the engine."

With this lie, I was able to nudge my sullen son into the pew between my father and me. The church building was new, unlike my girlhood church, Cathedral of the Sacred Heart, which rose solemn and majestic across from the fountain in Monroe Park on Richmond's north side. Its style alone, Italian Renaissance revival, was enough to summon the awesome power of God to a young girl's mind.

This new building had none of that. I had never been inside of it or any other Catholic church in this town. The narthex smelled of new carpet and fresh paint. Inside the sanctuary, the artwork stuck out from its white walls—more art gallery than church. Perhaps the secular mood of the building should have comforted me, but it didn't. The stained-glass windows were shockingly modern, and the statues of Mary and the crucifix looked almost temporary, as if they were on loan from a nouveau riche West Coast art collector. Against the monotone of the rear of the church, the green exit lights repeated their eerie visual incantation.

As a young girl, I had urged my parents to sit close to the statue of Mary at our church. It was a glorious depiction of the Virgin, carved out of warm marble. That Mary, the color of hon-eyed milk, pressed her hands together and looked to the heav-ens. She towered on her own altar, atop tabernacle doors that depicted her sacred heart. I couldn't take my eyes off that statue. Once, when the older kids were taking their first communion, I had been gazing up at Mary when—I fainted for a few seconds. My mother had rushed me outside past the procession of girls in white lace, boys in suits, and into the spring air.

"Barbara Jean, do you feel sick? Are you going to throw up?"

"No, Mommy."

"You feel a little warm. What happened to you in there?"

"I could feel the heartbeat," I had said, not knowing how else to explain the warm rhythms that had come over me, the gentle hum in my ear, and the utter stillness I felt standing amidst all those around me. And I had seen it, too. Mary's heart reaching, as if drawn to me by my little-girl wishes.

"Your heartbeat? Was it going really fast?"

"No, Mary's heartbeat. First it was in the box—the one that she was standing on. Then it was inside of me. I could feel it, Mommy, I could."

My mother had touched my chest and my lips, not daring to guess whether I was a prophet or a blasphemer. She was always at a loss in this church, not knowing whether the Holy Spirit overlooked her because she was not worthy or if she couldn't recognize something she had never been exposed to as a child. Not having grown up in the church, my mother held her silent doubts to be so sacred that they often took a higher seat to creeds we recited at each mass. For fear of drawing attention to her family or exposing her sacrilege, my mother had never repeated the story to anyone. Though repeated narrations did not reinforce the memory, I had remembered.

The last time I had seen that statue had been at my mother's funeral in January. I wasn't supposed to worship the statuary, seek solace in graven images, but as an artist, I couldn't stop my impulse to give meaning to objects. Or remove meaning. This new church didn't have a heartbeat; it had only a belly. New carpet incense, green exit mantras, and a garish Madonna all in the belly of the domed St. Stephen.

As I sat with my father, I repeated the familiar liturgy. I didn't need to consult the missal. The words cascaded from my mouth in a rockslide, persuaded so cunningly by the force of gravity that the flow seemed like free choice. I could handle this part of church, the rote catechism, the simple poetry and cadence. The congregation speaking as one, pulling together, surging to forget. The act of saying "Lord, have mercy" and "Hear our prayer" and "I believe in . . ." Even if the words weren't accurate, the communal speaking of them was tangible. I relished the mechanical chant, because it seemed to require so little of me. But once the sermon began, with ludicrous coincidence, on the subject of forgiveness, my mind awoke with a permission to wander. I wished once again for the liturgical freefall, but at the word *transgressor,* the priest afforded me the certain freedom to think about Bryce.

Oh Bryce, what have you done to me? Nothing could be so simple as irreconcilable differences or the latest catchphrase of Hollywood publicists, "an amicable split." His girlfriend, his baby. They were nothing to me, but soon would be the reality of the man who defined my adulthood—and the reality of my son who would spend future summers with his father's family. The woman? She would be there, too. Her image would grace my son's photo albums. But at present, she was nameless and faceless before me—utterly at the mercy of my imagination. I could conjure any features I wanted for this other woman. Squinty-eyed or long-legged or tagged with a grim sophistication that made her unapproachable. She was more beautiful than I was; she had to be. To coexist with all of my understanding, she needed to be stunning, and I needed to be shrewd. That's how I would gain my sovereignty over this situation. I was smart enough to get out, and she was not.

I closed my eyes to flee from this woman, the ultimate transgressor. I pressed my mind to take me back to the Cathedral of the Sacred Heart. Anything to conjure a real God into this artificial space, but all I could picture was the Mary statue with her colorless, sculpted face: a screen on which to project the very features I imagined my husband's lover to have. And this new icon was both the seductress and the saint. *Eve/Mary. Every. Everywoman.* Here at last, in my mind, was someone I could burden with real prayers made up of my own words. I watered the dry Sunday and the dry sermon with my prayers for a better life, my hopes for my sullen son, for peace with Bryce—may he find what he is looking for—and comfort for my widowed father. I circled these prayers again in a dizzy attempt to fortify them. But by the time the sermon was over, I didn't feel that God had heard me at all. My prayers were a vanity, and I felt vacant and robbed of my own thoughts.

Holy, Holy, Holy, Lord God Almighty. Reluctantly, I opened my mouth for the wafer. *The body of Christ, given for you. The blood of Christ, shed for you.* The port wine stung my tongue with its sweetness. I turned to see Sam. He sat alone on the pew, outside of the circle of communion. I rose and followed Dad. My father genuflected before the temporary statue of Mary, mother of God, but I didn't even bow my head.

EveryMary could have my father, my mother. She could have my husband, his mistress, and his bastard child; but if she wanted me, she would have to follow the green exit sign to a place where Sundays were damp with perspiration and lake water and light beer. With the taste of the Last Supper growing stale in my mouth, I renounced Catholicism and welcomed a different kind of quest.

· 27 ·

1983

THE MORNING OF Macy Killian's wedding, Karen drifted back to me like a noblewoman in a marriage of convenience. It didn't matter how we felt about each other; we needed to put on a good show for society.

Karen was not at all interested in helping with the cake and the photographs. She forgot her station at this event, but I was treading carefully around her since our blowup, so I said nothing.

My ultimate salvation came in the form of Macy's younger brother, Bill Killian. Pimple-faced and tuxedoed, he sought out Karen at the reception, since the bridesmaid he was escorting was too pregnant to dance. She sat at the head table, fanning herself while she unceremoniously readjusted her maternity pantyhose.

I told Grandma Lena to get a picture of Karen and Bill dancing together, a move that put me back in the friendship.

Next to them, the bride and groom danced in celebration of their union. Macy played the bride role well, just another evening-gown competition. She was keeping her last name, which seemed an easy decision because the groom's surname was Kometacalski. Even at age thirteen, I knew that my endorsement of feminism was superficial. If my future husband had a better sounding last name than Foley, I was going to take it.

Hyphenation remained a possibility, but I recalled one of my first weddings with Grandma Lena. The bride was Alicia Varey, and the groom was Jonathan Groce with the resulting hyphenation being Varey-Groce. She had since divorced and married a man named Ken Valentine. I think she took his last name. I know I would have. BJ Foley-Valentine. No. *Bobbi Valentine.*

Photographing this reception was a harder job than most. The outdoor venue meant we had to cover more ground. Grandma Lena was more physically fit than Nonna, to be sure, but she still had difficulty running from one side of the farm to the other. I did most of the legwork. I got us pulled pork sandwiches from the chuck wagon and notified the DJ when we were in place for the cake cutting.

With our constant relay, Grandma Lena and I neglected Karen. What harm could come to her here? But I was wrong. Bill had been sneaking her drinks from the four champagne fountains near the bar. He was underage, too, by at least five years, but his tuxedo gave him license to ignore state law. Karen had been dancing in the hot sun, not daring to eat anything she might drip on her linen outfit. By five p.m. when we were fulfilling Macy's dream to be photographed with her husband next to a black and white cow, Karen was throwing up next to the dance floor.

We apologized repeatedly to the backbeat of Karen's moans. We had taken as many photographs as we could without embarrassing the growing number of drunken guests, so Karen slumped into the back of the station wagon, and Lena drove us home.

At the house Nonna brewed up a wicked concoction to ease Karen's symptoms. I called Mrs. Sewicky to ask her if Karen could stay overnight. It was a mistake to think I could get off the phone that fast. Joyce wanted to hear all the details of the wedding, which I supplied for her sans her daughter's introduction to champagne. She asked to talk to Karen, but I lied and said that Karen was in the darkroom with Lena.

"Lena got a shot of her dancing with a cute usher, and I think she is really anxious to see it."

"Okay then, have fun. I'll see the picture tomorrow?"

"Of course."

Karen draped me with drunken apologies and oaths of undying friendship for the rest of the evening.

"BJ, you are my best friend. Even better than Beth and Tina," she slurred. "I'm sorry I said those things about your grandmas. They are the coolest lesbians I know. I am sure that God will forgive them like he forgives the Jewish people. You don't think Bill is Jewish, do you?"

I comforted her by reminding her that Bill was not wearing a yarmulke, and then I directed her to bunk in my mother's old bed. A mile away, Scott Baio and Rick Springfield pictures hung unkissed. I grabbed a Harlequin Romance from under the bed and went to the porch to read by the light of the bug zapper. The diamond clad clown hovered over the cover art. I opened to the first page of the story, then flipped back to the tantalizing blurb that preceded it.

Lena was in the darkroom developing the photo I had lied about. She didn't want the blame of Karen's antics to fall on her, so she willingly wed herself to the lie under the red light of her studio. In the parlor, Nonna was watching television in the dark. I could see the blue glare of the screen flickering through the window.

Somewhere, Macy Killian, weather girl and beauty queen, was having her wedding night. I had seen the sheer negligee when she showed it off to her bridesmaids.

"Just don't end up like me," the pregnant one had said. "Ooh,

I got to pee again." She had run off, urgently lifting the skirt of her behemoth bridesmaid's gown.

If Macy Killian ever got that big, she'd surely block the weather map, but on her wedding day she had been slender and blond, tanned and glowing. She was the epitome of bridal beauty and my personal image of a romance heroine.

When Dane Miles saw Therese in the doorway, her hair a gilded halo, he thought twice about the bargain he had made with his brother before he died. Standing before him was the woman who had run Carson down on a stormy night last autumn when her car hit his. Dane brushed one golden strand of hair away from Therese's cheek. How could he avenge his brother's death, when his adversary was so tantalizing and sweet? Dane lowered his mouth to cover her lips. Then again, he thought, revenge could be sweet as well.

· 28 ·

2000

AFTER CHURCH, DAD AND I worked to finish Sam's swing set. My use of power tools in the jewelry studio translated into an ability to make constructions of any kind. I used larger muscle groups with this project than with my intricate jewelry, but my skin glowed with the same satisfaction in my craftsmanship. Sometimes from his perch in the playhouse, Dad would smirk at me when he thought I wasn't watching. I took pride in his smile. I knew my father worried about me even more now that Mom was gone. I hoped our afternoon working together would not only ease his mind but also help to replace any shame he felt as a result of my separation.

In late afternoon, Travis made an appearance. I had not invited him, and his spontaneous arrival, in conjunction with my father's presence, unnerved me. I didn't want to be rude to Travis, but I really didn't want my dad to read anything into his presence.

"Dad, you remember Travis, Lena's nephew."

"Good to see you, Richard." Travis nodded. The two would have shaken hands if Dad hadn't been holding a cordless drill.

"Travis, this is a surprise. Barbara Jean didn't tell me we had contact from the MacKenzies. How's your mother doing?"

"Good, sir. I'll tell her you asked about her." Travis pushed on one of the upright supports of the playhouse. He seemed satisfied in the structure.

"You should have called me to help. I love this kind of project."

I patted his back in an attempt to look casual. "Dad and I needed some quality time together." I am sure that Travis detected my aloofness, but whether he was confused by it, I couldn't tell.

My father turned back to his work of sinking the screws below the plane of the wood. I had to believe that Dad hadn't noticed anything untoward in my greeting of Travis. I sensed tacit and reproving questions in my father's actions. His silence wasn't always a good thing. Part of me wanted to tell my father, flat out, that nothing had happened between Travis and me; we were just friends. But an unsolicited denial often confirms rather than refutes a claim. My father wasn't stupid. The advantage I had in this face-off was the possibility that my father didn't want to ask a question that could be turned around and asked of him. I had heard whisperings, from friends of the family, that my dad had started seeing someone only months after my mother's death. *Let him squirm.*

But supposing Travis was to become part of my life. Was the idea so far-fetched? I considered it for a moment—Travis and I playing house. I had not so much as kissed him, but here he was handing my father the new battery pack for the drill. It added a certain domestic quality to the encounter that I couldn't help but consider. It was an easy leap for my mind to make. I imagined the lazy mornings of two people who had no bosses to please, no clocks to punch. We would socialize with other couples, maybe Karen and Shelly, inviting them over for alfresco dining in our gardens. And talk. Undoing the mistakes of my first marriage, I would be open to Travis, easily expressing my fears and my needs.

I shook my head, appalled that I had actually committed such a crime of fantasy. I was worse than my college roommate who had bought the current issue of *Bride* magazine after every first date.

"Peach moiré," she would say in reference to her bridesmaid dresses du jour. I grimaced. Lynne was twice divorced, and here I was, still married, and having a peach moiré moment over Travis.

But in spite of my misguided musings, I couldn't help wondering, *What would my dad think of him?* I almost wished I could ask him. Dad always spoke plainly when it came to my friends. His insights would have saved me much heartache if I had only learned to accept his accurate character assessments. I could take months to see what my father did at a first meeting.

My father, with his scrutiny, would discover a different kind of man in Travis than the one he saw in Bryce. If I could ask him for his opinion of Travis, I would know for sure. But just the fact that King Richard stayed his judgment gave me some assurance. If he had anything negative to say, he would have pulled me aside and told me at once. Neither one of them seemed as bothered as I was. *Maybe it's about time I relaxed, too.*

Travis and I covered the playhouse with the old tent that Sam had used previously in his play. We would have an unveiling after he woke from his nap.

"Dad built me a swing set when I was little. It was nothing like this, though. It was a shiny metal type," I said, trying to spark informal conversation.

"Yes, and I cut my leg on one of those metal pieces, and had to go to the emergency room on a Sunday to get a tetanus shot." Dad tied the tent string around a post.

"I think that is the day I learned how to cuss." I laughed at the memory of my four-year-old self running up to my mother and repeating *Dammit all to hell.*

"That's why I don't work on a Sunday," Travis said.

"So you won't swear?" I asked.

"No, so I don't get all uptight."

"You don't need to pretend you are religious just because my father is here."

"Unchurched doesn't mean I'm not religious. A man must have a Sabbath."

I waited for Dad to lecture Travis, but he didn't. "Aren't you going to give him the speech about church?"

"I'm just getting reacquainted with Travis, Barbara Jean. Besides, he knows what he thinks. I worry more about the folks who can't seem to make up their minds about God."

Once again, Dad managed to focus on my failures. He had this ability to manipulate my beliefs by trapping me with my own words. Once, after a semester of philosophy, I came home from college espousing the tenets of fatalism. Dad rebuked me by saying that the Bible then could be accepted as truth because God had fated it to be. I never won an argument with my dad. I looked to my mother for support. But Mom couldn't (or wouldn't) save me. She had married my dad and all his beliefs. And my youthful self had hated her for it.

I had always wanted to trick her, to ask my mother how she could grow up in a household with a lesbian couple and then turn around and embrace the religious conservatism that surrounded Dad. I never did ask that question, though, and it boiled in my thoughts now, quite unexpectedly.

"Dad, how did you feel about Grandma Lena and Nonna?" I asked before I could censor myself.

"What about them?" He shrugged, noncommittal.

"You know what I mean."

Travis answered. "Mom never approved of the two of them together."

"Really?" In the years before the split, Margot had at least seemed congenial.

"My grandfather was a minister, after all. He was really steamed when Lena broke off her engagement and took up with Anja. My mom grew up hearing how corrupt they both were."

"Lena was engaged?" I asked. "Then that was her wedding gown in the attic."

"I don't know about the dress, but, yeah, she was engaged. It was some eleventh hour deal. She didn't leave him at the altar, but close to it."

"Do you know anything else?"

"No, that's about it."

I looked at my dad to confirm what Travis just told me.

"News to me," Dad said. "As people, I liked Lena and Anja, just fine. But I probably know a little more about the situation your mother grew up with, and I know she struggled with it."

"How so?"

"Being different from other families, not feeling she fit in. I think she craved an ordinary life, and I was just the ordinary guy who could give it to her. So in that way, I am grateful to your grandmothers that things were the way they were, at least until you came along."

"What do you mean?" I asked.

"You weren't rebelling against them. You were rebelling against us. If you had thought that I harbored any negativity toward them, I would have lost you to them forever. I just tried not to make a big deal about it."

"I'm pretty sure I wouldn't have become a lesbian," I said, intentionally avoiding Travis's gaze.

"I don't know," Travis said. "I hung around them a lot in my youth, and I have found that I am really attracted to women."

The humor smoothed away any uneasiness of our conversation. In the thoughtful lull that followed, I excused myself to wake Sam. I didn't worry about leaving the two of them alone to talk. Neither of them could trump the dialog we had recently concluded. Sex, religion. We had traversed all of the taboos of conversation, save politics.

Sam was asleep in his bed. The sweat of his afternoon nap glazed his temples. I watched as his long eyelashes fluttered in response to my presence in the room. He sat up and talked as if he had fallen asleep in mid-discussion and now was resuming where he had stopped two hours ago.

"Hayden wants to see the playhouse when it's finished. Can you call his mom?"

"Sure, bud. It's finished now."

Sam vaulted into my arms with a force that caused me to fall onto the bed. We crashed in a warm pile of arms and legs, just begging to be tickled. I pinned Sam to the bed and started my torture, but he got loose and found a ticklish spot under my arm.

"You're going to get it now, you scalawag."

Our laughter carried outside to the two men, who I imagined to be stuck for conversation and awaiting distraction.

· 29 ·

1983

THE PORCH SWING GROANED as I turned. I had spent the night in its cradle but awoke before even the early July sun had a chance to prod me.

Nobody else was awake when I entered the house. I checked the clock, five a.m. Back home, my mother would be waking for early church in another hour. I missed her. On Nonna's desk, a black phone beckoned. It had a hard, rotary dial and a thick, ropy cord that was on its way to extinction. My fingers knew the sequence, and soon I heard my mother's voice, rough with sleep.

"Hello."

"Hi, Mom."

"Barbara Jean, are you okay. What's wrong?" I heard my father in the background, echoing her concerns.

"I'm fine. I just wanted to talk to you."

To my dad, "It's okay, Richard. Go back to sleep." To me she said, "What are you doing up so early? Aren't teenagers supposed to sleep until noon?"

"I fell asleep on the porch. My friend Karen is in my bed. She wasn't feeling very well last night." I told my mother the story of Macy Killian's wedding, including the parts that Karen couldn't tell her own mother.

We laughed in hushed tones, and my mother confided how she had once drunk too much at a college party and had peed in her best friend's bed. "That was before your father reformed me. You won't do anything so stupid will you, Barbara Jean?"

"No, I promise," I said naively.

"So your friend Karen has her eye on someone. What about you? Anybody special?"

"Not really," I said. I could talk freely to my mom, but there was nothing to tell.

I heard footsteps in the dining room. Nonna entered the kitchen and made a beeline for her coffee percolator. After she plugged it in she mouthed, "Who?"

"Mom," I mouthed back.

She took the phone from me. "Judy, I didn't even hear the phone ring."

"Oh, she called you. I'll have to deduct it from her pay." Nonna winked at me.

"Well, yes, we did have quite a situation yesterday. Barbara Jean took care of most of it. I was proud of her." Nonna raised her voice intentionally for me. "She knows if she ever came home in that condition we'd hang her naked from her toenails."

I laughed and put some bread in the toaster. Nonna was a talker. Lena was the disciplinarian in the family. Nonna conversed affectionately with my mother, but ended the call when the perfume of dark-roast coffee filled the room. Nonna always drank her coffee out of a small bowl, no handles. She liked the feel of the warm liquid cupped in her hands. She poured two such bowls, lacing mine with plenty of cream and sugar, the way I liked it; hers, she dressed merely with sugar.

We took the toast, some marmalade, and the coffees to the porch rockers where we cradled the warmth and invited the sun to join us. The morning was chilly, but not unbearable, with the warm coffee resting on my cool thighs. Birds were starting to wake with their usual noisy banter, announcing the light as it peeked out from the roofs of the neighboring houses. Nonna and I sat in silence, enjoying the sunrise, but we had a comma between us where my mother should have been, where her voice still reverberated.

· 30 ·

2000

I MANAGED TO GET one solid day of studio work while my dad was in town—he took Sam to a fishing hole he had heard of at the lumber store. Finishing two commissions was my first priority. I needed to take them with me when I drove Sam back to Michigan. Both were necklaces, classically draped without the distraction of stones. They were easy pieces, but time-consuming all the same. Tyler School of Art had asked me for a representative work to showcase in their alumni show in early fall. I had not even begun to design that piece, but that would have to wait, at least for now.

For a job like this, I had to clean up the cast components and construct decorative links to join the pieces. I had hired out the cast portions. Initially I had carved wax into the shapes I required, but the casting company now had the mold. At any time, I could call in an order and have it shipped to me the following week. It was efficient, both in time and money, to let commercial jewelers handle that part of my craft.

I attached an abrasive wheel to my flexible shaft and cleaned the surfaces, especially around the area where the sprues had been snipped and filed. Most of the task went smoothly until I started to let my mind wander while working on one of the smaller elements.

"Damn it," I said after I gouged a fingernail with the rotating disk.

Looking down at my hands I saw what others must see—the dingy nails, chipped and dirty. I tried soaps and lotions and occasionally polish, but my hands were a résumé for my crafting profession.

I evened out my nail with the same abrasive tool that had cut into it, as close to a manicure as I was likely to get. I resumed my work, acting swiftly, turning the ugly gray scraps of metal into things of beauty, miniature sculptures. The Talking Heads blared from my portable CD player. It was one of those songs I could not get out of my head once it was there. I had listened to the Heads during my college studio days. *Don't you want to make him stay up late? . . . Make him stay up all night.* They, along with the Eurythmics and 10,000 Maniacs, had pulled me through the all-night working fogs that ended in harsh morning critiques.

The necklace required two kinds of links, one long and twisted, the other classic round. I wrapped wire around the mandrels and slid off the coil. Then I clipped and twisted the pieces where appropriate. As was the practice, I soldered the first links with the hardest solder and a little flux. The smallest tip of my acetylene torch worked for the delicate undertaking. I took my expertise for granted and coupled all the links quickly, not losing any of the precious links to the heat of the flame. After turning the torch off, I threw the chains together into the pickle, a warm chemical bath, where they would brighten in anticipation of the final polish.

I stretched and rubbed my neck, trying once again to familiarize my muscles with my workday. Reaching for a door that pushed out instead of in. Carrying the huge skeleton keys around in my pocket. And figuring where I had located everything in this new studio of mine.

"I can't lose these again."

Carefully I replaced my pliers in the red tool cabinet, but I knocked something over on the shelf above it. I righted the toppled picture frame, a drawing of the goddess Brigid. *Why had I brought this with me from Michigan?* It had probably gotten mixed in with my important tools or fallen into a box. The picture had been a gift from a gallery owner in Detroit. Della Kaminiski was her proper name, but her pagan name, as well as the name of her gallery, was Dawning Moon. I was wary of any religion that took Catholic saints and fashioned them into personal goddesses.

"You Catholics took your St. Brigid from us," Dawning Moon hastened to say.

But I heard the need for acceptance in her voice, and I disregarded her testimonials until a week later when, at the opening of my show, Dawning Moon handed me a present wrapped in blue paper, freckled with stars. I tore the paper to find a picture of a woman with red hair and three faces—only one of which turned to confront me. Beside this triple woman sat a well of water, a flame, and a spotted cow. The title read, "Bride."

"Bride?"

"Bri-dee. Another name for Brigid. She's Irish. Of course, you know that. But did you know that she is the goddess of crafts, especially smithing? I thought she would consecrate your studio at home."

"Why does she have three faces?"

"She's a triple goddess. In addition to crafts, she is the goddess of healing and writing."

"And is she the saint of those things as well?"

"You're the Catholic, you tell me. I am just a former yenta turned priestess. Ask me about Leah and Rachel or Lilith and Eve. I am not so good with mother Mary and her posse, though we consider Mary as a goddess, too."

"Mary?"

"Well, all except the ex-Catholics in our group. They are a little sore about having to grow up with that whole model of the Virgin Birth being shoved down their throat. Unattainable perfection, and all of that."

I looked at Bride, Brigid, saint and goddess. "I am Scotch-Irish on my father's side."

"Good, she's a match."

"Yes, thank you, Della." I couldn't bring myself to use my friend's pagan name.

JULES SCRATCHED AT THE DOOR of the lean-to. It had been three hours since he had been outside. I opened the back door for him. Grabbing a can of Diet Coke from the fridge, I followed Jules out into the yard. Immediately he ran to the fence and barked.

"Jules, no! Come back here."

Karen entered the gate, and I scrambled to pull Jules from his earnest intention to slime our guest. Karen didn't mind. She dropped to Jules's level and got in his face with a string of gibberish designed for dog ears only.

"Wazza good boy? Lookie zeze ears. Oh, you like when Auntie Karen rubs zoze ears? Zzyes. Dat feels so-o good." She looked up at me. "Where are the other boys?"

"They're gone for the day, so I could get some work done."

"I won't interrupt you then. I just came by to drop off the keys for Anja's safety deposit box. I forgot she had one until the estate received her yearly bill yesterday. I believe it just contains personal items, but if you have any questions you can call me."

"I don't see your car." I craned my neck to see over the bushes.

"I walked. The office is only a mile away, and I needed a break," Karen said. "You can walk me back if you are interested. The bank is only two blocks past my door."

I never wore a watch while I was working. The sun was high overhead. Noontime. I had accomplished more than I thought I would this morning. I could take a break and grab a salad from the farmers' market that resided in the former Woolworth department store.

"Let me crate Jules and double check my acetylene tank. Can I get you a drink?"

"No, I'm fine."

I locked the door to the house with the ancient skeleton key. I had wanted to get a locksmith out to the house to put new locks on before I drove Sam back to Michigan, but time was getting short.

Karen directed me west on Mulberry Street. The sidewalks were strewn with the berries for which the street was named. Neither of us cared, and we walked the pink-stained sidewalks as though the walks were red carpets, and we, the dignitaries. How many times had we traversed this path as teenagers? We used to walk barefoot and squish the berries between our toes until they reddened us as with the sacred oath of blood sisters (which we were). And with our sisterhood came the walking secrets of adolescence—secrets that, at the time, seemed so important, but now had faded with the other trivia of the times. The solution to the Rubik's cube. Lyrics from a Hall and Oates song. The date that John Hinckley shot Ronald Reagan.

"So what's new?" I asked Karen in opposition to these visions of the past.

"I'm buying my dad's practice."

"What about your brother?"

"He's moving to Atlanta. His wife got homesick. He just got a job as a corporate lawyer down there."

"So what does this mean for you?"

"Dad's going to stay on in a limited capacity for five years. Shelly and I are going to buy the house from him and live there with the office. It's not our dream house, but Shelly knows a contractor who works miracles."

"Isn't it funny, the two of us living in houses from our childhood. Please tell me that we are moving forward with our lives."

"Of course we are. So you are definitely staying?" Karen asked.

"Yes, I'm about ninety percent sure," I replied. "You'll have to give me the name of your contractor. I was thinking of putting a showroom into the house for jewelry sales. The woman down the block has a gift shop in her home, so I'm sure I have the proper zoning."

"I'll have Shelly check into it for you, but maybe you won't have to remodel. You could just sell your work at the gift shop."

"She has mostly country crafts, candles, that sort of thing. I'm not sure my jewelry would fit."

"You'd be surprised."

The walk was short. Soon we stood before Karen's office, a large brick dwelling with a gold-lettered shingle outside.

"Here's my stop. The bank is that large yellow brick building with the ATM out front."

"Thanks."

"Hey, maybe when I move in here, we can get together to walk or jog."

"Sure, that would be great. It'll have to be when Sam is at kindergarten, though. I can't afford a sitter just yet."

I continued down the street toward the appointed building. Business people scurried in an attempt to finish their errands on their lunch hour. Men in suits and women in heels brushed by me. They carried their sprout-laced sandwiches in white paper bags. Dressed in a T-shirt and khaki shorts, I felt diminished by their uniforms. I perched my sunglasses on my head and blinked away the sunspots as I entered the dark cool of the bank.

I handed the teller my key along with the notice that showed the terms of probate. The teller pulled a long, slim box from the vault and ushered me into a private booth. Several papers, deeds, and notebooks slid forward in the box. I removed them and was about to close the box when I heard the unexpected sound. *Clink-a-clink.* I reached inside once more. My fingers closed on the worn velvet of a jewelry box. I brought it out into the blue-tinged light of the room and opened it.

Inside two diamond rings and a wedding band glittered back at me. Wishing I had my jeweler's loupe with me, I raised each piece up to the light. The cut of the stones was different than those seen at jewelry stores today. I loved vintage jewels, the way they glittered differently than their modern counterparts, as if their facets reflected a different light source. It was as if they held the glow of a bygone era, like starlight that doesn't reach the earth until after the star has collapsed inward. Or maybe it was another source altogether. Another sun or moon or some forgotten fire, waiting to be rediscovered.

I weighed the rings my palm. The wedding band was an obvious match to one of the diamond rings. Nonna's wedding set, I surmised. The lone engagement ring? That inspired my curiosity. It had to be Lena's, although there was no inscription. Even without the accompanying band, the ring felt heavy, like a broken promise.

I twisted the rings onto my fingers. Nonna's rings, larger than the other, fit smoothly over my middle finger, while Lena's diamond assumed the traditional position on my ring finger. The artificial lights of the booth played darts on the surface of the gems. I clicked shut the empty ring box and put it along with the rest of the contents of the box into my bag.

"I'd like to close out this bank box," I told the teller. And with the increased weight of my left hand, I anchored the papers that I signed with my right hand. Barbara Jean Ellington. My smooth signature floated serenely next to the rigid X. I knew all too well that I was practicing to terminate a much bigger contract.

· 31 ·

1983

I SHARE MY BIRTHDAY with Kim Carnes, Natalie Wood, and Carlos Santana, but they are not the reason people remember my birthday. I was born at 11:08 p.m. on July 20, 1969, just twelve minutes after Neil Armstrong became the first person to set foot on the moon and before Buzz Aldren had a chance to join him. Moon Baby, the nurses dubbed me.

My mother didn't want to leave for the hospital for fear that she would miss the historic event. After the *Eagle* had landed on the moon at 4:18 p.m., she finally let my dad drive her to the hospital. He waited with dual anticipation in the waiting room. The nurses and hospital staff crowded behind him to watch the screen.

My mother refused sedation so that she would be conscious to hear the shouts when the astronauts stepped on the moon. She couldn't know that her own cries of labor would drown out the cheers. After the moment of impact, *One small step for man, one giant leap for mankind,* and Walter Cronkite's tears, my father sneaked past the distracted hospital staff to inform my mother of the news. He took one peek inside the delivery room, saw my blood-rusty head protruding from my mother's body, heard her cry, "Get it out! Get it out!" and passed out cold. A minute later I was born into a world where anything was possible, into a country united to make it happen, and into a family oblivious to it all.

When I turned ten, the anniversary of the moon landing dominated the news. But the day I turned fourteen was a year I could reclaim as my own. To celebrate, Karen suggested we meet Bill and Travis at the lake. Bill Killian had never spoken to me. I was reluctant to include him in my special day, but the alternative was the awkward threesome of Travis, Karen, and me, and I didn't want to encourage that scenario.

Karen gave me some red horn-rimmed sunglasses and black jelly bracelets as birthday gifts.

"They'll go great with your bathing suit."

I put them on along with my I'M A LOVER NOT A FIGHTER T-shirt, and we headed to the beach. Wednesdays were not particularly crowded at the lake. It was mostly kids and housewives, a few retirees. The weekenders, the ones who owned noisy motorboats, were trapped in office cubicles or behind assembly lines. The lifeguards grew apathetic and flirtatious in their downtime.

Because this was a special day, Karen proposed that we pay to be ferried to the small island on the north end of the lake. We could have a picnic and go hiking. A naturalist group maintained a trail and a bird observatory on the island, but it was known more as a haven for those with romantic intentions.

Travis arrived on time, but Bill was about twenty minutes late.

"Sorry I'm late. I got detoured. They are having preliminaries for a box car derby on Quarry Road," Bill said when he finally showed.

"Hey, that sounds cool. We should go there. Wanna?" Karen said enthusiastically.

I had a feeling that my birthday was becoming less about me and more about Karen and Bill.

"Why don't you two go, and we'll meet up with you guys later at Kampmeiers," I offered.

"No," Karen said. "This is your day. We'll do what you want to do."

"I insist. Go," I said. They didn't wait for me to change my mind.

"Would you rather go with them?" I asked Travis.

"It would be fun to see the derby, but I can take only so much of Karen. I know she's your friend, but she can be flaky," Travis said.

I laughed nervously, afraid that I was flaky by association.

Keeping with our original intent to explore the island, we rented a pedal boat. In my bag, I had the sandwiches and chips that Nonna had packed for us while she was baking the most magnificent birthday cake I had ever seen. (She had even conceded to red velvet.)

Travis reached out and held my hand while we pedaled the boat northward. His hand was sweaty and warm. I had an itch under my life vest on that side, but I didn't want to move my hand. The boat inched forward, and I tried to think of something to say. I had known Travis my whole life, but that did not prepare me to sit beside him on my birthday and imagine that my wish about kissing him might very well come true before I even had a chance to blow out my candles.

He stopped pedaling about halfway to the island.

"I didn't get you a present."

"It's okay."

"I wanted to, but with my lawn jobs and visiting my granddad, I didn't have time."

"I know."

"No, you don't know. I wanted to thank you for listening to me. You are the only one who understands what I'm going through. I couldn't have made it through this summer without you."

I took off my sunglasses, which had been sliding down my nose all day, and looked at him. I realized that I might truly be the only person who would understand. I knew how his father had been arrested for beating his wife after she turned him and his friends in for selling pot to Travis's friends. Travis had been only eleven years old. I knew about the divorce and the time his mother was hospitalized for depression and a botched suicide attempt. The doctor seemed to think it was a cry for help more than an actual attempt on her own life. She hid her bandaged wrists under the sheets when Travis came to see her. We waited for the razor blades to reappear, but the doctor had been right: the medication helped.

Travis had stayed with his granddad for two weeks while she recovered, but the Reverend Ernie Platz was past eighty, beyond his child rearing years. Grandma Lena took control. She moved Travis in with her, found an apartment for Margot only blocks away, and eventually taught them how to live together. Lena enrolled Travis in a private school and shouldered the bill. She even arranged for Travis to have a Big Brother.

Dave was an English and film major at a nearby college. Once a week he took Travis to the darkened theater on Fourth Street that not only showed current features, but oldies, indies, and foreign films. Dave taught Travis how to watch movies with a critical eye and introduced him to Shakespeare's vulgarisms.

"Chicks really go for the poetry of it," Dave said.

Travis had always been more mindful than athletic. With me, he never needed to apologize for his inability to throw a baseball or dribble a basketball. His vulnerabilities created nuance in his fifteen-year-old character that I had never known in another person. I knew how fiercely he guarded his mother, how closely he related to the great Shakespearean tragedies, the movies more than the written word.

I never pitied Travis, but not because circumstance didn't warrant the sentiment—it did. The fact was, he never required it. He loved his aging granddad. He was grateful to Lena and Dave and his teachers for their care. He was never a child in crisis when we played kick the can, or Ollie Ollie over, or flashlight tag. He was intense and solitary with some of his pursuits, but his isolation seemed intellectual rather than unfortunate. I squeezed his hot hand and wondered why I waited until my fourteenth birthday to fall in love with him. Maybe Karen was right. Maybe fourteen was the diamond age, when your nipples harden on either side of your heart's quickening pulse, and kissing is something you need to do every night even if it is just on paper. Paper kisses, like paper napkins, ephemeral and disposable, wiping your mouth clean to disguise an appetite.

I squeezed Travis's hand again. I didn't intend the action as an invitation, but Travis knew. His lips were as hot and moist as his hand had been and still was, but I didn't mind. Our orange life jackets bumped into each other, making the embrace cumbersome. Travis stopped to change positions, and then he kissed me again.

Before today, I had kissed two boys. Mostly my previous experience had been a fumbling of a lower lip or a tentative poke of the tongue, the result of a dare or mutual curiosity. But Travis kissed me for real, as my mind raced to think of adjectives for my diary. When we pulled apart, Travis looked at me with his ochre eyes, two suns burning my retinas. I felt my skin and organs blister, and I panicked.

"Come on," I said and let go of his hand.

I dove deep into the sweet lap of the lake. Once underwater, I wanted to scream, to mimic a siren's wail to unsuspecting sailors, but my life vest brought me too quickly back to surface. I would have risen anyway with a buoyancy of the spirit.

Travis watched me surface, and then jumped in after me. We floated in orbits around each other and kissed some more. After twenty minutes, we attempted the near impossible task of climbing back onto our boat. We were heavier, waterlogged and love-logged. Together we managed to push and pull ourselves aboard and resume our journey. The island greened before us. We didn't notice the clouds behind us.

· 32 ·

2000

I WAS ONLY THIRTY—five years younger than Cancer Society recommendations—when I had my first mammogram. A technician had flattened my breasts until the three dimensions I had cultivated for so long with a well-engineered bra became two-dimensional webs on film. I understood the language of two dimensions, the illusion. I had been a painting major for two years before I switched to metals. But to see my doctor point to the images before me and hear pronouncements of my own good health startled me.

My mother, Judy, had been forty-eight when she found her first lump—before menopause, when breast cancer tends to be genetic more than environmental. I had been adamant at my annual gynecological checkup, and my gynecologist finally bent to my demands, much to the dismay of my HMO.

Even with the clean diagnosis, I was vigilant about my self-exams to the point of compulsion. In the shower or prone on my bed, I questioned my fullness and my health and my losses.

Months went by when I did my exam only on the pink ribbon day, but those were rare. The more stressful my life, the more I reached beneath my bra, like a man compulsively checking his back pocket to make sure he hadn't lost his wallet.

The evening before I was to drive Sam back to Michigan for the rest of the summer, I read him three books and lightly covered him with a sheet. I closed the door to his room despite his sleepy protests. Then I went into my own room, flopped backward onto the bed, unbuttoned my cotton shirt, and undid the front clasp of my bra.

The valley between my breasts pooled with the night's perspiration. I dipped my middle finger in it as if it were holy water. But this was no self-blessing. I moved my fingers to the place where my skin became softer and the flesh yielded to the pressure. This exercise had never been erotic, but it had never been strictly medical, either. I thought of this probing as an emotional crutch even when the repetition suggested psychological malignancy.

My fingers traced a spiral on each breast, tweaking each nipple in turn. Sequentially, I checked my underarms, velvety with the day's hair growth. *Nothing.* I was dissatisfied with my lumpless condition so I repeated the process, twice, three times.

I had nursed Sam for almost two years after he was born. I felt the smocking of stretch marks made during those days when I was so full of milk that I burned. Here, under my shirt was an account of pleasures I had received and nourishment I had given. With my fingers I checked the balance on these accounts.

I didn't want to find my mother here. Or did I? I longed for the days of daughtering, receiving comfort. The shared acts of shopping away a disappointment or sipping cups of coffee together. And what of my days as a wife? The cellular level of my marriage memories haunted me. The way Bryce had cupped my breasts, my bottom, even my ripening belly. The bowl of his hand opened with supplication. And in the remembering, I felt the all too familiar ripple that told me exactly how long it had been since I had been touched, measured, calmed, worshiped.

In the bright light of a ballerina lamp, my body's betrayal disgusted me. I lay in the lamp's glare, stroking my breasts for the world to see through curtains as shadowy and transparent as mammogram films. I buttoned my shirt and rolled onto my belly. Reaching for my pillows, I rejected the comparison between the softness I had surrendered and the one I was seeking.

Fuck! Why did I have to take Sam to Michigan tomorrow?

I punched the pillows in a visceral need to connect with something other than myself. Karen had volunteered to take Jules so Sam and I could get an early start. Now, I missed him terribly. I wanted to run my hands over his tawny coat and let him lick the salt of tears that I wished would flow. I left the light on hoping the glare would cause my eyes to water, but it only burned my eyes. The bed creaked as I reached down and grasped the mattress, trying to pull myself into sleep. As I pulled, I felt a foreign object, and recovered from between the mattress and box spring, a paperback.

Lord of the Treasure. I smiled. That book must have been under the mattress for seventeen years. I fanned the pages and scanned the back cover.

Chase Maverick wanted nothing more than to find the ancient shipwreck that his company had spent years searching for. But now with funds diminishing and contracts running out, could he really put all his faith in the new marine scientist he had hired, especially one so lovely as Dr. Laura Primm? Even behind her labcoat and glasses, her beauty was apparent, but so was her mystery. Why was she so desperate for this job? Chase Maverick knew what he was after, but what treasure was Laura chasing?

I remembered the story. I couldn't recount the details of any of the important works I had read in English class, but I knew the subtleties of this plot. Or maybe I had read so many of these

novels that the formula was the cue. I opened the book and began reading. After about sixty pages the words started to mingle
and blur.

A few hours later I awoke to sense the vile damp of my own
saliva and the offensive brightness of the lamp. The book lay on
the pillow beside me. I straightened up and smoothed my shirt.
Two a.m. I wasn't tired, and realized if we left now, we could be
in Michigan by noon. I could grab a quick shower at the house
and relax before Bryce came home from work.

I lifted the sleep-heavy body of my son and loaded him into
the packed car. With any luck, he would miss the entire drive
through Pennsylvania.

"I love you, Mom."

"I love you, too, Sam. It's not time to wake up yet."

I propped his head on the pillow and strapped him into his
seat. He was still asleep. The skeleton keys weighed heavy in
my front pocket; the metal chilled me through the thin cotton.
I didn't look at the house after I climbed into the driver's seat. I
looked back instead—one last inspection of my son in the rear
seat. His head was tilted at what had to be an uncomfortable
angle. *Bryce would never take him from me.* It was more of a
hope than a thought. I started the engine, but I knew that fear
would be driving my car.

· 33 ·

1983

ONCE ON THE ISLAND, Travis and I held hands and hiked up the trail. It was a rocky path, and I had to look down to check my footing. Even then I stumbled a few times into Travis's tilting body. He held me tight. In those instances, I felt how tall he had become. My head was not even as high as his shoulder, but I could still feel his breath as it quickened during our upward climb. We didn't speak. Our silences were less clumsy now that we had gotten our first kiss out of the way. I was grateful for that.

We were almost at the lookout point when a breeze parted the trees. I smelled a summer storm first before I saw the rain-heavy sky. When we reached the top and stepped out of what should have been the shade of the trees, the darkness remained. Against the graying horizon, the leaves waved their silvery undersides.

"We have to find cover," Travis said.

I leaned into him. He would not let anything happen to me. "Will the boat be okay?" I asked.

"I tied it tight. It'll get a little wet."

We had seen a few people walking down the trail but did not see signs of life at the top. We were alone. A deserted island. I was too eager to see the romance of this moment.

Beside the lookout deck sat a tiny picnic pavilion. We ran for cover just as fat drops of rain began to kick up the dust of the trail.

"Want a sandwich?" I asked once we settled ourselves on top of one of the picnic tables. The sandwiches were more than a little squished, but Travis took one out of the sack. At the end of the pavilion that butted up against a maintenance shed, a Coke machine glowed an eerie red. We dug quarters out of our bag and fed them into the machine. The cans clanked out.

"I can't believe someone lugs up cases of soda to refill this machine."

"There's a service road over there." Travis pointed down at the view of a bridge. I immediately flushed with stupidity.

"Oh," I said. I didn't need to ask about the electric supply.

The storm that followed was nothing short of spectacular. Thunder cracked behind us. Lightening struck down a tree nearby, and we felt an underground current that shook the table on which we were sitting. The red Coke machine, a bright heart in the storm, suddenly darkened, and its hum stopped. I scooted closer to Travis.

Even in the cool of the afternoon I knew this storm for what it was—a poltergeist, the spirit form of my reluctance to enter adulthood. I was in love with Travis and eager to find out if our relationship would mature, but I was unwilling to move into a future that in all probability would tear us apart. And it would happen—sooner rather than later. For the forces of nature were at work not only on our island but also in a hospital room, miles away. What we witnessed as shards of electricity, lightning, and a loss of power was also the soul of the Reverend Ernie Platz, testing its belief in the afterlife.

PART TWO

Dredging the Blue

· 34 ·

My second homecoming to Mulberry Street was no less wary than my first. While rains greeted us after our arrival in June, my July welcome came in the form of a wet heat that tattooed a permanent sheen to my skin. In an ordinary July, I would have succumbed to the heaviness and slowed my work, but solitude plays tricks on an unoccupied mind.

Even in the torch of midday, I kept busy in the metal studio. I allowed nothing to penetrate my thoughts except for my work, a masterful set of silverware I was creating for the alumni art show. I would not think of my last hours with Sam at the pool or the as yet unpacked trailer in the barn or the divorce papers that I had signed cordially enough. *Too cordially,* Karen had said (even though she had advised me to do just that).

My new table setting was everything to me in this hard sequence of moments. I was an alumna with a reputation to uphold. I had been that student who put a glow on a teacher's face. The pupil to brag about. My teachers did not realize this until my final semester, however, but my bachelor of fine arts show had changed all of that. It had spawned a yearly event that continued to this day.

Even I will admit that I had not been a remarkable artist. I did have a unique perspective, however, and more important, I knew what words to spew at our critiques: *form, flow, elemental, juxtaposition, functionality, aesthetic.* I could recite lines of poetry and recall reviews of similar pieces and say all the things that my stumbling craft could not. My art professors, more realists of snug academia than artists of the world, came to admire my commentary. I would have walked away with a B average and a beginner's anonymity had it not been for my thesis show.

Right before my final semester was about to begin, my mother discovered the lump. It's probably nothing, her gynecologist had said. *You're so young.* But before I started classes, the C word hushed all of us.

Bryce and I had been married for six months at that point. Not that it mattered. Bryce was studying for the bar exam, and I was spending most of my nights in the metals studio. We met each other for frenzied sessions of lovemaking that sometimes had to be combined with a shower for the sake of time. With damp hair and a damp crotch, I would return to my rolling stool at the studio where I hunched, bleary-eyed, over pin findings and bezel settings.

During one of my all-night studio sessions, I found my inspiration. In a corner of the studio, freshmen and sophomores were playing cards while waiting their turn to anodize aluminum in the huge tanks by the back door. The sound of the shuffling took me back to the summers I spent at my grandmothers': the card clubs, the poetry readings, women talk.

Then it hit me. I would turn my bachelor's degree show into a card party. I would serve tea, invite the brightest poets from Philadelphia to read, and showcase my art. The idea flowered in the hours when my critical mind was already sleeping. I outlined a plan of action to make this event into a fundraiser for breast cancer: FemininiTEA.

Lana Franklin at the local cancer association had been invaluable. She set me up with letters asking suppliers to gift me with art supplies so I could auction my pieces for the cause. Female poets clamored to be included, and I found three like-minded artists to fill out the program.

For my part, I crafted dozens of unique teaspoons to be used during the tea, auctioned off at the end of the evening. The spoons were a beautiful parade of figures with the hollowed scoops as faces and the handles as flowing bodies. I duplicated some of them as cast forms, but some I cut and forged as one of a kind.

Of my fellow artists, a ceramist made teacups, a fiber artist contributed table linens, and a graphic designer did the promotional work. When the university staff got notice of this happening, publicity became a nonissue. I, known by then as Bobbi Ellington, became the star of the art department. Recruiters used me as an example of the kind of dedicated artists for which the school was known. The *Philadelphia Inquirer* even covered the story in the weekend section.

My parents came up from Richmond for the event. Nonna supplied all the pastries, even though she was officially retired. And Bryce came for the opening night only, which was just as well because he bristled at one poet's allusion to man as "woman's poor counterfeit."

The success of the event resounded for months. Orders for more spoons overwhelmed me. And though I got plenty of money from the transactions, a percentage of the sales went to fund mammograms for women in a low-income bracket. From there, I branched into a line of pins and rings. Occasionally, when asked, I contributed articles to magazines such as *Ornament* or *Metalsmith*. *American Craft* included me in a collective profile of emerging new talent.

For five years, even after we moved to Michigan, I continued to host FemininiTEA each year in Philadelphia, and extended the event to Detroit. Student and professional artists alike donated their efforts. In 1997, three years after Sam was born, the American Cancer Society honored me at a national awards banquet. I took Mom, beaming in her newest wig, as my guest. In my acceptance speech, I thanked baby Sam, my mother, my father, and my grandmothers. It wasn't until later that I realized I had neglected to include Bryce. He wasn't in the audience, so it didn't seem to matter.

The idea for this new place setting had come to me on my first evening home from Michigan. I was fumbling with four diamonds, almost juggling them with my fingers. I had removed the two stones from my grandmothers' engagement rings, one from my mother's, and the final one was my own. Those diamonds represented the range of possibilities: a broken engagement, early widowhood, divorce, and a long and happy marriage.

I wanted to use the stones to represent the lives of my family members. I considered jewelry, but these diamonds had said all they could as rings. I decided to take them out of the realm of the ornamental and bring them to purpose. A place setting would bring me full circle and remind the art community of my service. Most importantly, the project was challenging enough to keep me from missing my sandy-haired son.

I would have worked well into the night if my senses did not perceive the heavy, succulent smells of grilled meat. The scent brought me back to my corporeal self. *When had I last eaten anything?* I walked into the yard with Jules at my heels. Travis was standing as governor over Lena's ancient grill. I did not register surprise, but thought myself a very powerful conjurer to have him before me. I had wanted so much to see him, but without the ploy of my son, I felt shy about calling.

"I didn't want to disturb you," he said.

I walked over to him, and as if it were the most natural thing in the world, Travis leaned over and gave me a light kiss on the lips. Then he poured some cabernet into a small wineglass.

"These will have to do. I couldn't find any red wine glasses."

"That's because they are still packed away with all the other goodies I got in the settlement."

"It went well? You signed? He signed?"

Was it my imagination or did Travis seem pleased?

"You would not believe how well it went. We even went out to dinner afterwards as a family—like we were celebrating. It was surreal." I took a sip from my glass, the tannins of the wine playing softly on my tongue.

Travis looked quizzically at me. "I was really nervous for you. I guess it's because my own experience is still pretty new. Are you okay?"

"Travis, I don't even want to think about it. I may be in denial, but I can't think about my divorce. I have to spend all my energy not missing Sam, you know?"

"I can imagine what you must be going through; the bond between parent and child isn't something I know much about," he said quietly.

He was right, of course, and I felt stupid for talking about Sam.

"I'm sorry, Travis." I didn't know what else to say.

Travis could not possibly know. He understood the lessons of a failed marriage, but he had never had the opportunity to miss a child.

"It is quiet around here without my little buddy." He smiled, a seduction unto itself, and I knew that even though Travis had been nursing his own childless void for years, he could share my pain. *Beware this man; he is sensitive.* Travis flipped the steaks on the grill. The loud hissing filled the silences so neither of us felt obligated to speak.

I traced the edge of my wineglass with my finger. I wanted to trace my own lips, but that would betray exactly what I had on my mind. I had signed the divorce papers. Sam was not an issue. Why wouldn't Travis want to test the boundaries with a kiss? But maybe he wasn't testing. Maybe he already knew.

I looked at the man standing before me. *I could have handled his attractiveness, even basked in it, but why did he have to be so generous and emotionally available?* Already I could sense the complications of having a mere affair with such a man. Something about him already had too much depth for that.

I was not ready for the alternative, a serious romance. I felt that my skin was barely intact over my delicate organs. What would it be like to brush up against someone when I felt this raw and exposed? The friction alone would send my body into agony. Red wine did not help. I could already feel the warmth as the tips of my ears colored.

"So your trip was okay? You had no troubles?" Travis asked.

"Actually, I did get busted for speeding on the way back," I answered. "When I told the cop I was just returning from getting a divorce, he commiserated with me. I am not sure, but I think he asked me out."

"If you think he asked you out, he probably did."

"He won't get my address from my Michigan license. Still it would be funny if he called Bryce."

Travis chuckled, and I laughed, too. The flush spread to my cheeks.

I hadn't told Travis everything, which would have added a new level of humor to the anecdote. But I wasn't ready to share that side of the story, filled with my foolish superstitions. On the drive to Michigan, I had noticed the St. Christopher medal stuck to my dash. The patron saint of travelers, a gift from my father, had been with me since I bought my first clunker in college. It was still working its charm four cars later. The craziness was that I had renounced God and Mary, but I could not rid myself of the lesser saints. Mine had always been a religion built on details, smaller parts of the whole. In the past, whenever I misplaced my keys or purse, I petitioned St. Anthony, the saint of lost objects. And when I met a particularly steep hill while jogging, I had cried, "Little Flower, give me power," a prayer to St. Thérèse. Though I tried, I could not shake those habits, those superstitions, any more than I could stop brushing my teeth.

I knew I was being silly, especially with St. Christopher. I could not travel without my dashboard protector when Sam was in the car. It felt too risky, as if I were provoking God—in whom I had lost faith—to strike down my firstborn. When Sam was no longer a passenger, I put St. Christopher in the glove compartment. I considered throwing the medal away at the first rest stop in Pennsylvania, but I didn't, and the cop stopped me twenty miles down the turnpike. My first driving offense, ever.

After the police car drove away from me, I had pulled the charm from the glove compartment.

"Okay, you can stay," I had said to the medal. "But let's agree on some terms. From now on, none of this saint stuff. You are just Chris. Got that?" The remainder of my drive home transpired without incident.

TRAVIS SLICED THE STEAKS and layered them on top of salads he had prepared earlier. Lettuce, tomato, grilled peppers and onions, cheese and ranch dressing. I would have been more impressed if my hunger had not been such a distraction and if my head had not been swirling from the wine.

"You do realize that I am totally at your mercy, don't you," I teased Travis, hoping he would catch the guardedness of my voice.

Travis didn't smile. "You signed your papers, BJ. You won't be at anybody's mercy ever again."

"Divorce hardened you that much?"

"If it didn't harden you, you didn't do it right."

"Well, Karen tells me I had it too easy."

Easy. It had not been easy to sign those papers, on my birthday no less, but the pain was lessening. How easy it was to sit with

Travis and wait for August to wash over me with the return of my son. Travis would make such a lovely distraction. I reached up and touched his face, unaware that the action had become something other than pure notion. When he looked at me, I panicked and pretended to remove a trace of dressing from his mouth.

It had to be the wine. I scrambled to remember the saint to call upon to keep me from drunkenness. Amethysts were stones that were said to have such power, but I didn't own any. Dionysus came to mind. The god of wine. Was there one drop of Greek blood in me that caused me to enjoy the ceremony of a good meal and its accompanying drink?

Travis and I ate and talked, but mostly we ate. The food was nourishing and delicious, like the meals I used to eat on Mulberry Street. I recounted details of my trip, and Travis told me about his activities during my absence. He had found a house to buy, but he had yet to put in an offer. We didn't discuss the reasons for his reluctance, but I knew. Divorce had a way of making you second-guess yourself, like driving a car after a bad accident, when you are too skittish to even make a left turn ever again.

The day's sky began to fade; the horizon wrinkled with purple clouds. I hoped that somewhere in Michigan, Bryce was reading to Sam from the collection of Thomas the Tank Engine stories he had brought along. I hoped Bryce would make sure Sam brushed his teeth before bed, and I prayed (to nobody in particular) that none of Sam's little teeth would fall out while he was away from me. No scabs. No haircuts. I wanted wholeness to return to me next month. Wholeness and the perception that I had missed nothing in Sam's young life. Travis sat observing me from across the table. From the sympathetic look on his face, I knew he must have been reading my mind.

"Come on," he said at last. He grabbed Jules's leash from the hook by the door. "Don't worry about the dishes. We'll get them after our walk."

In silence, we walked toward the lake.

· 35 ·

AFTER I HAD UNLOCKED the security box and found my grand-mothers' diamonds, I had overlooked the remaining contents. Four weeks later I emptied my bag and found twelve savings bonds, Lena's death certificate, an additional life insurance policy, three Indian head nickels, a driver's license that expired in 1968, and two spiral notebooks wrapped in a newspaper article, bound with a rubber band. I immediately recognized the newspaper article. *What serendipitous force had brought it into my life at this time?*

I removed the old rubber band. It crumbled into dust. The newspaper article wasn't just yellowed; it was brittle and unreadable in the spots where the print rested against the metal spirals of the notebook. But here it was, nine years later, the article from the school newspaper on my BFA show. Was Nonna sending me a message from the grave? How strange that it should appear now as I was planning my college homecoming.

I opened one of the small notebooks. The pages crinkled in a way that comforted me. I had a different reaction to the content.

I did not want to see Nonna's lilting script as it laced each page.
I had only to recognize two words at the top of the first page to
know that the stuff inside would rust away the remaining armor
I had worked so hard to position.

Dear Judy. This was a letter to Nonna's daughter, my mother.
It might contain thoughts that Judy would have passed along
to me as her daughter, but then again, this might be the kind of
thing that a mother would take with her in death. Now, I was
holding the notebooks in a queer leapfrog of information. If the
contents of these epistles were not for the generations, then I was
trespassing on my mother's grave.

But when I spotted my name as I flipped through to the fourth
page, I read it as an invitation. The notebooks had been wrapped
in an article about me, after all. I sat down at the kitchen table
with a strange sense of anticipation.

April 29, 1991
Dear Judy,

   I am writing to you on the first anniversary of Lena's
death. Under normal circumstances, I would expect you'd
remember and call me with words of comfort, but you are
fighting your own battle, in which dates only have the sig-
nificance of various doctor's appointments. Today, you start
a new cycle of poisons designed to promote health. I struggle with the knowledge that you are following in Lena's
path. You are younger than she was, and I must believe
you will pull through. I can't sustain another loss, just yet;
I have not recovered fully from the first one. Maybe you'll
remember the anniversary when you are lying in the inner
chambers of the new treatment center, or maybe you won't.
Regardless, I suspect (and hope) that today, Lena's spirit
resides less with me in my grief and more with you in your
ordeal, but I am thinking of her all the same.

It has only been a year since I made her a promise to take our story to my grave, but it is a promise I am not sure I can keep in light of new developments. Your cancer is a weight I feel, a stone on my heart. Like all mothers, I worry that I have caused your battle with this heinous disease, not based on genetics, but toxins of the spirit that I have knowingly and unknowingly passed on to you. Perhaps I am giving myself too much credit.

I wanted so much to be close to you, as mother and daughter should be, but we always had an unnamed distance between us. Was it this, I wonder, the secret that I have been carrying with me for fifty years? I was protecting you. Lena and I both were, but when I see you withered by disease, I have to ask myself—from what were we protecting you? The only answer I have arrived in the mail today.

Barbara Jean sent me the newspaper that featured her art show. Our Bobbi Ellington is all grown up. Not only have you raised a talented artist but a woman of conscience. You have given that flower everything she needed to grow. Things I could not give you, you cultivated for the sake of your daughter. I could not be more proud.

However, and this is what burdens me, directly across from the story of our girl's success was an obituary of an alumnus who bequeathed a large portion of his estate to the university. His name is Henry Littlehail, though I knew him as Hank. My eyes crossed from the picture of Hank to Barbara Jean and back again. Their features blurred. I focused again on Hank and I spat on the bastard whose image kissed Barbara Jean's picture every time I closed the paper.

I turned back to the newspaper on my lap. I unfolded it to take a look at the man Nonna was describing. He was an older gentleman with glasses and a beard. Nothing in his features would have caused me to look at this picture if I hadn't been directed to it. He was just a man, as anonymous as he had been when I first dismissed his face.

Who was this man? Why did he matter? And what was this all about? The grandmother I knew was never as stiff and formal, almost cold, as the narrator of this epistle. Granted, the letter was not meant for me, the granddaughter with whom Nonna had always connected effortlessly. I thought back to the relationship between Nonna and my own mother. I knew my mother had a difficult childhood, but the gulf in her relationship with Nonna had closed over time, hadn't it? Yet here in this letter, Nonna seemed to be detaching herself more; holding my mother at arm's length. *Why?* The only way to answer my questions was to read further.

Briefly, my anger turned to gratitude. If Hank had not been so vile, my life would have taken a different road. Then, I turned once more to rage when I remembered how this man snuffed out sweetness to replace it with sweetness. How does he get the power to sentence me with one life over another? How dare he play God?

Hank Littlehail is a character in the story I must write. He is introduced somewhere in the second act, but maybe I will move him up to the first act where villains are typically introduced. This is my story, and perhaps when I have finished, you will find that the only monster in this tale is not Hank, but your own mother.

I need to preface this account with my history. It is important to me that you know how this story was played out before me. My great-grandparents were immigrants from Sweden. I don't know the *hows* and *whys* of their exodus, but their son Gustaf, the first in our family born on American soil, had riches and smarts enough to buy a tract of land. He built a stone house with sandstone he quarried himself. This is my current residence, the house in which I was born.

Mulberry Farm was named for the native trees that my grandfather cursed every time he pulled another sapling from his fields. The farm and its occupants experienced seven years of fertility. The harvests were heavy, and my grandparents were blessed with three daughters. Like the mulberry trees, the daughters vexed their father with their need for constant attention. Gustaf had a favorite in the youngest, my mother. Ada was fair with an impudent chin and a jutting jaw that flaunted her stubbornness as if it was a new hat bought for no reason other than she fancied it.

When Ada was four, at the tail end of the seven years of prosperity, a fever passed through the house, enfeebling all the females. It was at little Ada's bed that Gustaf prayed, and it was to her that God offered relief. The illness rendered her mother, my grandmother, barren, and the barrenness made her peevish. Ada's oldest sister Sara died, and her second sister Anja lost her hearing and some of her mental faculties. Ada grew more beautiful in body and mind as the years passed, but Anja regressed to a point where she required constant care. My grandmother tried to give her what care she could, but in the end, it wasn't enough. One fine spring day about three years after the fever had ravaged the family, Anja wandered out of the house while my grandmother and Ada were doing the laundry. The family, along with the few close neighbors and a hunting dog, searched for her for three days. At dusk on the third day, Gustaf pulled his daughter's swollen, purple body out of shallow stream on the property.

Ada became all the more precious to her father, but his affections suffocated her to the point of rebellion. She didn't want to marry a suitable man with a strong back and an even stronger sense of business. She didn't care that Gustaf's prayers had saved her from death. She countered Gustaf's prayers to God with some of her own.

Every evening after the supper dishes and the last milking, Ada would go to the lake to absorb its calm. Every evening a young painter would sit along the shore and paint by the diminishing light. During the day, Sid Stevens worked at the gristmill to earn money for his passage to France where he would paint with the masters. The moment Ada danced into his painting, he knew he would have to work twice as long as anticipated so he could purchase two tickets for the boat.

Sid painted the vista of the lake for Ada, asked her to marry him, and promised to take her away from the sandstone and mulberry farm and back to the continent of her ancestors.

Gustaf raged at the hasty match. His dream of a slower life vanished the day Ada boarded the boat. He hated Sid Stevens for taking away what God had given him. Before they embarked, Gustaf pulled his new son-in-law aside and told him, "If you are not a success in three years, I will bring Ada back myself."

"And what is your measure of success?" Sid goaded.

"You will never reach it."

May 1, 1991

Despite the threat, Sid and Ada stayed seven years in Paris and the surrounding countryside. Ada danced in the homes and landscapes of Picasso and Braque. She chatted on occasion with a few aging Impressionists. Sid loved being surrounded by such greatness, but he had a wife who was too lovely and daring for comfort. Jealousy began to crowd the other emotions in Sid's mind. His art was always one step removed from recognition, and his wife was one step too close.

For money, Sid worked at a gallery where all day long he touched great art, framing it not only with wood but also with envy. He lost his job after slashing a work by a lesser-known cubist. He claimed it was an accident, but he tasted blood in his cheek as he watched his wife talking to the artist. The knife slipped in his grip.

Ada's father paid for their passage home. War had broken out in Europe, and he wanted his daughter on his own soil. With a heavy heart, Sid and Ada obeyed the summons. When Ada saw her parents, she gasped at the sunken faces that had blanched in her absence. Her mother was toothless and nearly mad. She talked to people who weren't in the room and ignored those who were.

Gustaf wasted no time in tethering his son-in-law to the plow. Dirt replaced paint under Sid's fingernails, and he grew to despise the colors of sienna and umber, vowing never again to let them touch his palette. Farm work did not come in shifts like millwork. Sid had no hours off for painting. His resentment escalated, and he found his only release in making noisy, rambunctious love to the farmer's daughter while the farmer lay in his bed across the hall.

Sid didn't stop his feverish lovemaking when Ada announced she was pregnant. His ardor continued without restraint until Ada started to bleed in her sixth month. She lost the baby, a son, but soon became pregnant again. This time she moved into the bedroom down the hall. Gustaf could not hide his pleasure at Sid's symbolic castration.

In those final days when Ada was too heavy to dance, she tried to make amends to her husband but to no avail. I was born in a big bed in the back room of the house and named Anja Augusta Stevens after my aunt, the one who drowned in the stream. The year was 1917, the same year my father enlisted to fight the enemies of the United States and France.

In doing so, he called a stalemate to the war at home. Gustaf had no son-in-law to manage his farm. Ada had no flight from her father. And Sid pointed an Army issue rifle at the European countryside instead of his sable brushes.

I closed the notebook. The letter continued with more dated entries, but I could decipher only so much of Nonna's scrawl before my eyes strained. I lifted my head and looked across the kitchen to exercise my eyes. Sid Stevens's painting drew me into its theater. I imagined the lake the way it was before the county had mistakenly given it the name of Blue. This piece of water had meant so much to my family. Though Nonna's letter hadn't confirmed it, I knew that the lake had attracted my great-grandfather to his farm. His fields did not border the water but he must have had quite a vista when he was plowing the upper acres. I refused to be sad that this painting, along with the others, belonged to Travis. Nonna had been perfectly clear in her intentions.

But what had made her change her mind? I had yet to figure that one out. When Karen had told me that Nonna had changed her will the previous September, I had excavated my design journals and day planner.

What had I talked to Nonna about? I had been planning Sam's October birthday party. Bryce had been representing a rich client in Detroit. He hadn't been around. That was the other strange thing. Bryce had drawn up Nonna's previous will. Why didn't she ask him to handle the codicil? Granted, the Sewickys had been Nonna's main legal team since the seventies, but the codicil would have taken so little of Bryce's time, and he would have been glad to do it.

I again grabbed my sketchbook and flipped through my hasty notes and careful sketches. Stuck between the pages was a postcard from my parents. They had taken a cruise in September. Mom was dying, and the tour of the Virgin Islands was their last hurrah. A lump formed in my throat. Yes, Nonna and I had discussed my parents' cruise. I remembered clearly now. My parents were so giddy about the trip, even my mother, withered by disease. My father had alluded to the possibility that he might never return. They would just sail away together until the water could carry them no farther.

"Nonna, can you imagine having a love like that?"

"Honey, I did have a love like that."

I had sighed, not realizing the insight I must have given about the state of my marriage. Could that have been the sentiment that troubled Nonna?

Nonna may have guessed that my marriage wouldn't last. By that point, Nonna may have known that Travis's marriage had failed. Was she giving Travis the paintings as a way to bring the two of us together? Nonna knew that I would balk at the bequest—that it would create animosity, not attraction. Maybe Nonna wanted to keep us apart. I was as confused as ever.

Whatever Nonna's intention, she would have known the results. Years ago, Nonna had revealed that she could often predict the future.

"We all have the gift, BJ, but some of us lose it along the way."

"Okay, Nonna, what is my future?"

She had correctly predicted the birth of a son. "You are the last in the line of beatific women. The last of the storytellers and mystics. It is up to you to leave other hints of my legends and our existence. I will have no more daughters to do it for me."

"Oh, Nonna. You don't need a great-granddaughter to carry on. You will live forever," I had said, but Nonna's prediction had sent shivers down my spine and through my belly.

One year later, Sam had been born male even though the sonogram technician had proclaimed him a girl. I had wanted more children; I still did. There were months that Bryce and I had halfheartedly tried to conceive again, but we were quick to put our efforts on hold at the slightest provocation: a new house, a new car, a vacation, a class reunion, a foot operation.

There were no more daughters. Nonna had been correct. So what? It was a lucky guess that proved nothing. Surely Nonna would not have changed her will based on clairvoyance. Or would she?

I put aside the notebooks and resumed my work on the silver forks. These were the representations of my grandmothers. The prongs, wavy in their design, expressed Nonna's and Lena's hair. The two forks fit together like a puzzle. The diamonds glistened on the interlocking hands of the handles. I was pleased with my progress on the place setting.

I polished Nonna's fork to a reflective finish, a mirror. On the Lena fork, I used a sandblasted surface in a curvy pattern to echo the tines and hint at the scales of a mermaid's tail. As sculpture, the forks were satisfying, both separately and as a unit, a credit to the endless cardboard mock-ups I made in preparation for these pieces. I smiled as I ran a silver cloth over them for the fifth time.

I derived pleasure from this moment, when creation was complete, but I had yet to share my work with anyone else. Sometimes I succumbed to my inner critic and reworked a troublesome element, but for the most part, those issues were dealt with earlier in the designing stage. My art was good; I was confident of that. I needed no confirmation other than my own satisfaction.

· 36 ·

As I was becoming more absorbed in my work, I was keeping later hours and subsequently sleeping later each morning. Jules did not necessarily agree with this new schedule. Six-thirty a.m., feeding and elimination: that was his schedule. After the sun had been up for about an hour, Jules dug his nose under the sheet and into the back of my thigh.

"All right. I am getting up," I muttered.

The dog stood back and waited for me to pull on my robe. He cocked his head to the side, and I realized that my hair was sticking up in the back. Leave it to Jules to announce a bad hair day. I grabbed my brush and gave my hair a quick run-through. Straight and brown, it hung limp to my shoulders, except on those special occasions when I dug out my curling iron and flipped the ends up to give myself a little attitude.

"Better?" I asked, fully realizing the desperation that shows from seeking approval from a dog.

Jules followed me to the kitchen where I prepared a bowl of dog food sprinkled with some leftover chicken. I poured myself some orange juice and leaned against the counter. Travis had asked me to go on the boat today, but first I wanted to update the accounting ledger for my business. I would be forever grateful to my father for insisting that I take those business courses.

As I set my glass down, I noticed the light blinking on the answering machine. I had turned the phone off last night as I often did when I was working on a particularly delicate technique in my studio. I pressed the button.

The monotone voice announced the time of the call. "Eleven-sixteen p.m." Who would call me so late on a Saturday night?

"Bobbi, it's Bryce." *Oh no! Something's happened to Sam.* I knew it instantly. "Sorry to call you so late. I just got back from the emergency room with Sam. It's nothing to worry about, but he fell from the golf cart tonight and broke his arm. Left arm luckily. A buckle fracture. Very common for kids his age. He's going to be fine. You don't need to drive out here. The ER doctor put a splint on it until we make it in to see the orthopedist, who is a client of mine, on Monday. He's working us into his schedule, first thing, with no appointment. Give me a call when you get this message."

I panicked and had to redial the phone number three times until I got it correct—the phone number that until recently had been my own. Sam answered on the second ring.

"Hello, Ellingtons." He sounded so grown up that I wanted to cry.

"Hey, bud, it's Mommy. How are you doing? I heard you broke your arm."

"Yeah, and Daddy says I can get a green cast on Monday."

"Why green? I thought your favorite color was purple?"

"No, it's green now. For Michigan State colors and to go with the new shirt Daddy got me."

He changed his favorite color? I tried to hide my disappointment. "Go Spartans. Does your arm hurt?"

"Only a little. I got a lollypop, but it was the yucky orange kind so I gave it to a little girl who was crying."

"That was nice of you."

"Here, Mommy, talk to Daddy." Without warning, Sam concluded our conversation.

I heard some shuffling and Bryce's voice talking to Sam. "I paused your DVD. Just press the arrow button on the remote."

We never owned a DVD player.

Bryce picked up the phone. "Bobbi?"

"Hello, Bryce." I made my voice sound as sunny as possible to disguise emotions I could not even name.

"I don't want you to worry about us boys. I am taking care of Sam. This just happened so quickly. We were out at glow golf—"

"Bryce. It's okay. I know it was an accident." *Sunny, sunny, sunny.* I breathed. "He is five. These kinds of things are going to happen. I just wish I could be there for him."

Bryce sighed. "Oh, good. I was so worried you would freak out over this."

I pictured him raking his hand through his hair in relief. "I am capable of rational moments, Bryce." I tried hard to hold my tongue, but the retort slipped out. I quickly recovered. "What did the doctor say?"

"It's a buckle fracture on his ulna. Very common with kids his age. They said that most often parents don't come in until the third day, when the kid is still complaining about it. I didn't want to go into the emergency room on a Saturday night, but I erred on the side of caution because I knew you'd never let me live it down if something happened to Sam while he was with me."

"Well, you got that right."

"I called Mike, an orthopedist I represented last year. He said to bring Sam in any time on Monday morning, and they'd squeeze him in. He even got on the phone with Sam and told him he could pick out the color of his cast and that he'd still be able to swim with it on."

"How long will it be on?" I asked.

"Mike said about four weeks, which means he'll still have it on when I bring him back. He says he has a friend from med school in your area. He'll get me his card."

"I guess that's good. Can we get copies of the X-rays?"

"I'll look into it. I'm sure it won't be a problem. And Bobbi?"

"Hmm?"

"I just wanted to thank you. I know I was a jackass, and you had every reason to make things difficult. I can't thank you enough for keeping things clean, good for Sam."

"I needed to move on, too, Bryce. I didn't do it for you."

"I know, but I admire you. I think if I would have known how gracious you would be, I would have had second thoughts about going through with the divorce."

"You have a new life now, and so do I." I kept my voice clear and unwavering.

"Is that why you weren't home at eleven last night and didn't call back until this morning?"

There was a pause. I almost told him that I had been at work in my studio until well after midnight, but I caught myself. I wasn't interested in playing games and making him jealous, but I wanted that line of separation between us.

"Yes, Bryce."

He took the hint and was quiet. Without either of us having anything more to say, the conversation came to an awkward and abrupt end. When I hung up the phone I felt unsettled and somewhat agitated. After I showered and dressed, I tried to sit down with my account books and receipts, but I could not concentrate. Nonna's notebooks sat opened on my desk. I reached for them and turned to the last page I had read. Nonna's birth.

May 5, 1991

I was nearly three before my father came back from the war. I had seen his beautiful paintings, but this broken man bore no resemblance to the sensitive artist I imagined. Now we had the madness of two people in a house reserved for only one lunatic. One of them had to go. My grandmother died the month following my father's return.

My mother was stuck between two grieving men with shattered dreams, and she aligned herself with my father. She nursed and loved him. Demons visited him after dark, and my mother's nightgown grew damp with the sweat of his remembrances.

I had always slept with my mother, and this man displaced me. My mother did not allow me to use the word hate about anyone, but I felt the emotion toward my father even if I could not speak it. Sometimes, at night when others were sleeping, I would climb the attic stairs off my bedroom and view his paintings by moonlight. I imagined myself in those square hills, running and jumping. These could not be the works of the madman sleeping beside my mother.

I learned to stay away from the men of the farm, especially when circumstance brought them together. I spent many dinner hours looking for crayfish in the streams or playing in the loft with the barn cats. My grandfather would grumble that I was undisciplined and wild, but my mother could not bear to punish me and have one more battle on her hands. My father couldn't have cared less. He all but ignored me. I made a game out of spying on him throughout the day as he talked nonsense or worked at tasks that weren't real. He did things like stacking the hay bales into magnificent structures or mowing serpentines in the front lawn. My grandfather was livid. He resided more each day inside the terrible pit of his anger.

In 1925, when my mother told me that we would move to France, I shouted hurrahs into her hair. We would finally get away from my angry grandfather, and I just knew that the painter would replace my imposter of a father. Ada suffered greatly for her alliance with my father; Gustaf disowned her.

"Mama, will Daddy paint me into his pictures?" I asked one evening while she was brushing my hair. I wanted him to paint me. It would mean the painter had returned and that he recognized the daughter before him.

My dreams for Europe did not come true in France. My father's nightmares increased the closer we came to the deep slashes of earth that my mother called *trenches*. None of my father's old friends recognized him on the street, or if they did, they looked away in embarrassment. Day after day, he painted black canvases, and by nightfall, he threw them on the fire. My mother kept the windows of our chalet open even in winter to help disperse the noxious fumes of our hearth.

Finally, the black paint ran out. In 1927, we took a holiday to visit some of my dad's distant cousins in a seaside village in Greece. (He held to the weak claim that our family name had been Stephanopolis.) We never returned to Paris. It was in Greece that I glimpsed my father, the painter. For the decade we stayed, he painted my mother, the land, the sea, the fruits of the field, and me, over and over again. Those paintings sold well; I don't own a one. In those magic years, I could touch my father's face and cause him to smile. He embraced my mother passionately and unabashedly in front of me. Motherhood had softened her beauty, made it touchable instead of threatening. I don't think I was ever happier.

May 6, 1991

Our relatives were not gypsy people, but I surmise that they could be the lost kinfolk of the wandering strain. These were the sons and daughters of Zeus. They still believed in Dionysian festivals and the power of wine and cathartic theater.

The land and sea, as well as its people, welcomed us into their folds. The flavors of Greece were strong and earthy, the likes of which I had never tasted. My own perspiration took on the flavor of olive brine. This, I discovered at play. As I came of age, I, too, drank the sweet wine and enjoyed the love games with both boys and girls. There was no shame in this world where hedonism had no name.

I had many lovers, not all in the typical sense, but enough. With one girl, we washed each other's hair and then anointed the parts on our scalps with olive oil. We braided our locks and let them dry in the sun until, unplaited, our hair crimped and glowed like the edge of a coin. With another youth, a boy, I splashed naked in the sea and built fires on the beach. We looked up at the sky and identified obscure constellations. Not all of my encounters were so innocent, I assure you, and I enjoyed the caresses of boys and girls alike. It did not matter that I came home smelling like sex and the sea. They were the same scent.

In Greece, I learned as much about cooking as I had about making love. My mother and I baked enough breads and sweets for not only the villagers but also the sailors who followed the heavenly aromas from their ports to our ovens. I became very proficient in my art. My pastries rivaled those of Old World grandmothers. You have heard that boast before. It was true, and soon our kitchen overflowed with natives and travelers alike.

The foreigners, mostly men, brought with them the scent of unrest. They were quick to look over their shoulders, and eager to quarrel. Many of the village women had the gift of second sight, but we did not need their foreboding. In 1937, I was already an adult. Though I had received many marriage proposals, opportunities to marry and settle there, I knew that I was not of this place. The rest of Europe was encroaching on our haven.

We set out for America, the forgotten land of my birth. For years afterwards I wondered if Greece ever really existed or if I had dreamed the entire experience. We had no paintings or possessions to show for our time there, only a few recipes, not written on cards, but quilted into the hemispheres of our brains.

Our original plan was to open a bakery in New York City, but my grandfather died as we made our voyage. He willed Mulberry Farm to me. Although I didn't want the property, my parents decided it would be best if we settled nearby so I could manage my inheritance. We found a suitable tenant, and opened our bakery in Philadelphia, around the corner from Temple University. (Do you remember when I pointed the building out to you? The building is red brick with a blue awning. Barbara Jean tells me it's a photocopy place now. Kinko's, I think it is called.)

After so much time in Greece, I found America to be cold, narrow, and dark. My limbs slowed in the cold, and my tongue tripped over the thickness of the English language. I had no accent; English was my native language, but the words did not flow easily.

I hated the college students who frequented our shop. The girls played different love games than the ones I knew. Their approach was all about offering a prize and then snatching it away. The boys begged for their kisses in a manner that was too humiliating to watch. I wanted none of this scene. I served them coffee and doughnuts, powdered with disdain.

America did have one advantage over Greece, and that was the cinema. I went to the movies every afternoon, after the bakery closed for the day. I didn't care if I had seen the movie before or that I was sitting alone. All that mattered was that for two hours I was transported to another dimension. I began to play my memories of Greece back in segments like movie scenes, until I convinced myself that I must have been wearing Judy Garland's ruby slippers. Greece was Oz in Technicolor, and Philadelphia was the still gray world of Kansas.

May 7, 1991

The same year as *The Wizard of Oz*, 1939, I met your father. It was a golden age for films. They say that more great movies were made in that year than any other. Is it any wonder I met your father in a movie theater? You have heard that bit of trivia before, but I never told you that he was on a date with another girl. I sat behind him and to the left. He had his arm around this girl, but he kept stealing glances at me. He had the round face of a youth, even though he was twenty-one, one year younger than I. His blond eyebrows and his dimples made him appear even more boyish. I was not impressed by his attentions. I am sure I wore my trademark schoolmarm scorn as he tried to catch my eye.

The next day, he came into the bakery alone.

"Hello," he said.

"What can I get for you?" I pretended not to recognize him. His white-blond hair was flipped back into a smooth wave above his forehead.

"I would like to take you to the movies."

I didn't respond and showed no interest. I refilled the coffeepot.

He kept talking. "Preferably a movie you have seen before, so we can kiss, and get kicked out by an usher, and then go to dinner. You'll wear a red dress, and we'll go dancing for the remainder of the night. I will drop you off at the bakery in time for you to open the shop to work all day while I go back to the dorm to sleep until I can see you again."

Most girls would have been appalled by this speech, but I had not witnessed such truth in dating since I had arrived in America. It was refreshing and honest.

"Okay," I said without looking at him, "but my dress will be blue."

"Okay?"

"That is what I said." I finally looked at him. His eyes were a hue I had not seen since we had left Greece. Those eyes were the white arches of stucco churches that framed the azure of the sea. His pupils were the tower bells, darkened from copper to black by the saltwater.

"Your name is Anja."

"Yes."

"I am Charlie Graybill. I will pick you up at four."

While Charlie was honest with me, I was less than forthright with him. He was an architecture student in his final two years of study. His family was from upstate New York where they had a dairy farm. He was the first in his family to go to college. Charlie was Lutheran, devout even in his college years. He had even considered seminary school for a short time.

The talk about religion made me self-conscious. America as a whole was so much more religious than the places I had seen. I amended our life in Greece to read like a Jane Austen novel, proper and polite and more British than Aegean. The playacting did not seem like such a lie. In America, I was still a virgin; I had taken no lovers. I had lived as two different people in these two different worlds. Some days I believed that I had been twinned and that my double was still drinking wine and swimming naked in the warring seas of Europe while I rolled cold dough and watched the battles in movie theaters in America.

Our first date was quite pleasant and not unlike Charlie's prediction of it. My parents winked and nodded at each other as I nearly fell asleep frying doughnuts the next morning. My mother took over that job while I got the less dangerous job of cutting those circles out of dough. They did not say much about this new influence in my life. I never knew how they felt about Charlie, but I did know that they would do anything to keep from alienating me, even if that meant putting up with a careless employee.

May 9, 1991

I did not take Charlie to see my farm. I didn't want the property to influence what he felt for me. We continued in the strange platonic rituals of dating for two years. I hid my lustful tendencies behind an intense concentration. I listened carefully to every word Charlie spoke.

I had never met anybody so filled with passion about his studies, except my father. I wanted to tell him how I had played among many of the ancient temples that he held in esteem. My father and I often camped near these hallowed grounds, while he would paint me dancing among the white columns. I later learned the names of these columns—*Doric, Ionic,* and *Corinthian*—when I paged through Charlie's thick textbooks. I not only wanted to learn about the things he loved, but I also wanted to fill in the gaps of my informal education to be a better companion for him. Charlie, in return, took me to dance halls and to the movies. Not once did I catch him looking over my head at another girl.

Even he could not sit through enough movies to satisfy my appetites. I was alone at a Sunday matinee when the news hit the public that the Japanese had bombed Pearl Harbor. I was still trying to adjust my eyes from the dim theater to daylight when a stranger on the street rushed up to me with his high-pitched "Have you heard?" I immediately went to find Charlie in the room he was keeping on Market Street. By that time, he had graduated from college and had recently taken a job as a junior architect with the Willis and Ludwig firm.

Charlie was not in his room. Bob, his roommate and fellow architect, told me he had gone to find me to tell me he was enlisting. Somehow, I already knew. Charlie agreed to delay his registration until we were married. I wore a red dress.

I was so nervous on our wedding night, but it wasn't the usual bridal jitters. I was afraid that Charlie would find out the truth about my love-littered past. That night we made love in a manner I had never experienced before. We were in love. That made a difference, of course, but it was more than that. Our lovemaking was reverent. Afterwards, Charlie cried. I held on to my boy groom, my too-soon soldier, and tried to think of tender apologies for my bridal impurity. I was mistaken. He was not sobbing because I was not a virgin. On the contrary, he was crying because of the intensity of the beautiful act against the somber backdrop of war. "Why did we postpone our love?" he asked me. I knew the answer. We had waited for him to be ready.

· 37 ·

I CAME TO THE end of the first small notebook. I contemplated starting the next one, the thicker of the two, but Travis would be coming soon, and I had to get ready. I ran upstairs and swiped a brush through my hair. Carefully I pinned its length off my neck. One strand refused to cooperate, and I traced its path on my neck as it fell.

It was obvious that Nonna had a reason for telling this story to my mother. There was a purpose to this tale, but what? Nonna had hinted at bits of her past all these years. The passion was no surprise, and yet her telling of it was. I had longed to know my grandfather, the blond soldier in the photograph, and here beneath the uniform was a man and a lover. As I read the letter, I experienced the sensuality in the story, felt born of it.

I let my mind wander. How would I tell my own tale of love? What images would I choose? I closed my eyes and instantly saw water rippling on the screen before my mind's eye. The light danced along the surface, and I felt the warmth on my neck. I imagined a man's beard grazing my shoulder with its coarseness, replaced a moment later by the softness of lips against my skin. I jerked my eyes open and looked around my bedroom.

Travis. Of course, Travis. It was only natural I would choose him. He was the one who distracted me from the pain of missing my son. He took me on his boat, coaxed dark confessions from me without judgment, and shared openly from his own book of disappointment. We were two imperfect souls, floating together over living waters. And if that wasn't enough to sway a woman's heart, he was the man who held secret the mysteries of my youth.

When Travis appeared at the door minutes later, I was vulnerable to him. He kissed me lightly, and I opened to him. The moment I did it, I knew I had caught him off guard. Travis squeezed my shoulders, and I released him. He studied me, but I wiped my mouth and looked away. The last thing I needed was for him to see any desperation on my part. Outside, the truck engine was issuing a guttural reminder, an urgency that superseded any desires I might have.

"Um . . . I have lemonade or pop. Which would you like?" I asked hoarsely.

"We call it soda here in this part of Pennsylvania."

"Okay, wiseass." I buried my face inside the refrigerator. "Do you want lemonade or soda?"

"Lemonade is fine."

In fact, everything was fine. My divorce was final, pending a court date. Sam was injured perhaps, but okay and happy. And I would be alone with Travis all day. I smelled the familiar scents of the earth in full flower and the promise of waters. It was the prelude to a dance that was older than the ancestors, yet viable and current.

I had no doubt that I would share my bed with Travis before the day was over. I had even gone so far as to make the bed with fresh sheets. While I still wasn't sure if I was prepared emotionally for such an exchange, I knew what to expect: the arch to meet each other's expectations, the shy morning, the plan for a new rendezvous. I set the stage with the grazing touch of my arm and a certain edge to my voice when I made offers of drinks and sandwiches.

Travis felt the momentum, too. The boat outing was just a convenient way to pass the time until the polite, darker hours of consummation. And it would be dark regardless of the hour. I almost wished that Travis didn't mean anything to me so I could fully experience the anger I felt toward Bryce and relish the sweet relief as I evened the score in my shattered marriage. I wasn't using Travis exactly. I did want to make love to him for all the right reasons, but I also had my shadow purpose.

An afternoon storm expedited the inevitable. We returned to Mulberry Street wet and eager with the excuse to remove sodden clothing. It was a fast coupling, heavy with the weight of waiting—racing to beat the downpour. Travis was rough, not just with his beard and callused hands, but with his expectations. It was exactly the way I needed it to be, tormented by things we labeled only as passion. There was the noise. Thunder notwithstanding, the old bed in the back room groaned under our rotating bodies. There were other sounds, too: the creak of floorboards, swaying trees, whirring rain, and the slash of a branch beating against the siding of the house. In addition, I heard the foreign sound of my own cries in concert with the weather. Travis did nothing to hush me, and I cried out again before succumbing to the gentle pant of breathlessness.

The storm weakened, and our lovemaking slowed with the rain. We explored like new lovers do, pausing over body parts often ignored by long-term partners. We were as clumsy as drunks, bumping each other with knees and elbows, and offering soft apologies under our kisses. I was conscious of my body in a way that I hadn't been earlier. I knew what it was capable of, the soft places and scars that made me feel insecure. Travis traced the faded stretch marks on my abdomen, and I knew he was thinking beyond the imperfection to what it had meant for me. My shyness vanished then, and I folded myself around his body. The sun made an appearance just as the last of the raindrops fell. If the end of the storm brought a rainbow, neither of us noticed.

We were both hungry. Travis padded downstairs and grabbed a bag of pretzel rods from the pantry and a quart of strawberry ice cream from the freezer. He brought only one spoon, and he fed me ice cream, satiating the ravenous parts in me that our lovemaking had missed. In those quiet moments of revelation, I showed Travis Nonna's first notebook, and I read aloud the vivid descriptions of Nonna's early life.

"She's your grandmother. Isn't that weird for you?" Travis asked.

"You're my cousin. This is weird." I motioned to the bedsheets in disarray around our naked bodies.

"We're not related, BJ." He kissed the top of my head. "Not yet, anyway."

Jules whined at the door, and Travis stood to let him out. I couldn't help staring at his body as he pulled on his shorts, still damp from the rain. I wanted to pull him back into bed, but he had left the room. I did not have a chance to explore Travis's comment. Truthfully, I didn't want to ask what he had meant by "not yet." Whatever question I had, the answer needed to be "not yet."

· 38 ·

"ALL RIGHT, IF YOU AREN'T going to tell me, I'll have to ask you again louder," Karen said.

"Sssh. I'll tell you, but keep your voice down. Those Estée Lauder girls are staring at us." I sprayed Pleasures on my wrist, and then cringed at the overpowering burst of fragrance.

"Ooh, I sprayed too much."

"Here, give me a little of that." Karen took my wrist and rubbed it against her own. The deed mimicked our act of becoming blood sisters many years ago. "Okay now. You promised details. Spill."

"What do you want to know?"

"I want adjectives: fantastic, unbelievable, sweet mother of God."

"*Sweet mother of God* is a noun."

"Whatever. Tell me," Karen said.

"It was all of those things. Are you happy?"

"Are you going to see him again? Are you two shacking up until Sam gets back?"

"Hold on. I am trying to get out of one marriage. I don't need to jump into something else. You are in the wrong business. You need to stop writing up divorces and start a dating service."

"You are wrong about my job. You should see all the prenups I write."

"Really, around here? I don't think Bryce wrote many that I remember."

"Sure. And you would not believe the things people include. The law can be quite kinky."

"The law? Kinky? I can't seem to remember," I said with a sigh.

Karen and I walked past a sale on handbags next to the hosiery department.

"Hold on, I have to get some new support hose. One of my cases goes to trial next week."

I watched my friend as she fingered the samples. I could not help noticing the lingerie department across the aisle. I didn't care about the novelty of a new negligee, but some new underwear might be in order if this relationship with Travis continued. Luckily my bathing suit had saved me the embarrassment of exposing my worn underpinnings. Karen saw me looking.

"Honey, please tell me that you have already bought your divorce undies."

"Divorce undies?"

"Before I signed my divorce papers, I went out and bought twenty pairs of pure silk panties. I gave the bill to my ex as a final farewell message: *Kiss my ass!*"

"Silk undies? Was that what you put in *your* prenup?"

"Very funny. I am going to rise above your sarcasm."

I walked gingerly across the aisle to the lingerie department and removed a pair of red panties from the nearest display. I held them up to the light and gasped with delight at the sheerness of the fabric. With a hint of reserve, I placed the panties back on the shelf.

"I can't," I said unconvincingly.

"Come on, BJ. New trimmings, my treat," Karen insisted. "Call it the wedding gift I never got you."

· 39 ·

I LOOKED UP FROM my workbench every time I heard a lawn mower start. Travis had promised to come by later that day and finish trimming the yard. I had a feeling that he did only a small portion of the lawn each time so he would have an excuse to come back. Did we really need an excuse to see each other? At the sound of a car door, I squirmed again. Or maybe I was fidgeting because of the new thong I was wearing. With my every motion, my skirt slid across my bare butt and gave me a delicious thrill. I was cognizant of my sexuality, an awareness that had been dormant since Sam's birth.

Come on, BJ. Concentrate.

I filed the metal spoon in front of me. This one represented my mother. I intended to set my mother's diamond in a gold bezel and place it on the torso of the figure to signify the right breast. For the left breast, I had cut a jagged X into the metal.

My mother had a mastectomy in 1991 when it was determined that a lumpectomy was not an option. In 1998, the surgeon removed her other breast. She rejected cosmetic surgery, but she did have inserts for her bra. "I have decided that I would finally like to experience a C-cup," she joked when she showed me her larger prosthetics. She had made a similar joke about her blond wig. And I, B-cupped and brown-haired, tried to laugh as my mother transformed into something I was not. My own breasts became hot bull's-eyes on my chest.

I turned to my coarse sandpaper and continued to smooth the spoon. This was the part of my craft that I least enjoyed. I had learned to avoid shredding my skin on the abrasive surfaces, but my hands still had the worn look of a heavy laborer. I used to treat myself to paraffin hand peels at the spa attached to Bryce's golf club, but I had yet to find anything like it since my move. I hadn't been looking very hard. Until my finances were stable, I worried that such luxuries were in the past.

From outside my window, I heard the sound of a weed whacker. I pushed out the screen and looked in the direction of the noise. Travis was edging the side bed next to the fence. I didn't acknowledge him. Instead I quickly brushed my workbench clean of metal dust and put my tools away.

I turned the faucet on and scrubbed my hands with pumice soap. I liked the ritual of washing my hands. It showed the transition from one activity to another. It said, "I want to start anew." Even as a child, I never had to be told, I just did it. More often than not, I washed my face as well. Makeup wasn't an issue; I applied it only if I was going out. Clean and free, those were my vices. I didn't like the fancy soaps or gels. Even now, in the face of my transformation into a single woman, I refused all those samples that Karen was always pushing me to try.

Iced tea. I poured tall glasses for the two of us and loaded it onto a tray. I nearly stumbled out onto the lawn as I emerged from the dark house, but I caught myself just in time. Travis turned off the motor and motioned to me, and I put the tray down on the table.

"Hey. I hope I didn't disturb your work."

"Nope, just finishing."

He leaned down, and I kissed him.

"I'm done, too. Is that iced tea for me?" He always smelled like cut grass, even after he showered. I found I liked the green scent; it suited him.

"Yes, the iced tea is for you, but, as usual, I have no lemons," I said.

"I am getting used to it that way." Travis was bemused. He celebrated my little inadequacies. "What do you think of the annual border? These were left over from a client's house."

"Looks great. Did you just put them in today? You haven't been here that long."

"I've been here a little over an hour. You were just caught up in your work and didn't notice."

"I've seen this kind of plant before. They're certainly colorful. What are they?"

"Ah, my little brown thumb, they're called coleus. Their native to the tropics, but they make great annuals here, provided your soil is well drained, which yours is, thanks to your landscaper."

"The soil better be good. I pay my landscaper well."

"Yes, you do—all the lemonless iced tea he can drink. Let me wash up quickly, and I'll be right with you."

With Travis in the house, I used the time to survey the property. In a few short weeks, he had transformed the vista. Lena would have loved the new raised beds and the new rose trellis. It was a lot of work, but somehow, I didn't remember anything as a big project. Travis just dabbled in the yard. The biggest trick of all may have been making himself into a fixture. In gardening terms, he would be called the *hardscape*. Looking out over the lawn, I wondered how it would change with the seasons.

I had never seen much of this house in the fall, except for the occasional visits when I was in college. But now I had reason to be here and to contemplate that Travis would be here as well, in some capacity. I had been looking forward to autumn as Sam's return and the finalization of my divorce, but for the first time I considered that maybe my relationship with Travis might also have something to do with my optimism.

Travis bounded out of the house, letting the door slam behind him. It was the kind of thing I would have scolded Sam for, but my heart lurched, and I knew that I could and would let the transgression slide without an reprimand. I liked having Travis here to slam the doors.

"I have a question to ask you," he said when he reached the table.

"Shoot."

"Feel free to say no."

"What is it?"

"I would like to build a small temporary greenhouse in the back corner of your property. It doesn't look like I'll be able to buy property in time to set one up on my own land. I was hoping I could rent a spot from you. I checked into the zoning. You're fine in this area. We'll draw up a contract. It will be all businesslike."

"Yeah, sure. That's not a problem."

"Whew! I was hoping you'd say that."

"Did you doubt me?" I asked, searching his eyes.

Travis sat down and faced me. "I don't know," he said. "Sometimes, I'm scared for you and all this change."

I knew the point to his remark. We were moving fast these days, and sometimes I caught him looking at me. He was putting a great deal of faith in someone who just had her heart broken by another man. I can't say that I blamed him for his reticence.

"There are days when I feel so right here," he said, "like I've been here all along. It feels as though we never broke up as teenagers. Sometimes I wish we hadn't."

"What, and missed out on all those wonderful growth opportunities?" I asked trying to power a bit of levity into our conversation.

"Is that the sound bite that the spin doctors are using for failed marriages these days?" He wasn't sharing in my lightheartedness.

"It isn't so terrible. I'm glad things turned out this way. We are able to come to each other as adults. I doubt whether we would have lasted a month together when we were kids."

"Why do you say that?"

"Think about it. If things kept going the way they were going, I might have ended up pregnant by fifteen."

The mood changed, and I realized my blunder. "Oh, Travis, that was insensitive of me. I'm sorry. I forgot. It just slipped out."

"No, BJ, it's okay. I am glad you know. I'd hate to be dating a woman and trying to decide the right moment to tell her I'm sterile."

"Do you still want kids?"

"Yes and no. My childhood was not ideal—you know all about that—but I think I could be a good parent."

"You're so good with Sam. You'd make a great dad." As soon as I said it, I realized how it must have sounded, as if I were lobbying for a stepfather for my son. Part of me wanted to take it back, but part of me wanted to see what Travis would do with the information.

"Sam's a great kid. He makes it easy. You've done a wonderful job raising him."

"Thanks."

My heart melted. I could see it perfectly now. The pumpkins and Indian corn adorning the porch. The two of us walking Sam, backpack on his shoulders, to the corner to catch the bus. I may not have been able to say words like *love* or *commitment*, but I was starting to see the slide show in my mind. As long as Travis didn't ask for verbal confirmation of what I was feeling, I was satisfied developing my vision.

"BJ, did you ever think of me in all those years?" Travis changed the subject.

"You were forbidden fruit, how could I not?"

"My only love sprung from my only hate! Too early seen unknown, and known too late! Prodigious birth of love it is to me. That I must love a loathed enemy."

"Romeo and Juliet!" I clapped my hands.

"The English teacher in me is impressed." Travis straightened.

"Don't be, I had to memorize that speech in high school."

"You're ahead of most of my high school juniors then."

"That may be, but my knowledge stops there. All those poetry readings on Nonna's porch and I can't remember a single line."

"Still, I am pleased that you can identify the star-crossed lovers."

"Well, I'd hardly put us in that category."

"I said 'identify,' not *identify with*."

"Okay, Mr. English Teacher, but your stanzas just reminded me of something. I heard on the radio that they are having a production of *Romeo and Juliet* in the amphitheater this weekend. Shakespeare by the Lake. Do you want to go?"

"You know I can't resist the great bard."

"I am not asking you to resist anything." In the waning daylight, I leaned over the table toward Travis. As the Green Man that he was, he welcomed my invitation. I breathed in the verdant smell of his skin and kissed the poetry of his mouth. It was so easy—this romance, this relationship. *What had I been so scared of happening?* Maybe the better question was this: *What scared me still?*

· 40 ·

MAY 10, 1991

It is hard to describe the Second World War to those who didn't live through it. It was the first time in America that I felt united with the citizens of my home country. The feeling that we were doing something great pervaded the whole society. It did not stop the dread, but it gave the feeling some worth.

I was glad to have dough to roll and punch in those first nervous days of the war. The sight of Charlie in his uniform brought back memories of volatile men I had known in Greece. I had a taste of impending atrocities as we received the telegrams from Greece informing us of my slaughtered playmates. I could not cry for them. My tears were in reserve, dammed behind a stone wall for my future self.

Charlie trained in Virginia for an assignment in the South Pacific. He would be among the men who prepared the area for the troops. His tasks included scouring for land mines (a most dangerous occupation) as well as building bridges and roads and all the infrastructure of war. I hoped his knowledge as an architect would keep him away from the land mines.

Two weeks after he left for training, a small brunette woman walked into our bakery around closing time. I was the only one in the bakery; my parents had gone to a gallery that was displaying some of my father's latest paintings.

"Yes, may I help you?"

The woman, a girl really, was wringing her gloved hands in a way that said she was there for more than bread.

"You are Mrs. Charlie Graybill?"

I froze. "Yes."

"My fiancé told me I would find you here. He is in the same outfit as your husband. I don't live far from here. I am a student at the business school."

I knew what she wanted from me, and it was something I wasn't prepared to give away too easily, much less to a stranger. She wanted camaraderie, a women's circle. To give in to her would mean admitting that I needed support, and that my husband was in danger. Yet, in spite of the implications, I could not turn her away. "What did you say your name was?"

"I didn't. I'm sorry. My name is Lena. Lena Lefever."

I looked her over suspiciously. "How old are you?"

"Eighteen. I will be nineteen in March. I am getting married a week after my birthday when the men come home on leave."

That is when she caught my attention. "The men have leave?"

"Yes, they are coming home in March for a week before they get shipped out."

She had said the magic words. From that moment, I spent

every evening with Lena. I didn't want her company, but any bit of news she could give me was worthy of my time. We were not idle in our hours together; idleness would activate our terrible imaginations. Instead we used the time to knit. We stitched sock after sock for our soldiers so they would not get damp feet in the jungles of the Philippines. Lena chatted about her upcoming wedding and her plans for a home when Hank returned from war. Hank Littlehail. He was just a faceless name to me. Lena carried his picture in her locket, but it was too small for me to get a sense of the man. I did not know how small a man he really was.

On my calendar, March was the impetus for my every action. I was glad that February was such a short month, but Lena seemed to grow more agitated as the end of February neared.

We grew closer as we incubated ourselves for war. I did not reveal everything about myself, but I did ask Lena to proofread some of my letters to Charlie. My spoken English was flawless, but my written word needed help, and I did not want to appear uneducated in front of my new husband. (Remember, Judy, how I did grammar homework with you every night. I was not trying to teach, so much as learn with you. I think you knew that.)

Because of her task as editor, Lena was privy to some intimacies that women rarely spoke aloud. One evening, as I was rewriting my letter, making the corrections, Lena asked me, "How do you know if you please your husband?"

"Please my husband? What do you mean?" I had a good idea what she meant, but I didn't want to embarrass her if I was wrong.

"You know, in the marriage bed." She blushed.

I thought that it was a very naive question, but luckily I saw the look on Lena's face before I started to laugh. She

was earnest, and I could see how difficult this subject was
for her.

I could have said, "You will know when the time comes,"
or "That is not something you will have to guess," but Lena
required more. Her needles were shaking as she dropped
her knitting into her lap.

"Lena, have you kissed Hank?"

"Yes." Tears swelled in her brown eyes.

"Did you enjoy kissing him?"

"Yes."

"Could you tell? Did he like it, too?"

"I think so."

"Well, then start with that. Start with something you
know he likes. Then touch him. Touch his arm, his face,
and watch his eyes."

"What if they're closed?" Her innocence touched me.

"Then close your eyes, and you will feel it."

I don't know if I helped her, but she didn't broach the
subject again.

May 12, 1991

One week before the men were due, Lena came running
into the bakery.

"Anja! I have a surprise for you. Can you come now?"

Business was slow. Mama shooed me away with one
hand. I washed my face, applied lipstick (another American habit I had acquired), grabbed my hat and purse, and
followed Lena across town to a dress shop.

I assessed the clothing in the showroom while Lena disappeared into the back. When she did not reappear within
minutes, I sat on a Victorian era settee to wait for her. The
saleswoman was the first to emerge. "Wait until you see
her," she whispered in a reverent hush.

She pulled the curtain aside, and I got my first glance at Lena. She was wearing her wedding gown, a dress like those I had only seen in movies. It was made of white satin, cut smartly on the bias so that it draped her slim body beautifully. There were other details, lace collar perhaps or buttons, I don't remember. All I remember was the lovely look on Lena's face. I am sure you are waiting for me to say that I fell in love with Lena at the moment, but that would be crass and untrue. My heart belonged to an enlistee, not the imminent Mrs. Littlehail before me. I thought that Lena was quite breathtaking in her creamy satin, dark hair and flushed cheeks, but I can't say I had any rush of emotion. That would come in hindsight when I would experience gratitude because it was I, not Private Henry Littlehail, who got to see Lena in her bridal splendor.

"Do you think Hank will like it?"

I touched her shoulders and slowly turned her toward the mirror so she would know her own loveliness. Lena reached out to touch her reflection, but realized the glass was not her person. She stood with her arm in midair as if she were hailing a cab, unaware that the preferred mode of transportation for a princess was a carriage pulled by a white horse.

"You will take his breath away," I assured her.

She lowered her arm and turned to me. "Thank you," she whispered.

Lena went into the back room to change. She would never wear her wedding gown again.

· 41 ·

WE SAT IN THE TRUCK, neither of us speaking. The decision to drive instead of walk was a practical conclusion based on the number of things we had to carry: blankets, chairs, the thermos, and picnic basket. And now I fumbled with those props to avoid Travis and his words.

"You can't ignore me, Barbara Jean. I'll just say it again. I love you. It's not too soon to say it. I've probably always loved you."

After several days of conjuring pictures in my mind, the hour had come for words. I glanced at Travis and saw the dangerous yearning in his eyes—the blinking amber caution of a changing traffic light. I stumbled out of the truck. The crowds were thick through the parking lot. The play would soon begin. Travis could not possibly want to pursue this conversation here, surrounded by hundreds of people.

I tried to yank the basket from the back bed of the truck, but it caught on the lip of the built-in tool case. Travis caught up with me and coolly lifted the basket away from the impediment. With his free arm he pressed me into his torso.

"It's not too soon, BJ. Unless you are just using me to get over your divorce."

"No!" I exclaimed too quickly. I pulled myself from his grasp. "It isn't like that."

"Do you want to explain it to me?" Travis prodded.

"Not here."

We started walking. I reached out my hand as consolation for my missing words. Travis accepted it. Along the way, people, mostly clientele, stopped Travis to say hello or inquire about a job. I retained my anonymity under my baseball cap and dark glasses, and he did not introduce me.

"We're not finished with this," Travis said.

But I was perfectly willing to ignore the whole issue, so I busied myself with the details of the evening.

"What about there, beside the center aisle." I pointed to an empty section.

"It is too far away from the action."

After considering a few more possible locations, we agreed on a spot to the side of the stage. We could barely see the actors from this angle, but it was a private area off by some pine trees and away from most of the crowd. While the view was less than ideal, the sound was good: a nearby cluster of speakers issued a mix of oldies.

I opened the basket and spread its contents over the blanket. Brie, some grapes, assorted crackers, and cold fried chicken. All that food and I didn't really want to eat, but I didn't want to appear out of sorts. Loading my plate proved to be a sleight of hand. Travis grabbed a plate and followed my lead. He was hungry after his day of manual labor.

"So how many productions of Shakespeare by the Lake have you seen?" I asked between bites.

"None. They only started these a few years ago, from what I've been told. I thought maybe I'd try out for the production next year."

"Have you ever acted before?"

"Not as well as you."

I stared at him. He had that look again. He was not going to drop this.

I lowered my voice. "What do you want me to say?"

"I want you tell me what you feel."

"But what if I don't feel the same way you do?"

"Honey, you aren't that good an actress." Travis popped a grape into his mouth. "I know the answer; I just want you to admit it to yourself."

A song by the Temptations stopped midchorus, and the crowd hushed. When the stage remained empty, conversation resumed on a lower, anticipative frequency. Travis leaned over and kissed me on the cheek.

"Do you remember that time that last summer when I plowed the John Deere into Anja's porch?"

I gave him a little smile. "That's a hard scene to forget."

"I saw you in the window there, and the words, 'There she is,' popped into my head. And that quick, I lost control of the tractor."

"So you think we were fated to be?" I asked.

"I don't know. Maybe. All I know is that your husband didn't even wait for your marriage to be over before he decided to fall in love with another woman. Why should you yourself hold back? Don't give him that power."

"Do you really want to bring Bryce into this?"

"He's already here, isn't he?"

"Look, Travis—you don't understand. It was months ago, weeks ago really, that my husband of nine years came to me and told me he wasn't sure if he ever loved me. And now you are saying that you think you've always loved me. What am I supposed to think?"

"That's your problem. You are thinking too much."

A loose group of actors filed onto the stage. Daylight was failing just enough to warrant a spotlight, though from my vantage point, I couldn't appreciate it. Travis turned his head slightly to show that his attention had shifted. He was letting our dialogue die. Once again the audience quieted. The silence was a sharp chasm.

"Two households, both alike in dignity, In fair Verona, where we lay our scene, From ancient grudge break to new mutiny . . ."

"Travis?" I scooted closer until my face was brushing his ear. "I do love you."

· 42 ·

A NEW PROFESSOR was heading the metals department at Tyler School of Art. Though Greg Millhouse hadn't taught when I was a student, he was familiar with my work.

"I'm pleased to finally meet you. Your spoons have been held up as an example for me many times." Greg's reputation had preceded him as well. His use of cast elements and found objects had transformed fine-art jewelry. Shaking his hand, I couldn't help but wonder if I would be attracted enough to pursue this man had I not encountered Travis earlier this summer.

Greg had graduated from Cranbrook Academy of Art only five years ago, but he already had an impressive resume. The president of a Japanese-American conglomerate found Greg's work to be so worthy that he had bought a bracelet for his wife and commissioned the exact piece to be replicated at ten times the scale as a sculpture for his office. The commission had garnered Greg the cover of *Art in America*.

"The pleasure is all mine. I have admired your work for some time."

Many times during my marriage, I had the desperate wish I'd married someone who could comprehend the artist mind. Now that I was seeing Travis, a man who could speak in metaphors, that fancy became gratuitous. After my introduction to Greg, I felt a relief that I hadn't experienced in years. I had made physical contact with a handsome artist, someone I didn't necessarily fantasize about bedding (possibly after a long discourse on reductionism in twentieth-century painting that masqueraded as foreplay). Either I didn't need it, or I already had it. I sighed. Even *in absentia,* Travis was passing every litmus test I put to our new relationship, and I smiled thinking about him.

GREG WATCHED OVER my shoulder as I arranged my place setting in the showcase. The gallery curator had given me creative control over the space. I placed the utensils on a granite slab with two chalk-drawn circles on it to represent cup and plate placement. For a napkin, I folded a square of rough burlap. The rough textures played against the gleam of the silverware, enhancing the luster of the pieces.

"I like your use of the gemstones. Brilliant."

"Is that a pun?" I backed away from the case to critique my work. The arrangement was pleasing. The last two pieces held their own against the first three I had completed. The knife represented my father's image, stoic and steadfast, with a rigidity I'd come to expect. I had used the soupspoon as my self-portrait, depicting myself as mother, the role from which I took my identity at present. The spoon curved into the sculptural likeness of a bare-breasted mother nursing her baby. The baby's head obscured one breast. The other nipple was my engagement diamond.

Upon the completion of my place setting, Travis had languished praise until I blushed. I wasn't used to such enthusiasm.

"Stop. You are embarrassing me."

How could I explain that the first time Bryce had seen my spoons, he had asked, "Are people really supposed to eat with these?"

"They're a little lavish, but perfectly serviceable," I had countered, contempt in my voice.

These days, I didn't have to explain my whimsy or apologize for an idea that defied rationalism. Especially here, on Temple's remote northern campus, the population understood my undertaking. They should; they had nurtured my sensibility. I remembered the days when I tried my hand at performance art. In my junior year, I had dressed all in black and then proceeded to wrap myself in vinyl tubing and nylons, calling it theater jewelry. A jeweler by the name of Bruce Metcalf had been my inspiration.

"You need to come down and do a workshop with the students. We have a small budget for visiting artists. I could hook you up. They could really benefit from a demonstration of your forging techniques."

"I'd love that," I said, and I meant it.

Returning to this place afforded me freedom beyond that of divorce. Yet another reason to stay in Pennsylvania. The reasons were building, or maybe I was just more open to them.

"Can you hold on a sec?" Greg excused himself and jogged down the hall. In a moment he reappeared leading a young woman by the elbow.

"Lucy Divinko, this is Bobbi Ellington. Lucy is my graduate assistant."

Greg did not have to introduce me further. Lucy gushed and extended a newly manicured hand in my direction. I stared and then shook the younger woman's hand. As if she could read my mind, Lucy explained that her sister just got married over the weekend and she had been the maid of honor.

I laughed nervously. "You knew what I was thinking about your nails."

"I'm sure by the end of the day, they'll be gone. Call it my Cinderella moment."

I laughed again, more warmly this time.

"When you are done setting up, we should all have lunch. I

know that Lucy, here, is dying to pick your brain a little," Greg suggested.

"Sure, I'll only be another minute."

The three of us got a table at a crowded pub. Lucy wasted no time pulling me into a conversation about female jewelers.

"I don't know. I just feel with so many women in this concentration, we should have better coverage in the art magazines."

I refrained from saying that Lucy should have seen it back in my day, as if more than eight years separated us in age. Greg sat back with a bemused smile and let us rant and bond over the disgrace of the number of female goldsmiths compared to our representation in major shows and galleries.

"Oh believe me—the great gender divide has been broached at a number of SNAG conferences. I don't know which is worse, the artists who are in the dark about the injustices, or the ones who know about it, but choose to ignore it," I heard myself saying.

"I agree. We need more action. We've got to reach more of the art publications and get more galleries on board. Who do you know in the gallery world?"

"What do you mean?" I asked.

"Where are you showing your work besides the alumni show?" Lucy asked me.

I sputtered my drink and felt hypocrisy rising in my throat. "I'm kind of going through some personal stuff right now."

"Oh," the younger woman said. As if on cue, the waitress came, shouldering our order on a large tray.

I wiped my mouth on my napkin, but refused to be demoralized. I would never be able to defend my journey to Lucy. Some lessons need to be lived. But sitting in that pub, I held on to the certainty that my life *was* changing for the better, and it would soon be evident in my work, if it wasn't already.

Despite that moment of thorniness, I left the campus feeling uplifted. The opening of the show was fast approaching, and

I was eager. I still had a week; the extra time would give me a chance to polish my artist's statement, and perhaps I might even do something as drastic as highlighting my hair. For once in my life, I felt that my life was completely my own to forge. The effervescence of the moment made me giddy. *I don't have to be afraid of anything anymore.*

Traffic had not yet swelled with commuters. I turned off the radio to give my mind a chance to chase key phrases I wanted to use in my artist's statement. I definitely wanted to highlight the upcoming decade anniversary of FemininiTEA, but I also wanted to emphasize the new directions of my work. It seemed perfectly natural that my art should reflect the changes I was going through. While figures had always been prominent in my metalwork, I was starting to redirect my focus. My latest sketches had been less about people and more about place, architecture and landscape. I felt the pulse of my grandfathers through my veins. I had never known them, Nonna's father and her husband, but since I had caught glimpses of them in my grandmother's letter, I felt compelled to incorporate them into my life. It was as if their genetic code had just come out of dormancy, overturning the dominance of my grandmother's DNA. The architect and the landscape painter surged.

I had put Nonna's notebooks in my bedside drawer. I had been too busy with the fire of my torch, the heat of summer, and the passion I was experiencing with Travis.

And that was the order of it. I spent my mornings hammering metal. My biceps strained into humps that over the decade had become the envy of the gym crowd. By afternoon, the heat of the day drugged me with its call for laziness. Sometimes I would succumb to it as if it were a primitive beating drum—primal, old, instinctive rhythms. Repetition lulled my days and my nights. I could no longer donate my hours to unstructured activities like random cleaning or idle reading.

I thought back to the night of the play. Travis and I never really watched the actors onstage. We were content to lie on the blanket, away from the crowd, and listen to insects and Shakespeare in his iambic pentameter. *Her whip, of cricket's bone; the lash, of film.* Then water sounds. A heartbeat or a growl.

We lay together and tried to breathe with the words and the night and each other. I forgot about the grandmothers with the man-song drowning out more cyclical hymns.

How could I convey all of these impulses into my artist statement? Forget the paper; I wanted to put fresh meat on the slab of granite between the carefully arranged knife and dinner fork. And I wanted to leave it there to decay over the weeks my work would be on display. My art was passing, and in passing, it was becoming. *From meat and man, iambic, Yeah, I am.*

· 43 ·

"Don't be worried if he acts a little distant his first days home," Karen said. She was rolling blue paint next to the door. "My stepson holed himself up in his room for the first three days of our visitation."

"I didn't know that Shelly had a son," I said, amazed that she hadn't mentioned this before.

"Not Shelly, my first husband."

"Oh." *Shit.*

It had been Karen's idea to revamp my old bedroom for Sam's homecoming. Together we had stripped the flowered wallpaper and primed the walls. I had selected Sam's favorite blue crayon and taken it to the local hardware store to get a custom paint match. Then I picked two more shadowy shades to paint a silhouetted mural of spaceships, planets, stars, and comets. As the last detail, I used highlights of phosphorescent paint to outline the stars and paint lights on the spaceships.

"This room is going to make one little boy very happy," Karen said as she inspected the phantom images that were blooming from my brush.

"Yeah, I think he is going to like it. It'll look good once I move his furniture in here."

"I could get you some business doing murals if you are interested."

I sighed. "No, this is once and done. But thanks."

I was still nervous about the coming weekend. Bryce was personally driving Sam to my doorstep. He asked to stay until Sunday so he could rest before he repeated the ten-hour trip. That request had been made five weeks ago when I had dropped Sam off in Michigan. Naturally I had agreed to the suggestion. Bryce was still the father of my child. He would want to see where his son would be living, iron out details about insurance, among other things.

The last few days had been difficult with Travis. Expectancy was in the air between us. I wanted to talk to him, but I didn't know the words to say what I felt. I enjoyed being the things I was with him—lover, tease, and vamp—but I couldn't align those characters with my other roles of mother and disappointed ex-wife, which I needed to be while Bryce was there.

Later that evening, after I had scraped flecks of blue paint from my forearms, Travis drove me to the opening of the alumni show in Philadelphia. It was our first official function together. Travis dressed in a smart, collarless black shirt. He wore chinos and dark penny loafers. His forehead, out from under his hat, glistened with clean perspiration. I had never seen him dressed up before. When I kissed him in greeting, he tasted like a good memory, but not any memory that I had of him. His cologne seemed familiar, but not because of Travis. He was different.

With the summer air streaming around us and with the unrestrained volume of the radio, we drove without conversation.

The traffic was sluggish on the Schuylkill Expressway and slower still in the slender lanes of the city streets, but we were lucky in finding a good parking spot.

We had just entered the lobby of the building when Greg found us both and insisted on leading me away by the arm.

"I just want to introduce Bobbi to a visiting fabric artist who is here from Turkey."

"Oh, um, Greg. This is Travis," I said belatedly as we were walking away. I had not given any forethought about how I would introduce Travis. To call him my boyfriend seemed silly. The title of boyfriend was simultaneously an exaggeration and understatement—not to mention a bit bold, considering I was still legally married.

Greg signaled for Travis to follow us, but Travis just waved us away with a casual motion of his hand. I knew he would be fine on his own. He stood talking to the head of the chemistry department whose wife happened to be the exhibit curator. I sent Travis an apologetic glance from across the room, and he rebounded with a look of amusement. *Of course, Travis would fare well with academic types.*

I watched Travis all evening. He was at ease in the gallery even though the art that surrounded him was edgy and unsure. His stance projected patient authority as he talked to artists and professors, questioning them about their work, nodding when appropriate. Maybe that's what I loved about him. He could stand still and be himself when all else (the art, the artists—me) was trying to rebel. Nobody had ever exhibited that kind of patience with me before. I realized over the course of the evening that it was because Travis was a true independent spirit, a man who was at home with himself. He was so comfortable with his life choices that he could naturally allow others to come to their own conclusions at their own pace. With kudos unsaid, I found it was I who was dragging my date from the room. I could no longer stand still with elements of my past when my future was demanding attention.

"Come on, cowboy, let's ride."

"Cowboy?"

The ride home was quieter than our ride into the city. We listened to the college jazz station and turned the radio off when the music started to fuzz. We exchanged the straightaways of the express lanes for the curves of the country roads. Travis slowed the car at the dangerous turns, those marked by animal carcasses. Funny, how they were always present, with a warning in their decay.

"Are you cold?" Travis asked. "I can close the sunroof."

"No, I'm fine."

Travis reached for my hand. It was clammy.

"What's wrong?"

"Nothing." I didn't part with my emotions readily, as Travis was well aware. He typically scrutinized my every facial expression to gain insight as to my feelings. I kept my face impassive to keep him from reading my mind, though I didn't know why. My brain was currently measuring data, trying to find balance.

My control proved ineffective.

"I can tell you are thinking about something. Is it the show?" he asked.

"No. I'm not thinking about work. I think the show went really well, don't you?" I didn't wait for an answer. "I got some excellent contacts I can use when I move my business here."

"The show was great. But if you weren't thinking about the show, what are you thinking about?"

There was a silence before I spoke. "Us, I guess."

Travis winced and waited for me to continue.

"I'm so happy," I said finally.

"And that's a problem—*why*?"

"I don't want it to end."

"What do you mean end? This wasn't just a summer fling to—?"

"I don't mean end as in *the end*. I just meant end of an era."

"It doesn't have to be the end of an era."

Travis kept his eyes on the road. I sensed he didn't want to read my facial cues.

"Of course not, but things *will* change. Sam is coming home. We can't just roam naked around my house anymore—"

"I own a robe."

"—or drop everything and drive an hour to those foreign films you love. Did you say a robe?" I realized what he had implied. "We are not going to be doing the sleepover thing. I can't. I'm going to need a little space for the next couple of days. I'm a mother first. I can't explain this whole thing to Sam. Not yet. We need to slow this down a little."

I didn't elucidate further. Telling Travis that Bryce would be spending three days with me was a risk. Travis was an understanding man, but I didn't want to test his limits. I had communicated my need for space; he would respect the distance I was putting between us.

Travis was silent the rest of the trip. When he pulled the car to the curb on Mulberry Street, I invited him to come inside. I knew he would not turn me down, but I also understood the complexity in his acceptance.

· 44 ·

IN THE EARLY MORNING, I listened from the bedroom window as Travis filled Jules's bowl on the patio below. I had pretended to be asleep when he left the bed. He leaned over and kissed me on his way to the bathroom. The sun rose into a depressingly clear sky, and he had no excuses not to attend to his landscaping customers. I would not have given him any excuses, anyway. What was the use? I could not stop the lark from singing. I knew Travis felt it, too.

The night before, our lovemaking had been disappointing. We went through the motions but without satiation, and we fell asleep with more need than ever. And I could not discern if I was the source or the result of all that neediness. We had tried again, later, to quell the frenzy, but ultimately, sleep rescued us, offering only a restless trance as a poor alternative to our gratification.

Downstairs, the screen door whined and snapped shut. Jules was back inside, but I wondered on which side of the door Travis stood. I didn't have to wait long for my answer—I heard the truck engine. I sighed, uncertain if I did so in relief or in disappointment.

I got out of bed and stretched. No need to look out the window; Travis was gone. I rustled the bedcovers, presumably to straighten them, but the reality was that I was searching for something Travis may have left behind for me. When my search revealed nothing, I threw the bedding in a pile and scanned the floor for anything, a small sign to make me feel less alone. My gaze locked on something wedged between my nightstand and the wall, and I bent to investigate. Nonna's notebooks. They must have fallen when Shelly and Travis helped me move the furniture into the back bedroom. I picked up the notebooks without hesitation. Here was my sign. Nonna had something to tell me, and desperate for anything to fill the abyss, I could no longer escape from Nonna's words.

I dressed and made myself a thermos of hot, sweet coffee. With the notebooks tucked under my arm, I walked to the lake. I had spent few if any mornings by the water, and as I slipped so comfortably into the pocket of dawn by the shore, I found it curious that I hadn't. The water lapped at my toes with more sound than it did during the hectic days, and I could hear my own heartbeat as it studded my chest. In the light blue of the morning, I could still make out the pale outline of the moon, and I could feel its pull on the lake and all the fluids in my own body.

I had always considered myself to be born under the sign of the moon rather than the sign of Cancer. Everybody had looked to the moon on the day I was born, so it seemed to govern me in a way that the constellation of the crab could not. Who wanted to be under Cancer's domain, anyway? It sounded like a curse. I didn't know any other Cancers with whom I compared, so when asked, I told the zodiacally curious that I was born under the sign of the moon.

With the watching moon and the prostrating lake in attendance,

I poured myself a bowl of coffee and opened the last of Nonna's notebooks.

May 15, 1991

I cannot tell you how wonderful it felt to have Charlie home. Wearing my red dress, I greeted him at the door. Mama and Daddy left us alone for the evening. We wasted no time in finding my bedroom on the second floor of the tiny row home. In our passionate, tumbling reunion, drive replaced reverence, and I reenacted the love play of my youth. If my husband was surprised at my assertiveness, he said nothing. We didn't waste words or actions during his short leave.

It was with heavy heart and still-heavy loins that we left my small bed to dress for Lena's birthday party. I touched my abdomen as I tied the sash of my dress and imagined those clairvoyant Greek grandmothers nodding their heads. I felt the power of their vision with the truth of my womb. Some women knew. Charlie embraced me from behind. He let his hands slope below my waist. I would like to believe he had the gift of second sight as well.

In the two months I had come to know Lena, I had never been inside her home. She lived with her stepfather and mother, Rev. and Mrs. Ernest S. Platz, in a brownstone just two streets away. I cannot say I was even curious about her life. I was too absorbed in my own plight.

Lena's reality engaged me in a series of shocks, the first of which came when Mrs. Platz answered the door. She was petite and dark like Lena, but her stomach swelled over her legs like a hot air balloon over a basket. I estimated that the baby she carried would be born within the month. Lena, who had no siblings, had never talked of her mother's condition. It was a condition that was about to change, and soon.

Mrs. Platz led us down a hall to the dining room where the Reverend, Lena, and Hank sat drinking sherry. The Reverend stood to greet us. An inch taller than Charlie, he had a booming voice that had a slippery edge to it, more salesman than preacher. Then again, I supposed him to be God's salesman.

Lena's mother did not join us. I rose to help her in the kitchen, but Rev. Platz urged me to sit. Then he elbowed Charlie and said, "Your pretty little wife needs to conserve her energy for other things. You boys are only home a week."

It took me a second to complete the innuendo. I did not expect such talk from an American minister, but that was mild compared to the conversation to come. I felt as though I was in a reality perpendicular to our own, where people were the opposite of expectation and events were curiously jumbled.

I did not take notice of Hank at first, and when I did, the eerie pale of his blue eyes unsettled me. He sat quietly with a proprietary arm on the back of Lena's chair. I would soon understand why. Every time Mrs. Platz left the room, which was often, the Reverend, a little more intoxicated with each exit, would lean over to Hank and say something crude about his stepdaughter. He would remark on her high bosom, her compact buttocks, and the glorious pleasure that Hank could expect from such a "tight, little package." Hank's eyes remained expressionless.

When Mrs. Platz rejoined the party, her husband repeatedly bragged of his role in her present condition.

"Is this your first child?" Charlie asked, trying to turn the conversation.

"That we know of." The Reverend's laugh was loud.

Mrs. Platz disregarded her husband's lewd behavior.

"Shall we turn out the lights? I am bringing the cake now. I hope everybody likes chocolate."

In darkness we sang "Happy Birthday" to Lena, and when she blew out her candles, we all thought that the Reverend Ernie Platz might evaporate into the fulfillment of her wish. He did not, and Charlie thanked our hostess in a speedy exit speech. We were excused with a wink and a knowing command to "Go enjoy yourselves." We couldn't get away fast enough.

"Have you ever seen anything like that?" I asked Charlie once we were down the block.

"I wish I could say she was moving up in the world."

"You don't like Hank?"

"He's nice enough. Let's just say he will be receiving some letters from Virginia when we are overseas."

"Other girls? That's terrible. Are you sure? Because if you are, I can't let my friend marry such a man."

"What are you going to do? She'll end up marrying him anyway, and hating you."

I thought of Lena, wanting to please, wanting to be beautiful. It broke my heart, but I knew that Charlie was right. I hugged him close with a sureness that I had married well.

May 16, 2001

I didn't have a thing to do with it, but the wedding was off. The note came by messenger to our bakery. I immediately ran to the Platz residence. A sober Rev. Platz answered the door.

"You can talk some sense into her," he said, pulling me through the door. "She is up in her room."

His voiced trailed me up the steps. "And you can tell her that if she thinks I will support her, she has another think coming."

Lena's door was open, and she was busy writing announcements and notes for returned gifts. The woman before me was efficient and steely, where before she had been thoughtful and endearing. Again this house was muddling my expectations.

"Don't worry about me. I am fine. It's a mutual decision, really," she said before I asked her a question.

"It's just as well," I replied. Had she found out about the other women? I could not ask. "I will miss my support line. Who will follow news of Charlie's squadron with me?"

"Oh, Anja. You will be all right. You never needed me. Charlie will come home to you. He will build a fine house for you and your five children."

That is how we left it. Not only did Lena sever her relationship with Hank, but she ended our friendship as well. She no longer needed my reassurance, and she would not accept my pity. When I closed the door to her bedroom, I heard her wedding gown swish on its hanger on the other side.

I felt the vibration of footsteps on the pier before I saw them walking toward me. The three of them had the same red-gold hair. The father, the son, and their dog. Together, they appeared like a vision of glowing riches. As happy as I was to see my son, I couldn't stop feeling that his presence was interrupting something important. I stood and walked toward them, leaving my empty bowl to weigh down Nonna's notebook.

"Sammy. Look at you. And this cast? You have a green, alien arm. Oh, I missed you." I hugged my son who returned the gesture with half his strength.

"I missed you, too, Mommy."

"Hello, Bryce." I turned to my soon-to-be-ex-husband. "You're early. How did you know where to find me?"

"Actually Jules led the way. Your car was still in the driveway. Your neighbor said he saw you walking toward the lake. We needed to stretch our legs anyway, so we took a chance."

I picked up my shoes and the rest of my belongings, then joined them for the return walk. We exchanged pleasantries about the weather, their trip east. As we got closer to the house, Bryce touched my shoulder lightly with his left hand. He did not move his arm until we maneuvered through the back door of the house.

· 45 ·

KAREN HAD BEEN WRONG about Sam. He did not move shyly
through the house and my life. He was full of life and energy.
When he discovered the new bedroom waiting for him, he pulled
Bryce up the stairs to show him.

"This is even cooler than my bedroom at home." Those words
splintered through me. I looked away as Bryce delicately explained to Sam that this *was* his home now. "Remember what
we discussed, buddy?"

"Yeah, I know," Sam said. "Let's go see your room now,
Daddy."

I was not sure that Sam understood. They walked down the
hall, and I followed with Jules at my heels. Bryce would be sleeping in the room next to mine. I had arranged towels on the bed,
and put a flower in a vase on the bedside table. I had not added
these touches to be homey reminders, but rather the opposite. I
was making a statement that Bryce was a guest in my house, a
guest who was not allowed the privilege of rummaging through

closets. The room also had a fresh coat of paint and a new toile bedspread on the double bed.

"You didn't need to go to all this trouble for me," Bryce said.

"I want you to be welcome here." I had practiced those words, but my voice cracked when I said them. "You are still Sam's father."

Bryce backed out of the room and turned to look around the corner into my room.

"And this is your room?"

"Uh, yeah."

The bed was unmade, the bedding in a heap where I left it. I had planned to strip the bed later that morning and wash the sheets. I had not counted on Sam and Bryce's arrival that morning. The rumpled sheets were a reminder of the night I had spent with Travis. I blushed at the evidence.

I took a step closer toward the memory and closed the door to my room. "I didn't get a chance to straighten up in there." If Bryce suspected another man's presence he said nothing, but his gaze was hard as he studied the closed door. I could not help but conjure the image of a dog marking his territory.

I continued giving Bryce the rest of the tour. He'd only been to Nonna's house once during the course of our marriage, and that was some years ago. I concluded the tour with a show of my studio space.

"Wow," he said, "this is a much better setup than the one in Michigan. I can see you working here. Are you working on anything now?"

His interest in my work surprised me, and I realized that somehow, during the last few weeks, he had released me. We didn't need to hurt each other any more.

"As a matter of fact, I just finished my pieces for the alumni show, and I am about to break the mold, so to speak, and take my work in some different directions. I guess you could say that the last couple of months have been rather liberating."

"That's one way of looking at it." I was not sure, but I thought I noticed an edge to Bryce voice and a slight frown on his face. I had to be imagining things. He was experiencing the liberation, too, wasn't he? I showed Bryce my latest sketches.

"That is a departure for you," Bryce commented. "I am used to your figures, but this is exciting, too. These seem more like constructions."

I was surprised by Bryce's perception. I had never thought that he had given my artwork much thought. Now he was admiring my new projects and making astute comparisons with my past work.

"Um, yeah," was all I could stammer before I slid my sketches back into my portfolio. Suddenly the room seemed small and the hot air of August too tight to breathe.

For a moment Bryce looked as if he had something important to say, but he just tapped his fingers lightly on my workbench. "Is that the end of the tour?"

"Yes, I guess."

"It's just that it has been a long drive. Would you mind terribly if I went for a run to get the kinks out of my legs?"

"No problem. I think I'll sit outside and let Sam run around, too. Maybe later we can go for a late lunch. I didn't get to the grocery store quite yet. It was on my list of things to do today."

"Yeah, I know how much you like to go to the grocery store," Bryce said with a laugh. He looked as though he was going to lean down and kiss me, but he stopped himself. The funny thing was that I felt it, too. In spite of the divorce and my new romance with Travis, I wanted that kiss. *Old habits die hard.* Would we ever be comfortable around each other again? Would we ever get used to this new way of being together, this new dance that was no longer a dance?

· 46 ·

"No monkey bars, Sam." I said. "We have to wait until the alien doctor transfigures your arm back into human form."

Sam ignored me as he and Hayden climbed backward up the slide to reach the playhouse. I settled myself on the stoop. I guessed that Bryce would be gone for the better part of an hour with his run—enough time to read some more pages in Nonna's notebook. While I wanted to read what I could, I had a hard time turning the page. I distracted myself with my son's play, but the breeze caught the notebook and fanned its pages. I could not ignore the story I knew I must read.

June 10, 1991

I have tried to sit down and finish my story for many weeks now, but I have been procrastinating. I know why. Who wants to look into the mirror when they are sick or drunk or ashamed of their actions? Shame is a powerful thing. I know I must sit here until I finish or it will win. I have opened to a new page and filled my bowl with coffee.

Remember the speaker at Barbara Jean's commencement, talking of a life lived with truth? I know I must write this for me. I must put a face on my demons and a name to my sins. I have never been a particularly religious person, but there is something to be said about the power of cleansing one's soul.

The Ancient Greeks believed in the power of the theater to elicit catharsis. I agree; the theater is a holy place. I met your father there, and spent a good deal of my time at the movies, trying to escape my life. The war itself blurs in my recollection of it, but I remember the movies that came later: *Casablanca, The Longest Day, The Sound of Music.* It was not so with my personal life. I remember each of my transgressions and the authority with which I committed them. Movies could not absolve me of them; I can only hope that the telling will.

Spring of 1942, the weather was erratic, and so were my emotions. I missed my Charlie, and I missed my friend Lena, but with every day came a new sign that my intuition was correct. I was going to have a baby. I hid my condition from my parents. I wanted Charlie to be the first to get the news.

Every night I wrote to him. With Lena's help I had begun to correct my more glaring grammar errors. Without her, my letters still held hints of my ignorance with the written language, but I was getting better. I studied newspapers at night with a dictionary by my side. I cut out any article that described the happenings in the area of the Pacific where I knew that Charlie was stationed.

My parents tried to distract me with family card games, and I volunteered at the Red Cross two evenings a week. I kept busy. Often, I was tired. Never before had I taken such luxury in naps. On slow days at the bakery (the days were never slow, but everything is relative), I asked Mama if I could leave early. She never questioned me. I think she was afraid to say anything because the rent of my farm helped to float us financially.

One afternoon when I was home resting, I started to feel a strange sensation in my abdomen. It was too soon for me to feel the baby moving. I felt something warm and wet between my legs, and when I checked, I was bleeding.

How could I tell my parents of the miscarriage when they didn't even know I was expecting? The times were different then. These things were not discussed like they are today. How could I tell Charlie? How could he hear this news in a letter? I touched the dark blood. I know that sounds morbid, needing to touch it as it spilled from my body, but I wanted some tangible evidence of my loss. It was like the opposite of baptism. I was not receiving Father, Son, and Holy Spirit. I was losing husband, friend, and first-born child.

For one week I stayed home from the bakery. I told my parents that I had wrenched my back. They brought me hot water bottles, and tut-tutted about me being too young for such an injury. I wrote to Charlie, but I did not tell him of the misfortune I had suffered, that we had suffered. I wanted him to hold only joy inside when he read each of my letters. I not only hid the truth from him, I outright lied. In each letter, I wrote of my growing tummy, my nausea, and my exhaustion. I listed names for him to consider: Charles Jr., Nelson, Joseph. For the girls names I wrote down Alice (after his mother), Katherine, and Jane. I, myself, did not lapse into a false reality. The cramps were heavy, and I expelled small, unformed masses into the toilet. There was no way to forget.

I was recuperating alone one morning, when our doorbell rang. The sound of the bell always ignited the terror that was waiting in my heart. Was Charlie all right? I ran to the door, straightening my robe as I went. Though I was not dressed for visitors, I opened the door. Lena was standing there, or a shadow that looked like her.

She was pale and thin. Her lipstick was smudged badly, as if she hadn't even tried to put it on straight. Beside her were a tiny blue suitcase and a larger brown one.

"I looked for you at the bakery. Your parents told me you would be here."

"Come in. Did you carry these all the way here?" I asked, lifting the small blue case. It was light.

She walked instinctively to the kitchen where I put on a pot of water for tea.

"I am leaving town. I am going to Washington, D.C., to housesit for my cousin while he is overseas. I realize that I haven't talked to you in some time, but I wanted to tell you in person. Charlie, he's okay, isn't he? Forgive me for not asking sooner."

"Yes, he's fine, as far as I know. I jump every time I hear the doorbell. We only have a phone at the bakery, so I don't get too excited by the sound of the door there."

"Your mother said you hurt your back."

"Yes."

I guess I had been holding back my grief for so long, hiding behind my brave face. The teakettle whistled, and I started to weep. I expected to feel Lena's arms around me in an act of solace or at least hear some comforting words. The teakettle sang and sang. When it stopped, I stood up and removed the dry pot from the burner. That is when I saw that Lena was crying, too.

I did not get the whole story out of Lena in the kitchen that day. The narrative came later, during our months of seclusion in Washington, D.C. What I got was the headline.

On the evening of her birthday party, Lena Lefever succumbed to seduction, or at least that was her allusion, her illusion. I knew that a girl did not succumb to seduction and then call off her wedding in the same night. The only confirmed facts I got were that Lena was pregnant and unmarried.

"Does Hank know?"

"No. Please. You can't tell him. You can't even tell Charlie. My parents don't even know. I will go away to have the baby."

"I won't say anything. You have my word."

"Thank you." Lena was visibly relieved.

"Your mother, the baby, did she—?"

"Yes, a baby girl, Margot. She's beautiful, and another reason I cannot stay. I touch her cheek, and I remember the life that is growing inside of me. How can I love my sister and hate what is inside of me?"

Lena started to cry again. I handed her a clean handkerchief. I did not want to upset her by prying further. I would like to say that I did this out of friendship, but I was not that selfless. Before Lena had even finished confiding in me that day, I already had designs on her baby.

When my parents came home that evening, I had my own bags packed and waiting beside the door with Lena's two. Without going into detail, I explained that Lena needed me. They sensed the urgency. Why else would I abandon their needs when the bakery took so much work? They knew I was not a frivolous girl, and, too, they had prepared themselves for this day.

I kissed them good-bye that night, before we changed our minds. I gave them an address to forward any letters from Charlie. We called a cab, and the driver lifted our bags into the trunk.

"Don't let her lift any of those suitcases," my mother said. "My baby has a bad back."

For the first time, at twenty-five years of age, I was leaving my parents, for a life not entirely my own.

LENA SHRANK AWAY from the world as it was whizzing by our moving train window. I think she was still experiencing morning sickness. I could not feel sorry for her. I was still enduring cramps. Although they were lighter, I was afraid that they would become a permanent ache. On our trip south, I told Lena about my baby. I told her slowly, in droplets, like a leaky faucet weeping to fill a pail. I wanted her to have silences between my words to come to her decision, the decision I was mentally willing her to make.

She didn't say anything for the first two days we were setting up house in Washington. On the third day, she spoke with the deliberateness of someone who has taken time to think about her words.

"Anja, when my baby is born, I want you to have it for your own."

I had prepared myself. When she finally said her words I launched my planned silence, as if I were considering the idea for the first time. The pause went on forever in my head until I could no longer hold the words back.

"Lena, are you sure about this?" I asked her, but inside I was already accepting her offer.

"I have been thinking about this for some time, and it is the best solution. I can't very well raise it on my own. Maybe you and Charlie don't want a child that isn't your own blood, but I just can't give my baby to a stranger. I can't do it. Please say you'll think about it."

"What if the baby was of our own blood?" I chose my words carefully.

"What do you mean?" Lena asked.

"Charlie doesn't know I lost the baby. What if he never has to know?"

And with that, I revealed my plan. I acted as though I had just then thought of the solution, but in reality, I had been plotting since Lena first sat across the table from me in my parents' kitchen. Lena did not appear shocked, but pleased, and we made a pact. It was all settled. Lena would go to a military hospital to deliver her baby, and when she did, she would register as Mrs. Charles Graybill. Charlie would have his baby when he returned home, and I would not have to tell him how I had lost the child he had entrusted me to carry.

At the time, I did not see what a deception I was laying out for my husband. I did not think of the sacrifice of my friend. I only wanted the love of a child, and I was prepared to do whatever it took for me to overcome my own unspeakable loss.

When Lena was well into her fifth month, I shared the good news with my parents. Mama wanted to come down to Washington to see us, but the bakery was busy, as I knew it would be. She would not be able to make the trip. I promised to bring the baby home, as soon as we could travel.

All that was left to do was wait. Lena and I spent lots of time playing cards. I taught her all the games my parents had taught me. She had never been allowed to play cards in her house. Her stepfather would not allow it. He was a drinking man, a smoking man, but not a man of cards.

Slowly, card by card, hand by hand, game by game, I came to know Lena's story. The more I heard, the more I felt that we were doing the right thing, bringing the baby into our family instead of hers.

Lena was born near Pittsburgh. Her father worked in the

steel mills, and died in an accident there when Lena was only a toddler. Five years later, her mother went to hear a guest minister at her church. The Reverend Ernest Platz was a bachelor who spoke with such dynamism from the pulpit that all of the single women in the congregation set a course for him. Lena's mother did not enter the race. She shied away, though she was very interested in this young man, potent with thought and delivery.

A picnic followed the service that day, and the story that is told is that Reverend Platz took a bite of Lydia Lefever's cherry crumb pie and declared before the entire congregation that he would marry the woman who had succeeded in baking heaven into a crust. Less than a year later, they were married, and Rev. Platz was called to a church in Philadelphia.

Lena was ten when they moved. Knowing nobody, she spent most of her time reading books in her room. It was in her room that Rev. Platz first cornered his prey. At first it was just smoothing her hair and telling her what a beautiful girl she was. Then as he gained her trust (a feat he never quite accomplished), he would unbutton her dress and rub her back. "Sweet thing. Young girls can get themselves into so much trouble when they turn away from God. You love God, don't you, Lena?"

By the time Lena was twelve, the good Reverend was going to her room every evening to pray with her and read the Bible. He unzipped his pants, and ordered her to caress his flaccid penis. Lena had no choice but to comply. Her new daddy was a man of God. "You want to obey God, don't you, Lena?"

The Reverend Ernie Platz was nothing without his brimstone. His face turned dark with blood, unlike his genitals, white and limp in Lena's sweaty palm.

"You evil girl. You are not pretty, yet you tempt men. You do not walk with angels, but with Satan. You must repent before God. Feel the fires of hell. And if you cry out, you will be punished. God does not like ugly whores, bastard daughters of factory workers. Repent."

Lena would undress, and stand naked before her step-father. He would hold the lit end of his cigarette to her buttocks so she could feel the heat. If she cried, he would press it further until it burned full moons into her flesh. When he was finished with his cigarette, she would dress, and he would zip. Then, he would open the door to her room a crack, and they would kneel by the end of her bed to pray. Usually about this time, Lydia, finished with the supper dishes, would join them and pray aloud for her daughter's soul. She was so happy that her new husband and her daughter got along so well, and this fact she included in her "Thanks be" prayers as a postscript.

It was little wonder that it took the Reverend Platz eight years to impregnate his wife. The Reverend's sermons were the only evidence of any virility that Lena had witnessed. The Reverend's visits to Lena's room stopped when he discovered he had fathered a child by his wife. All those warnings against boastfulness and pride did not apply to him. At long last, after many prayers, his wife was pregnant.

Not long afterwards, Lena met Hank. She never had many friends at school, and never a boyfriend. She had started a secretarial course after high school. He was an engineering student. They met when he came to the business school looking for a student to type his term papers.

Lena volunteered to type his paper before she had a chance to think about the consequences or her own shyness. Hank loved the way he could leave his imprint on Lena, so innocent and willing to be whatever he needed in a girlfriend. They had only dated for two months when he proposed to her on the day after the attack on Pearl Harbor.

If you think it was difficult for me to hear Lena's story, you are right. She did not tell it willingly. After each installment of her story, I went to her and hugged her. She did not back away from my embrace, as I suspected someone might who had been victimized by a touch. I did not even know the worst of it, and wouldn't until later.

I asked Lena if I could touch her belly, feel the baby. I always asked, and she always let me. I marveled at the tautness of her smooth abdomen and the irregularities of little elbows and feet that greeted me. Her face registered delight each time I told her of the love I already felt for the baby. We had stopped knitting socks for Charlie and started on projects for the baby: a bunting, booties, and even a white baptismal sweater. I had promised Lena that we would have the baby baptized. Through all her trials, she still loved the church. It was literally her sanctuary. I had never grown up in church, but I was sure that Charlie would want to bring the baby up Lutheran. Lena and I discussed names. Graybill was a solid surname. It sounded good with most given names.

The nights were hot in D.C. We lived in the city where the heat never quite evaporated into the hills of Maryland and Virginia. The heat stayed flat and steamy along the river, between the buildings, and in our kitchen. I still baked breads to sell in Washington when the flour supply was reliable. The house felt like a brick oven in the evenings, and we needed to escape its torture.

Some nights Lena and I would find a secluded section of Rock Creek and walk beside it or dip our toes into the glassy edge. That was when I would tell Lena of the farm where I would take the baby until Charlie returned. I had received a telegram informing me that my tenant had been drafted by the army and could no longer pay rent on my property. Now the farm was an empty cradle, waiting for my baby.

"You should see it, Lena. It has hills and a stream, and the whole place is surrounded by these wild mulberry trees. We could raise chickens and maybe a have a cow for some fresh milk. We used to have fresh milk every day when I was a girl. Charlie's family owns a dairy farm."

Lena never talked of her plans for her future, after the baby was born. Of course, I invited her to stay with me until Charlie returned, but she was uncertain.

"We'll see," she would say and turn her face away.

I saw some softening in her when I described the lake near Mulberry Farm. "It goes as far as the eye can see, and in the evening the sunset makes dancing sparks of light on its surface. It is so peaceful—nothing like it. We can take the baby for walks; there is a path nearby. Or we can even go swimming."

"I used to swim at a water hole near Pittsburgh," she'd say. "I loved to swim. My mother says I could swim before I could walk. It is the only memory of my real father, floating with me on that pond. I must have been two or three because he died before I turned four. Do you think it is a real memory?"

"Of course, I do." I did not lie.

"I swam in pools, too. I got a blue ribbon one summer for swimming the fastest of any girl in our town, but that was before my mother married Daddy, and we moved to Philadelphia." Lena was shy then, as if she had spoken out of turn.

Sometimes we would hold hands on our walk. It was platonic, but the things we were about to share were so visceral that we needed to grab tight. Those nights were white with our fears, red with our dreams. We were both

expectant with so much more than a baby. We wanted the
world to be a good place where evil cowered not only in the
far reaches of the warring world, but also in the bedrooms
of little girls. Yes, I knew you would be a girl, Judy, for
how else would we be able to seek redemption? I knew, too,
there would be a Barbara Jean, for our demand was too
great for one generation to bear.

I was weaving ends back into a baby sweater when Lena
shared with me the second part of her story. She lit a cigarette, as she was in the habit of doing since we had come to
the capital. We didn't yet understand the health hazards of
cigarette smoke for unborn babies. I never liked the smell,
but I did like Lena's show of independence, so I never chastised her.

She blew the smoke out of the corner of her mouth. Perhaps she was reserving the rest of her mouth for her words.

"Anja, do you remember the night of my party?"

"Yes, of course."

"Do you remember the things that the Reverend said about
me?"

"He was drunk. I didn't pay attention."

"Oh, Hank did."

I remembered back to Hank's vacant blue eyes, and how
they absorbed all the drunken whispers from the Reverend. Hank looked every bit the soldier then, uniformed
and filled with the anger of a nation. Those eyes. I did not
see my own protection in them, but imagined them to be
rather like those of the enemy we were fighting. Blue eyes
for Hitler's Aryan race. I tried to shake off my feelings and
support this man who took a great cause upon himself, but
I still had my Greek ways. I still had my intuition, and that
was something the gypsy in me could never extinguish.

Oh, Hank did. From that statement came the story I
didn't want to know, yet I already did. Hank had walked

Lena away from the brownstone to the small room he rented near the college. He had to sneak her inside. His landlady had expressly prohibited smoking, drinking, carousing, and women. Lena was a bit lightheaded from the dessert wine we had used to toast her birthday and upcoming nuptials. She felt very close to Hank, and she opened up to him emotionally. My feeling was that she would have opened up to him physically, too, if he had given her the chance.

Lena told Hank of the abuse she had suffered as a child, and how happy she was that he was saving her, taking her away from it all. She told him of the zippers and the prayers and the cigarettes. Hank was livid. She thought he might be, and she tried to calm him by saying that she had survived. It was over. She had him now. However, Hank was not angry with the Reverend; he was angry at Lena.

He knocked her on his cot and twisted her arm. "How could you?" he asked.

She didn't answer, and he slapped her hard across her mouth. "You slut. You couldn't even wait for a date; you had to get your action with your daddy. And to think I waited patiently for you. Well, not anymore."

With one hand he held her down, and with the other he undid his belt. She tried to deny his accusations and resist his weight, but he just gagged her so she wouldn't be heard in the adjacent rooms. Then the man she had promised to marry, the man she wanted more than anything else to please, the man to whom she would have given herself in five days—that man raped her.

What did Lena know of sex? She only saw the limp cowardice of a child predator. Lena had not known that a man's organ could inflate against her, could tear her flesh. She backed herself against the wall and made herself very small, but not small enough. "Look at me," Hank said. He yanked her hair back until she could see the sweat on his lip and smell his breath, sour with the wine. She started to count inside her head the way she did when the cigarettes burned her buttocks and inner thighs. *One, two, buckle my shoe. Three, four, knock on the door. Five, six, pick up sticks. Seven, eight, lay them straight. Nine, ten, a big, fat hen. One, two . . .* Over and over, the mental rhyme numbed her senses. Eventually Hank's grip loosened, and he rolled off of her.

She untied the binding on her mouth herself. Hank did nothing to stop her. It was so dark; she had to feel around on the floor for her panties. Lena pulled on her underwear without doing anything to stop the blood. It spread until it was a map on the white cotton. When she opened the door Hank called to her: "I won't marry a secondhand bitch. Find some other fool."

Lena walked home alone. Like a conquering nation, the map in her panties flooded its borders. Each annexation brought a wave of nausea, and she grabbed the sides of a trash can and retched. Adding mockery to offense, Lena's diamond sparkled, winking the reflected light of a spotty streetlamp.

Nobody wants to hear about her own conception. We hide that messy business behind baby showers and baptisms and strollers in the park. Judy, I never thought of your beginnings in those ugly terms. How could such a gift come from such brutality? I never believed in original sin, and likewise, I never believed that you were born out of anything but my desire to hold you in my arms.

We did go to the hospital as planned. Many women accompanied other women to the delivery rooms, especially then. In the small room at the end of the hall, I waited with more female relatives than daddies-to-be. Each woman pressed a picture of a serviceman into my hands. My son.

My sister's husband. My neighbor. I had a picture of Charlie with me in the pocket of my dress, but I did not show it for fear that I would reveal our hoax. Instead, I fingered the photograph until its edges were sueded from my touch.

Lena's labor had started early on the morning of December fourth. We had walked around our neighborhood until the pains grew stronger and closer together. I, who had never driven a car before, had practiced driving Lena's cousin's 1937 Oldsmobile Club Coupe until I could drive it smoothly through the city. This was no small feat. The car was large, sold to Lena's cousin by the DuPont family chauffer. It had a built-in radio with two speakers, a luxury I could not enjoy for fear of distraction. When the hour came, my anxiety was compounded by Lena's labor, but I managed to drive us safely to the hospital. They whisked Lena away in a wheelchair. I watched her go. The attending nurse asked me for the patient's name.

"Mrs. Charles Graybill," I said.

"And you are?"

"A friend."

That same nurse returned to inform me of your birth, shortly thereafter. Lena named you in those woozy hours after you were born. We had never known anyone named Judy. It was a clean name, free from expectation, even though you were not. I was afraid that Lena would change her mind about giving me the baby, especially since, as a girl, you did not carry the mark of her attacker.

My fears were unfounded. The moment she handed you to me was her greatest triumph. Lena had wholly succeeded in pleasing another person, a feat she had never before accomplished. Did she fall in love with me the day I validated her existence? We'll never know, but she did accept my proposal to move to Mulberry Farm—as if to say no would have threatened her very life.

I COULD NOT FINISH the letter. I closed the notebook and looked at my son who in turn was watching ants move about in the dirt beneath the swings. I knew the truth about us now. Lena was my real grandmother, my blood and bones grandmother. Lena was my son's great-grandmother. Even Sam was not who I thought he had been an hour ago. I had no artist in the family, only a family history of cancer and incest. The late morning brought a chill, an intimation of autumn and my life to come. The past, this very house, neither could blanket me in its warmth, and for the moment I felt a loss greater than any of the many I had experienced in the past year.

Why had I never suspected? Those moments Lena and I had shared out in the garden together. Why had Grandma Lena never told me? She had let Nonna have all the glory. I wondered if subconsciously I had known it then. The lie had to be present at the cellular level, somewhere. Did my mother know or, at the very least, suspect? There had to be some code embedded in our brains. A child knows its mother. It is a matter of survival. Then again, my mother didn't survive, did she?

Bryce opened the kitchen door. He was wearing only a towel wrapped around his hips. His body was pink from exertion and damp from a recent shower. I had not realized he had come home from his jog. I must have been too absorbed in the notebooks to notice his return.

"I just wanted to let you know, I blew a fuse with that fan upstairs and my electric razor," he said. "I was going to fix it, but I couldn't find the switch for the cellar light."

"You shouldn't go down there without shoes anyway. I'll get it." Seeing his half-shaved face, I knew his concern was immediate. "If you can just stand here at the door and keep an eye on Sam, I'll be right back," I said. "Oh, and Bryce, please don't flash my neighbors."

Still clutching Nonna's notebook, I brushed past Bryce on my way to the basement. I felt the spark but denied it. It was only

Bryce's assumed familiarity that had unsettled me. His nakedness implied an intimacy that wasn't there. I would have to make certain boundary lines with him, just as I would have to make limits for Travis.

Travis. I opened the door to the cellar and stared into the dark vacancy of the stairwell. Had I suspected that Travis and I shared not just a story but also an ancestry? *My only love sprung . . . from my own family?* I pressed the notebook into my chest and fumbled for the light switch. I didn't reach it until I had descended the three top stairs. I pressed the button until it clicked. One naked bulb exposed the narrow stairway enough for me to negotiate the rest of my way. Not so with Nonna's story. With so many questions raised, I could almost be sure that I would have to read to the end before I found all the answers I needed.

· 47 ·

BRYCE HAD GIVEN SAM the option of where he wanted to go for lunch, and I had cringed when he said Chuck E. Cheese's.

"Maybe with his arm the way it is, we should . . ." I began.

"He's fine," Bryce interrupted in a way that told me the decision had been finalized.

I did not know what my real objection was. The three of us climbed into Bryce's 4Runner. I immediately wished I had driven. Everything seemed to be on Bryce's terms, and I wanted desperately to prove that things were different now—even if that difference was limited to the symbolism of taking the driver's seat.

The restaurant was less crowded than it had been on that rainy day in early summer. We ordered a pizza and sat down to wait while Sam scurried from one game to another.

"It isn't in our arrangement, but I am thinking of driving in for Sam's birthday."

"Yeah, we'll see. We have two months to think about it. I'd kind of like to get him started in school and see how that goes."

"It's no problem, is it?"

"No." I shook my head. "I am going to get our drinks. What would you like? Cherry Coke, no ice?"

"Yes, please."

I was anxious to get away from Bryce. Perhaps I could convince Sam to give me some tokens so I could play a few games before the pizza arrived. How silly it was that I was avoiding my ex-husband. Now he wanted to come in October for Sam's birthday. If I didn't negotiate my terms now, I was setting myself up for future difficulties. I returned to the table with the trio of drinks and a determination to set things straight. Bryce stood and took the cups from my grip.

"Look, Bryce, I don't have a problem with you coming in October, but maybe it would be better if we got you a hotel room nearby. Maybe the Holiday Inn with the indoor pool and miniature golf course. That way you could take Sam swimming."

"Am I in the way?"

"I think it's great for Sam, but we are getting on with our lives, and I don't want there to be any confusing issues from here on out."

"Are you talking about the towel, because if that's —"

"No, I just don't want Sam or anybody else to get the wrong idea about our relationship. We need some boundaries."

"You're right. A hotel room is probably for the best. Do you want me to get one for tonight?"

"No, you don't have to," I said much too quickly. I wished I had thought before I answered, but I couldn't take it back now. At least, I had stood my ground about future visits, and that gave me license to relax. I couldn't help thinking about the baby. Karen had said the baby was due in September. When in September? The beginning of that month was only days away. Would his girlfriend be so quick to allow him to travel ten hours away in the uneasy weeks of new parenthood? Was she okay now with Bryce traveling so close to the end of her pregnancy?

I searched my brain for a new subject. As flustered as I was, I resigned myself to the habitual questions about work.

"Work is good. I took a couple of weeks off to be with Sam and worked at home sometimes and quit working early during the other weeks he was there. I'll have a lot of catching up to do when I get back, especially with Larson retiring at the end of the year."

"Oh, Fred Larson is finally making good on his threat?" I asked, but I really wanted to scream at Bryce. Why did it take the dissolution of his family for him to finally take time away from the office? If he could have spared two weeks when we were married . . . I didn't want to think about it. The world of *could have* and *should have* was a breach to my sanity.

"Yes, Fred is going, but I think his wife's health was the clincher in the deal."

"Is Molly sick?"

"MS. She's had it for years, but she's going downhill fast. It doesn't look good."

I scanned the games for Sam. Only disaster could separate these men from their work: disease, divorce, death. Why did these high-powered, goal-obsessed men fail to find life where it really existed, in the bounds of their relationships? Family lawyers. Did they even know what constituted a family, or were they all jaded beyond care? My thoughts drifted back to July Fourth when I sat on the boat with Travis, each of us unveiling our marriages for the other to see. Travis and Liz had quit their jobs just to spend more time with each other. To me, the idea of working with Bryce was absurd. We had barely enjoyed each other's company in moments of recreation.

Was that true? Was I being fair? I looked back across the table at Bryce. Here we were at a family restaurant at our son's request. Maybe fun wasn't a word to describe our outing, but I could almost pretend that we didn't mind sitting across from each other in a spirit of codependence. In fact, I realized that I chose to be here at this moment with Bryce. And that choice empowered me.

Sam joined us when the pizza arrived. He was talkative. He wanted to inform me of his summer activities. Bryce nodded with pride and filled in the finer points of Sam's exploits when Sam's telling became too hurried. I stayed present in my lunch with Sam and Bryce. Not once during dinner did I look over my shoulder for the ghost of Travis sitting in the far booth. This is where the story of my summer had truly begun. Looking back on this moment, I would see the season fading here as well.

Though I wasn't mindful of the way my life would play out from this moment, I did have the realization that no matter how we compartmentalized our relationship, Bryce would never belong solely to my past. Bryce would come for Sam's birthday bearing presents. Then a month later, I would drive Sam to Michigan to deliver him for Thanksgiving. There would be school plays and graduations. Someday, maybe at Sam's wedding, Bryce would kiss me on my cheek, and say, "Our marriage didn't work out, but look at this wonderful kid we raised." And I would nod my agreement and say that our journey together had been worthwhile.

LATER THAT NIGHT, after Sam was asleep under the stars of his new room, I found Bryce sitting on the swing on the front porch.

I sat down beside him.

"I'm going to turn in early tonight. Do you need anything?" I asked.

"No, I got everything I need. I'm going to sit out here for a little while."

"No problem. Just lock the door when you come in. I am going to try to wake up early tomorrow and log in a few hours of studio time, if you don't mind."

"No, that's fine. Maybe I'll take Sam to the grocery store and pick up a few things for you."

"You don't need to do that."

"I just ran out of deodorant and need to get to Wal-Mart anyway."

"Okay," I conceded. "I have a list started on the—"

"Fridge. I know, I saw it."

And with that bit of information, I left Bryce to contemplate the Pennsylvania night. I had my own thoughts to attend to, specifically a story I needed to scrutinize. While the husband who wasn't a husband sat on the porch swing of a grandmother who wasn't a grandmother, I picked up Nonna's letter to uncover my own identity.

June 12, 1991

It was easier for me to relate the tragedies of Lena's life to you than my own. Even after fifty years, I draw a sharp breath at the remembrance of Christmas 1942. Holidays were a trying time for many families. Lena and I journeyed with you to my parents' house. It was perhaps too early to be traveling with such a young baby, but I was homesick and lonesome for my family over the holidays. If my parents found it strange that Lena was not staying with her own family, they said nothing. They were planning to help us move to the farm a month later.

My mother and father were so pleased to be grandparents. Lena and I took you to a Lutheran Christmas Eve service, not to relate the miracle of Christ's birth with our own new experience, but to pray for the servicemen. The minister read Charlie's name aloud, and I pressed my palm to your chest as if together, we were prayer hands.

The day after Christmas, when our bodies were sluggish from excesses, the doorbell rang. We weren't expecting anybody, but I knew who it was.

"No," I said when my father and Lena started for the door. I handed the baby to my mother and opened it myself.

I pitied the man on the other side of the door. He was a uniformed stranger who went around telling women that their sons and husbands were dead. I invited him in for coffee and old Christmas cake. I comforted him for the terrible job he had to do. Did he have more calls to make? We gave him bread and wine to take to the next houses, but I didn't imagine he took those loaves to the front stoop with him. The bread was dark, the wine red. They made for a black communion.

I do not remember the transition into 1943. When did the calendar change? At the funeral, someone gave me a flag. Charlie's parents and sisters were there. I had met them once. They didn't often leave the dairy farm. They had little interest in the baby. Could they sense you were not of their blood? "We have nobody named Judy in our family." I tried to embrace Charlie's mother, the other Mrs. Graybill, but she just looked begrudgingly at the flag. I should have given it to her.

All of Charlie's letters came back to me unopened. He had not received a one. He did not know I was pregnant, and had not been victim to my ruse when I was no longer expecting. He never knew about the baby named Judy. Then I cried, because maybe it was he, not I, who was holding our firstborn. I burned them then, lest Lena think our device was for naught. I wanted to save her from that stain.

Oh Judy, without you and Lena, I would have become powder, dry and crumbled and useless as chalk dust. Maybe you didn't revive me. Maybe it was hatred that watered me in those dry days, hatred for a man named Hank Littlehail.

The stories came back to me with wounded soldiers or

from their girlfriends or mothers. Hank Littlehail had been negligent with explosives. He was supposed to create a pass to build a road. Charlie was the supervising engineer on the project. He realized that Hank had done shoddy work, so Charlie went to do a field check. Hank followed after him to steer him away from the unfinished portion of the job. No witness is sure why the explosives discharged. The two men were down the road from where the actual blast took place, but Charlie must have seen the blast first. He pushed Hank Littlehail into a ditch and was rocketed on top of him. Charlie did not die instantly, though like Hank, he was knocked unconscious. The rest of the men in their patrol saw the explosion, but they were unable to reach the men for another hour. Hank lost his right leg; he came home in the crusty, crimson uniform of a hero. My husband wore a star-spangled burial shroud. You, Judy, wore your little white baptismal sweater. You were innocent in all of this bloodshed. I wore black, not of nuns, but of widows and thieves.

I closed the notebooks and tried to sleep, but my mind was restless. The more I tried to relax, the more agitated my thoughts became. Around midnight, I heard Bryce climb the stairs and enter the room next door. The moon, newly risen, shone brightly through my window, and I feared its coming would amplify my current state of sleeplessness. I could hear Bryce shuffling through his suitcases and the whisper of fabric brushing skin. The moon completely illuminated the room on that side of the house: I assumed Bryce hadn't turned on any of the ancient lamps in the room.

I listened in the lunar-lit dark for sounds of his breathing, but heard nothing. How strange it was that plaster walls and oak doors with cut crystal knobs now separated me from the man who until recently had slept beside me in our queen-size bed. The proximity of him to me made the division seem more contrived than it had been when we were displaced by several states. Before yesterday, geography had been our barrier. Now the obstacle was selection.

· 48 ·

FOR THE NEXT TWO DAYS, I watched Bryce move through my home. He moved with the grace of someone who belonged there, and it irritated me to watch the fluency in his actions. Sam, although oblivious to the undercurrent, seemed happier than I could remember. And it was easier for all of us to exist under the spell of late summer than to dismiss the illusion. Travis had not called once since Sam had been home, but when I unlocked the barn, I noticed that he had dropped off a couple of garden tools. He must have appeared while Bryce and I were at the lake, taking Sam for a swim. I was sure Travis would have noticed the car with Michigan plates. I had tried to call him, but his service answered, and I didn't know what to say, so I had hung up. Travis had caller ID; he would know I had tried to reach him.

Sam was taking his afternoon nap when Bryce sat next to me at the kitchen table. I looked up from my sketchbook. Bryce had a serious expression on his face.

"You're leaving?" I asked.

"I'd like to stay one more day if that's okay."

"Why?"

"Bobbi, look, this isn't easy for me. I need to talk to you about the divorce."

"What is it?" *Oh my God, he's going to renege on the custody agreement.* My heart lurched and fluttered arhythmically.

"It was so hasty. I don't . . ."

"I thought that was the way you wanted it. Your girlfriend being pregnant—"

"You knew about that?"

I flashed him a hardened look. "Do you think I am an idiot?"

"No. That's not the point." Bryce looked down at his folded hands.

"What is the point?"

He sighed and then straightened. "The baby wasn't mine. I threw our marriage away over a bunch of lies."

"And you just found out?"

"No, I've known since before you came to sign the divorce papers."

I exhaled, long and slow, as if to rid myself of months of toxins. I did not know what to say to him.

"I couldn't tell you when you came. You were so agreeable and honest when we looked over the contracts, and I felt so small, like I was never worthy of being your husband." He paused to arrange his thoughts. "Then these last weeks with Sam. I can't tell you. I knew when he left that I wouldn't just miss him, I would miss us. These last couple of days were a test for me. It isn't over, Bobbi, at least not for me. I see what we can be together. You have showed so much strength and integrity through this whole mess. I would be a fool to walk away from our marriage."

"Bryce, you already did walk away from our marriage." My voice was cold and even.

He looked up and into my eyes. I did not turn away from his

gaze. I had to be strong. Bryce took my hands in his. "Bobbi, I want us to stay married and work out our problems. I am willing to admit what I did was wrong." He paused before his final summation. "I will do whatever work it takes. I just need to know if you can find it in your heart to meet me halfway on this."

The breeze from the open door turned the pages in my sketchbook, and I pulled away from Bryce's grasp. I placed both hands on the book and gave it my weight. *Little Flower, give me power. Little Flower, give me power. Little Flower, give me power.*

Down the street a lawn mower sounded its gravelly call. I did not look up. I could not. I was using all of my energy to keep my book closed.

"I've shocked you, I know." Bryce stood up. "I don't expect you to jump at the chance to take me back, but if I know soon that you'll think about it, I can call the courthouse and stop the paperwork from going through. At least think about it for Sam's sake."

Bryce walked out of the room before I could answer. *No. You can't do this to me.*

· 49 ·

THE ATMOSPHERE AT THE dinner table was strained, but polite. We passed food across the table with such cordiality that even Jules seemed bewildered. Even when Sam spilled his juice, we each jumped up and said, "I'll take care of it," while our son marveled at his good fortune in not being reprimanded. After dinner, I asked Bryce to watch Sam for a little while. I told them both that I was going to sketch at the lake, but I did not even bother to take my supplies with me. After the bombshell that Bryce had dropped on me that afternoon, he would conclude I was using this outing to sort out my emotions.

The night was breezy. I had seen on the news that a tropical storm was dancing on a southern coastline and flirting with the northern weather. I had grabbed my favorite fisherman's sweater from a trunk of fall clothes that was, as yet, unpacked. Now with the wind scattering the leaves, I wrapped the sweater tightly around my body. I suspected that my chill had less to do with the breeze and more to do with my state of mind.

I tried to think about Bryce and his offer, but as soon as I lost sight of the house, I forgot about his plea. Instead I thought about the other revelation, that Travis and I were cousins.

I love Travis. I love him. I repeated the mantra over and over.

I summoned the image of my lover to my mind. *The dimple next to his burnished eyes. His full lips, soft in comparison to his strong, rough hands. The way his hands matched mine, callus for callus.* I walked steadily toward the lake. My gait was determined, as though I dared the sky to rain on me. The more I thought about Travis, the more I felt his presence. I could conjure him, I knew—not just in my mind.

The rain came in fat drops, slowly at first, then quickly. The gray sky dotted the sidewalk like a pointillist gone mad. I continued to walk away from shelter and toward the cumulative spill of the lake. The lake was everything to me. The waters pulled me by some force I had not known existed before this summer. I had tried to name this force in the past. Now that the names tripped on my tongue, my ability to believe wasn't contaminated by the left-brain labels. I wasn't thinking about what I needed to do or who I was. I just followed my imperative. With an elemental urgency, I started to run.

I knew before I turned the corner. I could feel his presence. My eyes flashed on the white truck at the water's edge. A mere confirmation. The parking lot was nearly empty. With the rain coming, the last few boats were coming into dock, but Travis was lowering his boat into the water.

Travis was part of me. The blood that we shared didn't separate us. It bound us together in a secret knot. I wouldn't even have to tell him. When he saw me, his shoulders straightened. I waved, and Travis waved back. I slowed my run, now, toying with him. Travis wound the rope around a post at the dock, and watched my approach.

I reached up and pulled his face to mine.

"I've been waiting for you," he said, wiping the wet strands of hair away from my face. "I'd almost given up hope."

I looked at him without speaking. My eyes darted back and forth across his face. I didn't find longing in his expression, but concern. *He doesn't need to know the whole truth. I will carry that burden.*

Travis cleared his throat, but his voice was still husky. "He's still here."

I nodded.

"How long do we have before he alerts the guard?" Travis asked.

"It's not like that." But I did not know what it was like. I didn't want to talk about Bryce.

Travis took a step backward, trying to distance himself in case I was here with bad news.

"Well, I'm taking her out. Are you coming?"

Again I nodded, though I wasn't sure of everything that my agreement had implied. Suspiciously I looked through the rain to his boat. It was the first time I had ever noticed the black letters on the bow of the craft.

"Tan-*gin*-ika?"

"Tan-gin-*ee*-ka," he corrected, accenting the long *e* sound. "It's African for *Goddess of the Lake*."

I was bewildered. I had never revealed to Travis how I used to worship Mary and God in these waters, how I now worshipped the lake itself. How could he possibly know of my sodden faith? "Why have I never noticed the name before?"

"I've had the idea to name her *Tanginika* for a while. I finally got around to doing it. The former owner named her *Bessie 2* after his cat. We kept that name because Elizabeth's dad called her Bessie when she was small."

"I seem to recall *Bessie,* now that you mention it."

"I thought it was about time for a change. That, and I had to keep myself busy these last—"

"Ssh." I cut him off before he could finish his sentence. I trailed his lower lip with my finger, and then kissed the spot my finger had traced. I didn't want to talk.

"Let me pull the truck into the lot. I'll meet you back here."

The rain slowed to a steady, but not bothersome, shower. Travis returned in a minute, and he helped me board the craft. The motor started on the first try, and Travis veered the boat away from the harbor. His was the only vessel heading out into the waters. When we were a good distance from the dock, Travis increased speed over the bumpy water. I didn't ask where we were going; I didn't care.

The wind and rain hit like pellets on my cheeks. The pelting marked me, but I kept my face high. I needed to feel the pain of the moment. It freed me from my emotions, and kept me firmly in the present. *This* moment, with *this* man, on *this* lake.

It was too noisy to yell, so Travis motioned for me to sit nearer to him. I did, and he ran a warm hand over my legs, covered in gooseflesh.

"I have a blanket around here somewhere," he shouted.

He reached behind me and pulled a plaid blanket from the storage locker.

I wrapped the length of it around my legs. I didn't want to talk to Travis about anything. As long as the boat was roaring I didn't have to, but that wasn't what Travis had in mind. He slowed the boat and stopped the motor. All at once, we leaned into each other. The rain had stopped stinging my face, but Travis, with his bearded kiss, rubbed my skin deliciously raw. We continued our rough embrace as the sky around us deepened. The boat rocked and drifted, but we didn't pay any attention.

Travis fumbled for the blanket but couldn't find it.

"Oh, hell," he mumbled and pushed me back onto a pile of wet life preservers where I waited for him to descend upon me.

We were alone on the lake, and it filled me with wonder. I

had never felt so connected to anyone or anything as I felt that moment with Travis and the rain and the lake. I knew the truth about our shared bloodline, and it didn't matter. It was something tangible that would hold me until I made my decision. I needed to be held and comforted, and not just by Travis.

"GOD!" I screamed, and the Goddess of the Lake rocked us both, like twins in a cradle.

I WAS QUIET on the return ride to the dock. Travis honored the silence. He had always respected everything about me. Was I worthy of such reverence? At the dock, I jumped out and helped to tie the boat. My legs were wobbly after the turbulent ride, and I struggled to find my equilibrium.

"When can I see you again?" Travis asked.

"I haven't decided," I answered. *Decided what?* I didn't know.

Travis looked up at me from his boat. "Bryce wants you back." He said it quietly as a statement, devoid of emotion. "That's why he hasn't left yet."

I looked away from Travis to the horizon. I crossed my arms in front of me to ward off the imminent chill.

Travis slumped wearily in his seat. "Every day I see his car there . . ." His voice trailed off behind his palms. I stared at him.

"Travis, this is the last thing I wanted."

Releasing his face from his hands, he looked directly into my eyes. "BJ, don't ask me to step aside. I can't be that strong."

"I can't be that strong either."

"Let me come home with you. I'll be beside you. We'll tell him together."

I focused again on the horizon. "No, I have to do it. I owe him that much. I'll tell him. I'll tell Bryce tonight."

· 50 ·

MY SKIN TINGLED traitorously when I climbed into bed. I had taken a warm bath and was now wishing for a drink of herbal tea, but I didn't want to risk it. A cup of tea would involve another encounter with Bryce who still sat at the kitchen table. My homecoming had been awkward, not as I had planned. I could not slip inside unnoticed. I did not have time to gather my thoughts or change my clothes. When I came in the back door, Bryce was pacing in the near dark. Obviously worried, he gripped his cell phone in one hand. The sight of me abated his fears, but did nothing for his anger. I turned on the light.

"Bryce, are you okay?" I asked.

In the harsh lighting of the kitchen, I noticed how wet and muddy I actually was. The muscles of Bryce's face clenched into a tangled expression when he saw my disheveled appearance. He turned away from me to take a cleansing breath and run his free hand through his hair.

"You'd better kiss Sam good night. He is worried about you."

He would not even look at me. I knew he was trying to quell his own inner storm.

"Bryce?"

"Just go to our son."

Glad for an excuse to delay our conversation, I made my exit.

I tiptoed up to Sam's room after a short detour to the wash basket where I found a towel to dry my face and a denim shirt to replace my muddy sweater. At first I thought Sam was asleep, but he sat up in bed as soon as my shadow crossed his doorway.

"Where were you? Daddy and I drove around looking for you," he said. "We went by the lake, but you weren't there."

I held my breath, waiting for Sam to mention seeing Travis's truck. Just because he had not remarked on it now, did not mean he had not pointed it out to Bryce.

"Mommy, where *were* you?"

"Mommy was taking a rain walk to clear all the spider webs from her head."

"Silly, Mommy. You don't have spiders in your head."

Projecting my own chill onto his sweating form, I pulled the covers up to his neck. He threw the covers back.

"Can you read me a story?"

"One short story."

Sam pulled *I'll Love You Forever* out from under his pillow. He had been waiting for me.

"Oh, bud, you know I can't read that book. It always makes Mommy cry."

"Please? You haven't read it to me all summer."

All summer. My boy had been away from me for so long; I could not deny him. I read the story about a boy growing up and moving away from his mother, and I cried like I always did. Sam dried my eyes with a hug, but the tears continued on the inside.

I avoided Bryce. He couldn't see me like this, and I definitely could not initiate the conversation we needed to have. Instead, I walked stealthily to my bathroom. I turned on the hot water and peeled off my clothes. As the water ran, I looked at my reflection in the mirror on the opposite wall. The signs were all there on my skin, the roadmap of my affair with Travis. The red abrasions did nothing to mask my glow. Critical of this woman I faced, I touched my arms and my breasts, and then I traced one nipple. I pinched it hard between my fingers, to the point of pain. Before tonight, I had been within my rights to take a lover. I was hurting nobody. That changed this evening. Now I was the one to tear the family apart. Bryce had taken everything from me now, even the role of martyr. He had turned the tables on me. *Why do I have to be the villain in our marriage?* I turned away from my likeness and the new labels that formed in my mind.

I used the time in the bath to think. I wanted Travis, in spite of all I knew. Then why did I suddenly feel sympathy toward Bryce? Was there mutuality in our affairs? I knew now what it must have been like for him to experience the thrill of new love after all the months of neglect in our marriage. *Who was I kidding?* Beyond neglect, we had actually put effort into its ruin. I could not lie to myself anymore. Bryce was right to flee when he did, though he was wrong to come back.

Travis touched something in me that Bryce never could. Travis and I knew each other the way poets know their own words. Like poets and words, our coming together was predestined. I lowered my head until I sank beneath the surface of the water. The warm water washed me in calm nothingness. Only when my lungs started to burn did I rise to the surface to breathe.

After my bath, I retraced my steps to check on Sam. He slept soundly. I brushed my lips on his flushed cheeks. It hardly seemed fair when I looked at his sleeping form. I had to make decisions for both of us. For the moment, we subsisted in Nonna's house, sleeping with the questions, waking with secrets. I decided to put off talking to Bryce. Let morning come—and with it, some clarity.

Once in my bedroom, I tried to settle into bed, but I was too restless. I sat up, took out the sketch pad I kept by my bedside in case inspiration came in the form of a dream. I opened to a blank page, and the marks came easily. Dark somersaults of charcoal jumped from the soft pencil. I didn't even recognize my own hand. At least now, I gave my subconscious mind a chance to tackle the problem. Swirling, stabbing gestures filled the page. I drew figures and shadows. I forgot about my mental fatigue and drew, as if in a trance. An hour passed, or two. I didn't censor myself.

Only the familiar creaking sound broke me from my trance. The noise told me that Bryce had already reached the top stair. I bit my lip. It was too late to turn off my light. He knew I was awake in my room. There was a pause as I felt his presence standing on the other side of the door. *Please, don't open the door. Go into your room, Bryce. Don't do this to me.* I was afraid not only that Bryce would want to discuss what happened this evening but also that he would try to seduce his way back into the marriage. While I didn't want him in my bed, part of me knew that even with everything we had been through, I was still vulnerable to him. Given the choice to open up to Bryce in conversation or to bed him, I'd have picked the latter. Ridiculous as it may seem, I was afraid I'd return to my husband solely so I wouldn't have to verbally desecrate my relationship with Travis by discussing it with Bryce. To tell Bryce about Travis and me would contaminate our love in a way that was unfair.

I heard Bryce fumble with the door to his room. The latch clicked, and I exhaled. For the moment my indecision was safe. I put my sketchbook down and tried to remain still.

Through the thin walls, I heard Bryce shift in his bed. As I listened for sounds of him, I knew the opposite was also true; he was listening for me. I needed distance, and I felt sure that Bryce would not follow me. I picked up Nonna's notebooks and carried both of them to the living room in the front of the house. The streetlights shone bright through the window, but the moon hid behind the clouds. I turned on the small lamp on the end table. Nonna's revelations couldn't hurt me anymore.

· 51 ·

June 13, 1991

None of our friends has ever asked Lena and me to re-count our love story. Maybe it doesn't matter, but in the silence of our story, I have lost many of the details, which is just as well. You had a difficult enough time living with the generalities of our love without mentioning the specifics.

Lena and I lived together platonically for the first year. The war brought shortages of men, meat, bread, milk, stockings. We had to live where we could find abundance. We moved to the farm where I became a plane spotter. Whenever an airplane flew overhead I would identify it and record the time in a small notebook I kept in the bread drawer. It was my personal contribution to the war effort.

Lena got a job in town at a silk mill. She worked on the third floor where she and other young women actually roller-skated, if you can imagine that. The room where she worked had wooden floors and two long tables where the women laid out parachutes. Skating back and forth across the floor, they folded the silk parachutes into packs for our soldiers.

That was not Lena's only contribution to the cause of patriotism. She carved out a victory garden at Mulberry Farm, and she helped to find a family who was willing to cultivate our barren fields.

In Lena I saw a goddess of fertility. When she was nearby, all life seemed to thrive. The baby in my lap learned to sit and clap her hands. Then she learned to walk and call me Mama. The few farm animals we had grew fat. Even my own body, willowy until then, favored a new succulence.

Lena felt safe with me, and with her I did not feel I was betraying my husband's memory. I won't trouble you with first kisses and embraces except to say that as the more experienced of the two of us, I maintained a level of reticence. I didn't want to scare Lena. She needed to be sure. Even when she was, we kept everything in the present tense. These were uncertain times. We did not know what the future would bring.

I suppose Lena fought her instinct to vilify our union. If she was taught that playing cards and fornication were such crimes, what was this love? I didn't carry these associations. If the lake had been a little bluer, the air a little saltier, I would have sworn I was renewing my barefoot youth by the Aegean Sea.

We could not have continued living this idyllic way forever; I realize that now. These were times of war, and we had little right to our strange happiness. There had to be an end for our free fall of love. In the world of dreams, we might have landed lightly on a cloud or a pillow and gone our separate ways. In reality, the fall was not gentle. A jarring event forced us to put a box around the things we felt, to tie our emotions with string and address our intentions.

In August of 1944, Lena received a letter from Hank. I was the one who pulled it from our mailbox and put it in my apron pocket. I didn't show it to Lena for three days. I considered throwing it away, but I just couldn't make myself do it. I carried the sealed envelope with me that whole time and let it burn its white heat through the thin fabric of my pocket. Every time I let my fingertips graze it, I felt a hot spark. Finally, when I couldn't stand the scorching any longer, I turned the letter over to Lena so I could watch her destroy it. When she opened the seal, she read the letter and didn't say a word. I searched every trash can for days, hoping to find the torn remains of the epistle. After almost a week and still no commentary from Lena about the letter, I repealed my fears.

We were in the habit of going to Charlie's grave each week with fresh flowers. I liked the ritual. Every Saturday night, after dinner, Lena would walk me through her gardens and show me what was sprouting or blooming or dying off. As we walked and talked, I would pick two bunches of flowers, one for the cemetery and one for the kitchen. Then on Sunday after the late service, Lena would hold your fat little hand, while I puttered around the gravesite, brushing away the dead grass and putting fresh water into the staked vase.

The Sunday after the letter came, however, Lena did not want to accompany me to the graveyard.

"I don't think my presence is appropriate," she said.

Because I had never forced her to go, her resistance scared me. Did it have to do with the letter? My fears returned. I tried to reassure her.

"Nonsense, Charlie liked you. He was so happy I had made a friend. I am sure he is glad I have you and the baby now." I squeezed her hand and smiled.

"Is he glad you have me, or is he just happy I'm not a man to toy with his memory?"

"What are you saying?"

"Nothing."

"No, you said it. What did you mean?"

"Forget it, Anja. I'm just cranky, a little tired I guess. I stayed up past midnight with canning the last of the pickles. I think I'd like to rest after church."

The next week, over the Labor Day holiday, I traveled by train to visit my parents in Philadelphia. I took the baby. It was the first time we had been apart from Lena, but she insisted on staying behind to care for her burgeoning garden and the animals. She promised us a pantry shelf full of preserves upon our return.

The visit with my parents was not as I expected. They closed the bakery over Labor Day, and we enjoyed a grand picnic in Fairmont Park. It was a happy time, but I sensed a darkness over my family. My father's wheezing concerned me, and my mother shrugged when I asked her about it.

"We are old," she said. "When a new generation arrives, it is no longer our time."

I told her she was being silly, but I could see the vibrancy slipping from her eyes. Only you could reverse the years. Every time she held you, Judy, I saw the twinkle of my mother's prime returning to her. Then again, maybe it was only the reflection of your youth coloring her age-grayed eyes. I was so absorbed in my family reunion, I did not think about what was happening with Lena, two hours away on our farm. I had no idea of the devious forces that were playing havoc with my family life.

While I was picnicking with my parents, a large convertible pulled up to Mulberry Farm. A man with a stateside military uniform got out and opened the passenger door.

Hank Littlehail propped himself on crutches and hobbled to the back entrance of my house. Lena was inside ladling the last batch of peach jam into the hot, steamy jars. With only the screen door separating the two of them, Hank Littlehail did not bother to knock when he entered the kitchen. He stepped into our lives and removed his hat. I know that there was some shock involved in the meeting because Lena knocked over the jar she was filling. The gooey jam spilled to the floor where the stickiness would remain even after Lena had attempted to clean the mess. I know enough of the details to be able to connect the dots with my imagination.

"Hello, Lenie," Hank said quietly.

Lena stood frozen, but her mind raced. Her first thoughts were to defend herself, but when she saw Hank's leg, cut off below the thigh she stopped. This man could not hurt her any longer.

"War does terrible things to a man," he said, covering her surprise.

"Yes, I suppose it does." Lena caught herself staring and turned to look for a towel.

"What are you making?" he asked.

"Jam. I am using up the rest of the peaches." Lena's voice quivered only slightly. She hastily wiped the spill.

"It heartens a man to come home and smell the perfume of a good woman's cooking. It's a privilege worth fighting for."

Lena didn't comment. That day she was a good woman, but the last time Hank had laid eyes upon her, he had called her *a secondhand bitch*.

I wish Lena had held on to those painful memories. I wish she had let them twist in her belly. I wish she had regurgitated them and spit them in Hank Littlehail's face.

But not Lena. She had a soft heart and a will to please. She wanted redemption even though she had done nothing wrong. She wanted her daddy to come back from the dead, she wanted Reverend Platz to tell her she was a good girl, and she wanted Hank Littlehail to promise he'd love her forever.

Hank played with the brim of his hat.

"I expected you would have married while I was off fighting this war." He felt Lena's hesitancy and added, "You're a beautiful woman, after all."

Lena was silent, her eyes downcast.

"You're not married, are you? I didn't see a ring."

"No, Hank. I didn't marry."

"No fellow?"

"No fellow." Lena blushed when she thought of me, but Hank interpreted her reddening as a sign of chastity.

"Would you care to sit down?" Lena offered him the closest chair.

"No, Lenie. This is a short visit. I'll say what I've come to say, and then I will leave you to finish out your task at hand."

"Well, I'll sit then." She didn't think her legs would hold her much longer.

"I don't know how to say this, Lenie, so I'll just come right out with it." Hank kept his eyes lowered to the floor. "We both know that we've made some mistakes in the past. I'm not proud. But honestly, Lenie, none of that matters to me anymore. War changes your priorities." He sighed and chose his words carefully.

"When I was over in that jungle and in that ditch, you were all I could think about. Just knowing that you were someplace in this world, a place I could return to, that thought kept me alive. I made a promise to myself that if I ever got out of that jungle, I would find you and ask you to marry me."

Lena turned white. Even though his letter had been full of friendly banter, this was the last thing she ever expected to hear from Hank's lips.

Hank continued. "I wanted to write to you from that hospital, but I didn't want you to come see me all helpless in my bed. I wanted to come to you as a man. I wanted to walk into your house, look down at your face, and ask you to be my wife. I've bought a little house in Norristown. Just like we talked about, remember? And Guy Chambers has promised me a job supervising his draftsmen."

Lena clamped her hands together, as was her custom when she was nervous. She had stopped listening to him and started staring at the window at a bird on the window ledge. It had a worm in its beak.

"Lena?"

She turned to look at Hank.

"Lena, I am asking you to marry me." His blue eyes implored her far more than his words.

Lena did not move. The silence that followed was awkward. After what seemed like an eternity, Hank put his hat on his head.

"I don't expect an answer today. I'll let you think about it for a few days. I'll come back again on Thursday for your answer. If your answer is yes, we'll go get our license, because, Sweet Lenie, I've wasted too much time already."

"Hank?" Lena spoke at last. "Hank, I . . ."

"Please, wait. Whatever you decide. I have to know that you've thoroughly thought about the possibilities—even if it is only a fraction of the time that I have thought about it."

And with that Hank Littlehail hobbled out of the house.

As if in a trance, Lena watched him go. When she heard the car door, Lena tiptoed to the window. The stateside soldier helped Hank into the car. As the driver turned to saunter to his side of the car, he waved to Lena behind the curtain. Hank lit a cigarette and drew a long drag. He did nothing to acknowledge Lena, just flicked a few ashes out the window. The soft scent of tobacco reached Lena's nose, and she inhaled deeply. As the car pulled away from the curb, Lena waved. Finally aware of her, Hank nodded.

The sound of the engine faded. Lena ran upstairs to the room we shared and went to the dresser where she pulled open the top drawer. She reached behind her nightgowns and unmentionables and retrieved a small box from its hiding spot. I knew all about the ring, where it was hidden. I know how she tried that ring on and watched the light dance off the gem. I know the movements she made when she twirled her fingers in the air. She filed her nails where they were rough from work. She hummed to herself. These things I know. I know all of it because when I came home late that night, she was asleep on our bed. The engagement ring was still on her finger.

I woke her immediately.

"Lena, I'm home." I turned on the bright light beside her sleeping form.

She roused slowly, not registering my worried look. Casually, without intention behind the gesture, she shielded her eyes with her left hand. "Oh, I had the most unbelievable dream. I dreamed that Hank came back, and he wanted me to marry him. Can you fathom that?" Her face had the look of a little girl.

I lifted her hand from her face and threw it on the bed in disgust. "Fathom what? You are wearing his ring."

Lena was quiet then. She didn't like to see me angry. She

scooted up until she was sitting in a little ball against the backboard of the bed.

"I didn't mean to upset you," she said.

"Why should you upset me? It isn't like you are going back to that bastard."

The room went silent. I swallowed and waited for Lena to reply. The silence grew until it was fabulous in its presence, like a lounge singer with a pink boa wrapped around her neck, scatting into the microphone. Then the scatting silence turned into a baby's cry. My maternal instinct rose within my chest, and I pivoted toward the door. As I held the knob, I looked at Lena sitting on the bed. She looked like such a child, like the older sister of the baby who was calling to me from the next room.

"Does he know?" The cries from the next room were getting louder.

"No, I haven't told him about the baby."

"I suppose he apologized and told you that he loves you."

Lena did not hear the challenge in my voice. She falsely assumed I was relinquishing her from any bond we may have shared.

"He said he couldn't stop thinking of me," she said.

"Hmmm."

I put the open notebook on my lap and turned off the lamp. I sat in semidarkness. The window was open, but there was no breeze. The night air, moist and hot, blurred the light from the lamppost. I closed my eyes to better concentrate on my own thoughts. Thoughts of the past swirled together with thoughts of the day. Lena had been approached with a proposal in the very kitchen in which Bryce had made his case. We were both being made to choose between the fathers of our children and the ones we truly loved. And the ones we loved were not those ordained by the populace. Why was it that history always repeated itself? Had Lena felt the same searing pain that was ripping through me now? I knew the outcome of the scene Nonna described. Lena turned away from Hank Littlehail, my mother's father—my own grandfather, and lived happily ever after with Nonna. But why would Lena do that? Why would she choose the hard love, the one that challenged society? Maybe there wasn't a choice. Maybe there was only love. If that were the case, if this letter was speaking directly to me, it reinforced my choice to turn down Bryce's offer of reconciliation and run straight into Travis's arms. But what if Nonna had written this letter as a way to issue a warning to the next generation? I could not read any more of Nonna's letter until I had the answers in my own heart. Whatever decisions I made had to come from within, not some omen from the grave. I closed the binder and let it slide from my lap.

I fell asleep on the sofa, but the sound of an engine startled me awake. Peeking through the curtains, I saw a truck turn the corner and go down Mulberry Street. Was it Travis? The light colored pickup was a later model than the one that Travis drove, or was it? My mind was playing tricks on me.

You must know the whole truth. Nonna's voice penetrated my mind. I heard the creak of boards and listened to hear if Bryce or Sam were awake. The noise stopped. It had been the musings of the house, echoing Nonna's sentiment. *The truth, Barbara Jean.* Both comforted and terrified, I turned on the lamp to help me find the notebook, which had fallen on the floor next to a sleeping Jules.

I touched the smooth cover of the notebook. My last communication from Nonna, and I didn't want to end. But I knew that somewhere in the end of this notebook was a beginning—my beginning. I continued to read.

· 52 ·

HANK DID NOT COME Thursday as he had promised. We both waited expectantly until the late afternoon made us skittish around one another. After dinner, Lena took a drink to the porch swing. I put the baby down for the evening and joined her out on the swing. We swayed a little; I reached across for her hand.

"I love you," I said. "You know that, don't you?"

Lena took her hand away.

"I want you to stay here with me, for always," I continued.

Lena didn't look at me when she talked. "This isn't exactly the kind of family a baby should have."

"You'd rather a rapist parent for our daughter?"

"He's apologized for his mistakes."

"Has he?"

"Anja, this is not even about Hank. It is about us."

"What about us?" I asked. "You were the one who pursued me. I thought this was what you wanted."

"Yes. I did. But was it what you wanted or were you just using me to get over Charlie?"

"NO!" I said. "No."

"Really, Anja? Think again. You don't like the fact that I am wearing Hank's ring, but you have Charlie's photo standing on your bedside table. Everywhere we go, you're always saying, 'Charlie this,' or 'Charlie that.' And going to his grave every Sunday . . ."

"I didn't know it bothered you," I said.

"How could you be so oblivious?" she said.

The swing came to a standstill. We stayed in that motionless place, waiting.

"I'm sorry," I said finally.

"Anja, I don't want your apologies. All I am asking for is my chance at happiness." Lena looked at me with surprising directness. "You suffered a great loss, but I promise you will get another chance, too. I'm sure of it."

"No," I said.

"Anja, the men are coming back. It's a new world. Don't you want a house full of children and a man to take you to the movies? Don't you want to sit down to a family dinner and host cocktail parties with other couples? Don't you want those things?"

"Do you?" I asked her.

Hank Littlehail showed up at ten o'clock the next morning. I did not want to see him, and I did not want him to see the baby, so with you balanced on my hip I hid behind the closed door of the stairwell. I held my breath, and listened as Lena greeted your father, the rapist, the man who murdered my husband. I knew his intentions since the hour I felt his letter in my hand. He didn't love Lena as much as I did; he simply wasn't capable of it. Of that I am sure. Before I sat listening to their exchange, I didn't fully believe that Lena would actually go with him. I heard him tell her once again that he forgave her for her past and wanted to marry her.

"There is something I need to tell you first," Lena said, and I realized she was going to tell him about the baby.

No! No! I wanted to shout. She couldn't be doing this. If I had considered the possibilities that she might leave, I had not fully accepted she would take my baby from me. *Lena, don't. This man wronged you, wronged us. Don't let him tear us apart.*

"I should have told you sooner . . ." she began. Lena's voice reverberated sweetness through the wall, and I could no longer stay hidden. I pretended I had just come down the stairs, and I opened the door with a good deal of commotion.

"Mrs. Graybill, Anja. Lena, you didn't tell me Anja was home."

"Hello, Hank."

"I've been meaning to come visit with you and express my condolences for your loss."

"I understand you were the last one to see Charlie alive."

"Yes. That's true."

He might have offered something to me, a crumb of kindness. He could have told me that my husband's last words were of me, or that he owed his life to Charlie, but he said nothing. He stood there, or rather, propped himself there, in his casual attire. He was holding his hat, and his hair, overgrown for a military man, was dressed with something slick. Around his crown there was an indentation where his hat had been, and his eyes still haunted me. I directed my gaze away from them, downward to where his leg had been. It was too soon for a prosthetic, I mused at the time. Looking back on the incident, it was more likely that he was using his handicap to attract Lena's sympathy. He wasn't crippled; he was spineless.

The space beneath his thigh hexed me for a moment. I would personally cut off his other leg to have my Charlie come back alive. I would butcher this man into ever smaller pieces of repentance. So engrossed was I in my mental knife-work, I almost didn't see him raise his arm to touch you, Judy, the babe in my arms.

"How sad that this little one will never know her father."

How could I dream of knives and axes and still hug a child? Judy, I pulled you away before he could touch you — before he could taint any more of my brain with thoughts of hatred. "She will never know her father, but at least she will always have her mother." I hugged you close to me, and I looked at Lena in a way that told her with no uncertainty that I would not surrender the baby. In those days there were no paternity tests. My name was on the birth certificate, as Lena was well aware.

"A woman's love can heal when nothing else can," I spoke my words to Hank, but Lena knew they were for her.

Lena looked from Hank to me and then finally to the baby in my arms. I knew I had to leave Lena alone to make her decision, but I had to make my last plea. I boldly walked over to her and kissed her on the cheek.

Lena remained at the farm. I never asked her why because I never wanted to hear her say that it was solely because of you. It never would have occurred to her to fight over you or to take you from me. I do think that she was happier with me than she would have been in the world where men swallow women like Lena. Whether or not Lena shared that awareness, I don't know. We have been blissfully content over the years. Ours was a great love. I don't want you to ever doubt that, but, in all honesty, this was not the life that either of us had planned.

As for you, dear Judy, I am not assured that our loving home ensured your well-being. What can I say? I don't know what kind of a father Hank Littlehail would have been, though I can imagine. I imagine he would have been tough and that the freedoms he fought for would not necessarily belong to you as his daughter. He would have made you walk a narrow line of self that is often imposed on girls. *Dick can run. He can throw. Jane says, "Run, Dick, run." She says, "Throw, Dick, throw."* But this compressed view of girlhood, with spartan paternal authority, was what your generation knew. It was the solidifying force among your friends, many of whom rallied to break down those barriers. I know that you needed to escape from the home we gave you and move toward normalcy, whatever that meant.

I watched you become a nurse, marry a steady man, and mother a rebellious daughter. I could see you holding back your own passions for fear that they would lead you to more ridicule. Remember when we quit our church after you had completed one year of catechism classes? You had asked to quit the classes and to your amazement we let you. The real reason was that Rev. Carroll asked if Lena and I would stop attending the same service together. Some of the parishioners were talking. We thought we were shielding you from the cruelties of the world, but I know that you shielded us from many more. You kept the taunts to yourself.

Maybe I should have let you and Lena go to live out your

days as Littlehails. Maybe then, your body would have rejected disease instead of welcoming it. Sanity dictates that I believe I made the right choice to keep you and Lena in my love. I didn't invent Hank's crimes, but maybe I garnished them with my jealousies and my losses.

· 53 ·

June 15, 1991

I wish that were the end of my deceptions and the pain I inflicted on Lena's family. Do you remember the day that Barbara Jean turned fourteen? I spent all day working on the perfect cake. This was the first time she had spent her birthday at our house, and I wanted it to be special. I wanted to give her the loving memories of a grandmother that I never had. More than that, I was competing with Lena for a legacy.

I remember the smell of the air as it turned to rain. My fears escalated. You arrived safely from Virginia, but the kids were out there in the storm. When the power went out, it nearly drove me mad. Margot tried to call us, but the telephone lines were down, so she drove over to the house to tell us that her father had died.

I felt no sadness for that man's passing. I spit on the ground. Lena told Margot that under no condition would she attend her stepfather's memorial service. You were shocked, but too worried about the kids to pay much attention to us.

Margot. How we worried about her when she was small. She was living under the same roof as Lena's abuser, and there was little we could do about it. We might have told Lena's mother Lydia, but she died when Margot was five. Then, it was just the word of the good Reverend against the word of two women, who may or may not have been living an immoral life. We invited Margot over to play with you as often as we could. We watched her in play to see if she seemed like a little girl who was in trouble.

Sometimes we invited the Reverend Ernie Platz over for dinner to watch the two of them interact. How I hated to sit at the table with that man. I listened to his slippery stories and watched him smoke his cigarettes. Lena turned herself to stone each time he came, and I needed to coax her to come out again after he left. It was like feeding a wounded bird.

One day when you girls were nine, Lena had taken you both to the park when Ernie arrived for dinner. I had never been alone with him before. He made a pass at me. Not just with words, but with his hands on my buttocks. I was astonished, but I still had my wits. I asked Ernie for a cigarette. He took one out for himself as well. Lena smoked until she turned sixty, but I never did. Ernie lit my cigarette. He was practically drooling.

"Reverend, do you believe in praying for souls?"

"Well, yes." He was puzzled.

"Well, then you'd better pray for mine."

He just blinked at me. I walked over to where he was seated. He had a look of sweet anticipation on his face. I blew smoke in his face, and then I positioned my cigarette right beside his white mustache.

"Reverend, you pray for my soul because if you so much as lay a finger on me or do the things to Margot that you did to Lena, I won't wait for the law to step in. I have friends from the old country. I will have you hunted down and dismembered. Your pulpit will be adorned with your body parts." I took his sweaty palm and turned it to the heavens. "And lest you forget we had this conversation, just look at your praying hands." With that said, I extinguished my cigarette into his hand.

I don't know if my performance was enough to keep Margot safe. We had little opportunity to ask her such delicate questions. She never understood Lena's hatred of her stepfather, so I have to believe he never gave her reason to hate him personally.

That July day, Margot went out into the rain to find Travis. She was angry with all of us because we could not absorb some of her grief. A half hour later, Barbara Jean came walking through our door with wet hair and a lustful gaze. We heard your sharp inhale as you noticed the graying love bites on her neck. I looked at Lena with horrified eyes. You, Judy, were afraid of your little girl becoming too adult before her time, but we knew something uglier, a story of our family's incest repeating itself for the generations. We were sick with our own secrets.

What could we do? I was afraid for you to find out the truth, that I was not your real mother. Lena did not want you to feel that she had discarded you. We were desperate to do what we could to keep Travis and Barbara Jean apart without revealing our own sham.

We chose to sacrifice Margot and the memory of her beloved father. We knew exactly what we were doing and the result it would have. She visited us again the day after Barbara Jean's birthday.

"Lena, he was the only father you ever knew. I know he

loved you. He always considered you his oldest daughter. I was sometimes so jealous of that. Can't you make peace with him?" Margot pleaded. Lena walked out of the room. Margot turned to me with an open mouth.

"You have no right to ask that of Lena," I said.

"I am her sister. I have every right."

"Just like your father had the right to berate his stepdaughter in the name of God?" I asked.

"I didn't say she had to agree with his religious views. I think he was a bit over the top myself."

"Oh, and did he expose his private parts to you while you were praying? Did he burn your thighs with cigarettes and tell you not to scream? Did he blame you for his impotence because you were too ugly to excite a man?" As I spoke, I made myself into ice—slick, cold, and clear.

"Did she tell you that?" Margot folded her arms around her torso. "My God, she is delusional. She needs help. My father was a minister in a church for over thirty years. His parishioners loved him."

"I am not talking about his parishioners."

"Why would he violate Lena and leave me alone? My mother was there in the house with them for God's sake."

"I don't care what you think, but it's Lena's truth, and she is not going to the funeral," I said, calmly. I was about to walk away.

"I cannot believe that I ever defended the two of you to him. He was all the time telling me about your perverted ways, and I defended you." Margot's voice was faltering. "And you. You are the mastermind. Lena does anything you say. You probably planted these things in her mind to lure her into your bed. You are sick. That's what you are."

I did not deny any of it. She talked herself into her own denial.

"Are you through?" I asked.

"Yes," she said.

"Then get out of my house."

"You can't throw me out. I'm leaving. And don't you ever come near my son or me ever again. You are a witch."

It was so easy. I cried for days in the privacy of my bedroom. Lena was braver than I was, unless, of course, she was feeling less guilty.

We tried to hide our emotions from Barbara Jean, but we didn't have to worry. She was sick with her own grief over the loss of love. She couldn't understand why Travis didn't return her calls.

Lena took her to the lake, but she wouldn't get in the water. She sat on the shore and sketched and sketched. Her pencil strokes were angry and aggressive as Lena's swimming strokes had been the first time I brought her to the lake. I didn't interfere, nor did I join them. Blue Lake was always a poor substitute for the Aegean.

At the time of BJ's party, we did not know that time was running out. When Lena got sick, I finally realized all that she had meant to me. She was the person who had stayed by my side through it all. I tried to give back to her all that she gave me, but the task seemed too vast, especially in the cancerous years. I took her to Greece after she lost her hair. We toured the places I knew, even though the landscape had changed. At last, I took her to the village where I had grown up. Magically, it was as I remembered it. Not only did I recognize some of my playmates among the time-withered faces, but some of the older citizens as well. Women who were grandmothers when I left were still making breads. I wondered if I had misjudged their ages or if time did not have the same hold on these inhabitants.

I took Lena to the water. She clasped her hands in delight at the cobalt surf. Immediately she began to strip, and I

followed suit. We were two old ladies swimming buck naked in the sea. I saw the burns and tattoos on Lena's body
where the radiologist had done her job. Her scalp, pink and
slathered in sun block, was beginning to show signs of hair.
It should have pained me to look at her floating there in the
last hours of daylight, but when I looked on her face I saw
only the markings of tranquility. We were not separate from
each other or the rest of the world. With water and sky,
and hope and pain, male and female, bigot and martyr, we
swam. This is the moment that I carry with me. It is how I
define my life.

Dear Judy, when you read this account, if you read this
account, I expect your first reaction to include judgment.
You may even think it is my due, but it is madness to think
you can judge others and not blacken your own spirit. I
speak from experience. Instead, I invite you to cleanse your
soul in the waters of the sea.

You may think you would have chosen a different life,
but I have come to believe that is not true. Life does not
happen to us. We choose our experiences. Whatever disease
you have invited into your breast, you have the power to
set it free.

> Daughter of my heart,
> Dare to depart.
> Come swim along with me.

As always—your loving mother,
Anja

· 54 ·

I DIDN'T RETURN to my room, choosing to remain on the sofa with my thoughts. I knew now that this letter had been too late for my mother—deliberately distanced from her. It seemed intended for me alone, existing as my birthright. But what was I supposed to do with this information? What was Nonna telling me with her message? My subconscious mind continued to process the letter even after I drifted into an uneasy sleep. At first my dreams were turbulent though unremarkable. But in the still hours when dawn grants dreams longevity, I dreamed I was with my mother. Mom looked as she did in those years right before cancer took its toll. Her hair was curly and graying slightly, but her eyes were still bright. She was walking up ahead. I called to her, but she didn't turn around, so I ran to catch up with her. We walked for a long time down a rocky beach without acknowledging one another. Then we reached a cliff and the beach stopped abruptly. Mom turned to face me, her daughter.

"You know you almost drowned once when you were a baby,"

she said. "It was in a neighbor's pool. Your father rescued you. I was always terrified of the water."

"But you swam all the time," I said.

She did not hear me. "I saw you first, but I wouldn't get into the water even though I knew you were drowning. I just stood there and watched. I could not believe how beautiful the water looked with the sun dancing on the surface and your hair swaying under the water."

I reached out for my mother, but she was already walking away in a floating motion over the cliff where I could not follow her.

"Mom, where are you going?"

"So beautiful." She kept on walking away from me, and then she was gone.

"Mom, wait for me," I called after her.

Feeling utterly alone, I turned around, hoping Mom would reappear. Nobody was behind me, but down on the beach, about a quarter mile away, Sam was standing. He was waving and calling to me, "Come on, Mom."

And then over my shoulder, I heard the sound of the surf. I turned to the horizon, but the sky and the sea were the same color. I couldn't determine boundaries, but as if by magic I saw three porpoises leaping in the distance. They were swimming away from the shore and I watched them until I could no longer see them, but at least now I had a line that could divide the sky from the water.

I WOKE BEFORE Bryce and Sam did, but I sat on the sofa for a long time just looking at my hazy reflection in the front window. *Who was the person I saw?* Was she wife or daughter, mother or lover? And the names? Which one fit this vision of pink faced girl/woman with the leathery hands and sun chapped lips? Out of the reflection came a craving, which I reached for and pulled to me until it nudged out all the questions of the morning. So many masks. Some I had chosen to wear over the years, but some were already there, painted in henna, decorating my skin with their deception.

My love for Travis went beyond the moment; it was past, and it was future. Our love was a continuum to which I belonged. But did it even matter? How could I break up my family? Would it be better to keep my time with Travis as memory where I could keep it protected, perfect, and whole? In that same instant I knew that there was no Bryce, only Travis, but how could I be the one to desert the life we'd promised to sustain with no thought to impediment? All my fears assaulted me, and I kept hearing Sam call to me over and over in my mind.

Come on, Mom. Where was he leading me?

I liked to believe there were two endings to my story and that either way I would be fine. But I didn't have two lives to live. I was Lena, standing once again on the brink of two possibilities. And still, I didn't know. How had she based her choice—on her love for Nonna or on her love for her child? I loved Travis. I loved my son. Somewhere in those great loves, my fate was waiting for me. I could breathe only because I held on to the surety that by this time tomorrow I would move forward with only one of my two lives.

As a warm-up, I turned my mind to easy determinations. *What should I do this morning?* Take care of the dog. *And after that?* Make breakfast. *What should I make for breakfast?* Blueberry muffins. I would make blueberry muffins.

Jules padded over to me, and I rubbed the scruff of his neck. He had slept beside me all night, a departure from his recent patrol beside Sam's bed. I rose and followed Jules to the kitchen where our morning routine awaited me. So much of life was routine, and I knew that whatever tomorrow brought or the day after that or next week, I would still be rising each morning and feeding this dog. I would dress and brush my teeth and feed my son and make jewelry. I would make love and cry at movies and open birthday presents and visit the dentist. I found a weird calm in my customs, and the thought never occurred to me that this was the eye of a storm, around which all my life's turmoil swirled.

Carefully, I washed the fresh berries. Bryce loved blueberries. I pushed that memory away. For the moment the tasks of rinsing the fruit and checking for stems was my mind's only design.

Bryce came into the kitchen first, pulling a sleeveless tank over his head.

"Come on, Jules. Inside, boy." He opened the door, and Jules bounded toward Bryce. *Oh, the love of a dog.* Bryce wiped Jules's legs with the towel that was beside the door, and the dog responded with a sloppy kiss. I looked back at the two of them, and tried to gauge Bryce's mood.

Bryce returned my gaze and saw the muffin tins on the counter. He walked over to where I stood by the sink. Reaching over me, he grabbed a large blueberry and put it into his mouth.

"I'm sorry I was in such a bad mood when you came home last night." He closed in behind and put his arms around me. "You don't have to talk about it. I won't ask that of you. I love you." I let him hold me, but neither of us knew what to do next. The embrace was wooden but not comfortless. Bryce kissed the hairline near my ear. He had often kissed me in just that spot. I didn't move. My heart fluttered in its cage.

Bryce spoke in a low voice. "I'm going to drive out to the track and go for a run. I need to work some things out of my system. When I come back, you can just put our cards on the table, okay? You can just give me an answer."

I didn't respond. Bryce gripped my shoulders and slowly turned me around.

"Please tell me it's not hopeless," he said.

I couldn't look at him directly. "Not hopeless," I repeated.

He kissed the top of my head and then lifted my chin.

"That's all I needed to hear." Bryce nodded. He grabbed another blueberry and checked his watch.

"I'll be back in forty minutes."

"Oh God, what am I going to do?" I asked aloud after Bryce had left. I looked at the calendar on the refrigerator. Sunday.

Sam entered the kitchen. "Where's Daddy?"

"He went running."

"He didn't leave, did he?"

"Leave?"

"For Michigan."

"No, Sam, he's not going yet."

"Is he going today? That's what he said last night."

"Did he say that? I don't know."

I pulled my son into my cotton nightgown. The rough edges of his cast caught me at my waist.

"I bet you'll be glad to get that cast off."

"Yeah. But I am a little afraid."

"Why?"

"I don't know. I just want Dad to be with me when the doctor saws my cast off."

If I could, I would have pulled him back into my womb. His head was right at my belly, and I stroked his hair with the same movements I had used on my growing abdomen when I was pregnant.

"My brave boy."

"My brave mommy."

I laughed and cupped his chin. Sam smiled up at me with more faith than I had in anything at the moment. Here he was, so real and trusting, the key to it all.

"I love you," I said.

"I love you, too." He squeezed my middle and planted a playful kiss near my navel.

"I kissed your belly button," he said.

"Yes, you did."

At that moment, looking down at my son, I didn't have the strength to split from Bryce. I couldn't break up Sam's world, my world, and rebuild it again. That was why I put off telling Bryce about Travis. He didn't need to know. Last night with Travis was good-bye. He would come to see it that way, and I hoped in time he could forgive me. I had made the vows to Bryce, and no matter how powerful the love I shared with Travis, it did not release me from fulfilling the obligation I had first to my son. I remembered my dream. It was so vivid now.

Bryce would try harder; we both would. We could make this work, I told myself. If we hurried, we could leave tonight and have enough time back in Michigan to register Sam for school. Karen could handle the house. I could resume my old life, and Travis would slip back into the places where he had always been—in my heart as a remembrance, in my blood as a cousin. Travis would understand. He had done much the same thing when he surrendered my needs for his mother's years ago. I had survived the pain of losing Travis once. It had changed me before, and no doubt would change me again, but I would survive.

Sam disappeared to play with his figures. I forgot about the muffins I was making, and instead entered the lean-to. My studio was tidy, as it had been when I prepared for Bryce and Sam to arrive. The concrete floor was cool on my bare feet as I shuffled over to the ventilation hoods. Normally I didn't enter this space with bare feet for fear of the metal shavings that dusted all surfaces, but the space was unusually clean, and if this was truly my decision, I had to stop thinking of this as my studio. I had to stop thinking, period; I had no choice.

I lost myself in action, my best narcotic. While packing, I didn't consider time. I unscrewed the tip from my torch and loaded my bricks and charcoal pads into an empty cardboard box that had never quite been thrown away. I sorted through a few random items, but mostly, I emptied whole drawers into that box without looking inside. I lost myself in my task until there wasn't much else to do. Bryce would have to help me lift my anvil. My tools were already situated in my red Craftsman tool chest. I spun to look at it and noticed the framed picture of Bride sitting on the shelf above it.

"Yes, Bride. Here we go again. Last time. I promise."

I turned her three faces down, deposited her in the box, and wove the cardboard flaps over one another to close the box. Just as I put the box atop the worktable, I heard a car door slam.

"Sam, Daddy's home," I called down the hall, and ran out onto the porch. But when I got there, it was Travis who stood before me on the sidewalk. I looked down to see that I was still in my nightgown. I had no reason to feel shy around Travis. He'd seen me in far less, and though it seemed ages ago in my mind, I reminded myself that we'd been intimate only the night before. Regardless of that fact, I felt vulnerable and awkward in the light of this morning and my recent decision. Here was my lover, come to claim me. He didn't know I was leaving, and I had to tell him. Somehow, I had deluded myself into thinking that this meeting would never have to happen.

"Hi," he said.

"Oh . . . Travis." My voice caught on the words. They sounded far away, like an echo.

"Were you expecting someone else?"

"I'm sorry. It's just that Bryce—"

"He's still here?" he asked with genuine incredulity.

"He went running." I scanned the road for any signs of Bryce. "He'll be back any second."

"Oh hell! When I didn't see his car I thought he went back to Michigan. I came to take you and Sam to the lake." Travis climbed the stairs to join me on the porch. He bent to kiss me, but mercifully Sam came barging through the door.

"Travis!"

"Hey, buddy."

Sam sprang into his arms. "Mom, are we going on the boat today?"

"It *is* Sunday," Travis pointed out.

I was quiet.

"It's okay, BJ."

"Yeah, Mom, it's okay!" Sam agreed.

"BJ, you did talk to Bryce, didn't you?" Travis asked.

"When I got home last night, I—"

"You didn't talk to him." Travis eyed me carefully and then shook his head. "Tell me what this is. Tell me why I am here, BJ."

"Not here. Not now." I looked at Sam whose smile had vanished. He looked at me with confusion.

"Mommy, can we go with Travis? We haven't been on the boat in a long, long time."

None of this should be happening. My thoughts swam. How could I get Travis off of this porch so I could get on with my life? I couldn't think.

"Mommy, please? Can we go?"

I didn't have a chance to answer; and my world got a little smaller. Bryce walked up the sidewalk from the barn. I hadn't heard his car. He stood on the curb; his flushed body glistened with sweat. He looked up at all of us on the porch as if we were players on a stage, acting out some comedy of errors. I was still standing in my thin nightgown next to the stranger who was clasping his son.

"Uh, hello," Bryce said.

What had he heard? My mind raced.

"I'm sorry. Oh, Bryce, you've never met my cousin Travis."

Bryce stood on the bottom step.

"Actually, I'm Lena's nephew," Travis clarified. He released Sam and reached down to grasp Bryce's extended hand.

Each man gripped the other's hand in a silent show of strength. I watched them step away from each other. Was it my imagination or had they bowed their heads as if offering the enemy respect before a battle? Then Travis turned his head, and looked directly into my eyes. *I didn't tell him.*

I had never ached for anything the way I ached for Travis in that moment. His gaze held everything: our future, the house, the greenhouse, the boat, the artwork, the lake, fireworks, poetry, stories for all the generations. We would have the perfect life; I could see all the cards spread before me like a good playing hand. I swallowed hard, and then I looked at Sam who had jumped down from Travis's hold and was running to Bryce. I looked back at Travis. His eyes continued in his silent appeal, but I just thumped my knuckles on the porch railing.

"Travis just stopped by to get the paintings that Nonna willed to him," I said, still locked in Travis's gaze.

Travis did not flinch, but his eyes softened, and I could see that he understood what I was telling him. *I love you.*

"BJ, you don't have to do this," he said.

"Yes, I do. They are yours. Nonna wanted it that way."

Travis nodded in disbelief that masqueraded as agreement before my husband.

"If you'll excuse me, I'll go get them."

I opened the door and slipped inside to the dining room. I touched the curtains as I passed the windows. They felt rough against my fingers. I heard echoes of the conversation between Bryce and Travis. Boat talk, mainly.

"Nice boat out there. Have you had her long?"

"I got the boat in my settlement. She got everything else."

I shrugged on a hooded sweatshirt that had been draped over a chair, and the fleece soothed my skin. I zipped the sweatshirt closed and sighed.

It's going to be okay. I can get through this.

I pulled the paintings from the walls. Small, bright squares of emptiness replaced the landscapes. I stacked the framed canvases carefully without looking at them. I'd rather not think about what I was giving away.

I was about to turn and go back outside when I remembered the picture hanging in the kitchen. I stepped lightly into the heat of the room and rested the other pictures on the table. There it hung. Brubaker Lake. I imagined it had graced that wall for at least fifty years. I reached up to remove the painting from its nail. It didn't budge. Although I had just taken it down from the wall a few weeks earlier, it held fast this time. I tried again, and it didn't move. Sweat dribbled down my forehead from the effort, and I fanned myself. I looked up at the image, undulating before my eyes. And then it hit me.

NO! Somewhere a voice within me screamed.

This painting belongs to me.

I didn't care about lines of ancestry or legalities, this was my legacy. Blue Lake . . . the brushstrokes . . . the blue of a promise . . . the sun . . . the water . . . the reflection . . . *Marry me, Ada* . . . Grandma Lena . . . God of Mermaids . . . the kisses . . . little-girl wishes . . . woman prayers. All of it came swirling down upon me, and I couldn't breathe. I leaned against the wall and hyperventilated. My head was spinning, and I groped for the table to steady myself. I tried to call for help, but words were replaced by all the images swimming in my thoughts. They were waves crashing over me, pulling me under the current. I kneeled on the chair to keep from falling. And here, under the tide of my fear and dizziness, I prayed the most important prayer of my life, a barter for my very being.

Tanginika, Goddess of the Lake, watery Mother, I need to breathe, again. Help me decide what to do.

I looked up at the painting—so blue—and drew in a full, calming breath. And as I did so, the answer came to me in the voice of my grandmother.

Daughter of my heart.

Dare to depart.

Come swim along with me.

· 55 ·

TRAVIS ENTERED THE KITCHEN. I felt his presence, but I didn't turn to look. My breath was no longer a struggle, though my heart was racing.

The frames clattered against one another as he picked up the paintings that were on the table.

"I'll be going now," he said quietly.

"Travis?" I was still facing the wall.

"Hmm?"

My painting looked down on me from its perch, and I bowed before it. Red is often the color of courage, but this time it paraded in blue. "Will you take Sam to the lake for a couple of hours this morning?"

Travis didn't answer immediately. At first, I thought perhaps he hadn't heard me. I waited for his answer. The silence became palpable. I pursed my lips. In our conversational ravine, I heard my son making engine noises and whistle sounds. The noises rose and fell—crescendo, decrescendo—and I guessed that he was following Bryce as he paced the block.

"I can do that," Travis said at last.

"Thank you."

He didn't wait for me to expound on the matter. If he had further questions as to my mind—and I am sure he did—he took them out with the paintings into that August morning.

I heard the low timbre of masculine voices in clipped dialogue followed by my son's squeal of pleasure. Sam ran inside and shot past me in an effort to get to his bedroom for his swimming trunks.

"Mom, where's my suit?"

"It's on the top of the wash basket," I called up the stairs after him.

He sprinted down the steps again with his green suit, inside out, the white net lining dangling over his cast like a waiter's napkin. As he passed by me, he graced the air with a missed kiss that had been meant for my cheek.

"Well, good-bye to you, too," I said.

"See you later, Mommy."

"Don't forget to wear your life jacket," I said, wanting to assert to my motherhood—the one frontier where I had fooled myself into thinking I had control.

The sound of the truck engine had been vibrating for the entirety of Sam's dash, and a minute after he was out the door, I heard the gears shift to signal Travis's departure. With the sound of engine fading down the road, I mentally began to count the seconds until Bryce would appear in my kitchen. After I had counted past twenty, the realization deepened: I could not wait another second for my life to happen to me.

Ironically, I found Bryce on the porch swing waiting for me. *I wasn't the only one trying to circumvent this conversation.* I dropped beside Bryce and noted the sharp, oddly pleasant, smell of his cooled perspiration. The swing moaned as he pumped it back to set it in motion. Because I didn't echo the action, the swing twisted and bucked until Bryce put out a foot and stopped the movement.

I leaned forward and braced my weight on my arms. My legs dangled down, with only my bare toes making contact with the porch. I looked at my feet, already dirty.

Bryce clapped his hand down on my knee as it peaked out from the hem of my nightgown.

I braced myself against his touch. *Dare to depart.*

"Sam and I are not coming back to Michigan with you, Bryce." I breathed in and steadied my quiet voice. "I am not in love with you anymore."

Bryce let out an uncomfortable little laugh. "Well, I don't have to state the obvious and ask if there is anyone else, do I?"

I felt my voice getting stronger, planted in resolve. "I think we can leave other parties out of this. This is about you and me."

"You're sleeping with him." *So much for removing the other parties.* Bryce had chosen a statement instead of a question. His remark was meant to elicit my defenses, but I didn't give him the satisfaction.

"Bryce, I signed your papers."

"Forget about the papers. Let me ask you this: If he weren't here, you'd give our marriage another try, wouldn't you?"

"If he weren't here, I wouldn't know all the things that you and I lack as a couple. I require more now."

"What do you require now that I can't give you?"

I didn't answer him. How could I say—*I want to smile uncontrollably when you walk into a room? I want to respect your choices. I want your patience with mine. I want you to enjoy an art exhibit with me and mourn losses with me. I want fidelity, whole and untouched. I want a connection so strong it can traverse years and secrets and still hold strong. I want to love and to be loved. I want to be part of something larger than myself.*

I couldn't say those things; Bryce would see them as judgments instead of requirements. I wanted to end it with Bryce, but I didn't want to put him down or start a fight. I scoured my mind for something positive to say.

"Bryce, I'll always have feelings for you. You know that. We share a wonderful a son—"

"Yes, Bobbi, and we owe it to Sam—"

"We owe Sam what? Two parents who are in pain?" My tolerance snapped.

"I am willing to work through that together."

Bryce wasn't going for subtlety. I lifted my chin. "Maybe we could work it out and maybe we couldn't. But I can't sit around and wait anymore to find out if my life is going to change for the better. I have a chance to make it happen, now, and I am going to choose to be happy. Happiness, Bryce. Contentment. Love. Don't you want that for me?" It was a trick question, and I was playing dirty by asking it.

Bryce could not answer, or would not. As an attorney, I'm sure he saw my trap. He kicked off the porch floor in reaction to me and in an attempt to move the swing again, but this time I joined him in his effort. We swung like that, in tandem, for what seemed like minutes, and then he put his arm around me and pulled me to him.

"Oh, Bobbi. I knew when I drove here that I was fooling myself. But I had to try. I just don't want to say good-bye. You. Me. Sam . . . The crazy dog," he added as Jules whimpered at the screen door.

We both laughed softly at the diversion of our canine friend looking so sorrowfully at the two of us. But though Jules's appearance gave us levity, it also added a poignancy to the moment.

"Bryce, you are going to be okay. I promise." I squeezed him gently.

Bryce looked out over my head to the expanse of Mulberry Street. "God, Bobbi, where do I go from here?"

I knew the answer, but I couldn't tell him.

Home, Bryce. You go home.

I knew the answer because I had made that journey.

· 56 ·

BRYCE SHOWERED AND PACKED the few things he had brought with him. He sat in the living room watching the early rounds of a PGA tournament while he waited for Travis to bring Sam home from the lake. I couldn't stay there with him, and I wasn't ready to face Travis, just yet. I changed into a pair of jean shorts with an embroidered shirt and started walking in a direction away from the lake. I wasn't conscious of a destination, just the need for air, but soon I was headed along Brubaker Road, a road on which I hardly ever walked. The sidewalks stopped after the first half mile, and I tramped the weedy edge, as the road curved back along the drying cornfields. The tall stalks obscured my view, so I was surprised when the road deposited me onto Vista Street. I had a choice of turning right, along which nested a small housing development, or turning left toward Blue Lake. I looked to the left and the location of Travis's boat. Though I couldn't see the lake itself, I could see the trees that surrounded it along with a portion of the parking lot. Upon further scrutiny, I could distinguish the peak of the bird sanctuary in the distance. Even though I felt the pull of the water and of Travis, I ultimately chose the path to the right. Only a smattering of houses, they looked like miniatures against the landscape. Even the churchyard of Lakeside Lutheran, which was vast in comparison to the crowded Cape Cods, seemed the stuff of O-gauge train scapes. My eyes followed the short midday line of the steeple's shadow.

All at once, I knew where I was headed; this had been my destination all along.

Stone masons were halfway finished with the renovation of a wall that surrounded the cemetery. They wouldn't complete the work today, being a weekend. The church parking lot was strangely empty for a Sunday. I noted the sign outside: CHURCH PICNIC, THIS SUNDAY AT 10 AM AT THE MEMORIAL PAVILION, BLUE LAKE. VISITORS WELCOME. I had the whole space to myself, and I felt oddly comforted by the fact that I wouldn't be bothered. I followed the familiar path, taken only a few months previously, to Nonna's grave, beside Charlie's. I had no trouble finding it. A tiny flag sat in a holder next to the caramel colored stone. As I knelt down, my notice tripped on the dark 2000, freshly chiseled into Nonna's side of the granite. It was the same stone she had chosen over fifty years earlier when Charlie had died. I thought about the corpse of a twenty-something soldier lying next to that of a lady octogenarian. Sharing a mere two years together, they hardly seemed compatible in death. But I supposed that was what made life interesting: you never know who will share your journey.

"Ah, Nonna," I said tracing the letters on her stone. I still found it hard to believe she was here, beneath the ground. Words. Stone. Grass. Earth. Wood. I tried to summon each layer of detachment from her now that I knew the truth, but, in reality, I only felt closer. Her love had been a choice, as was my love for her.

I wished I had brought some flowers from Lena's garden, but I hadn't realized I was on a pilgrimage to the family plots. I contented myself by clearing away the natural debris that accumulated around Nonna's and Charlie's graves. It was peaceful here, something I hadn't noticed during the burial. I could hear the sounds of children playing in the nearby neighborhood, but the sounds were joyful. As I worked pulling weeds, I thought back to how much had changed since last I stood here with Bryce by my side. Not the least of all the changes was that I had learned to trust myself. Whatever happened from here on out, I would be okay.

"See what you gave me?" I couldn't help but see the humor. Once again, I was doing the chore I hated the most, but doing it with a smile.

When I was satisfied with the state of the grave, I stood.

"Thank you, Nonna," I whispered, giving the stone a final touch.

Carrying the rubbish with me, I meandered across the cemetery to a trash can and then walked upward to Lena's grave on the hill. Lena's headstone, carved with delicate roses, was almost identical to my mother's grave marker in Virginia. I realized finally that it was not a coincidence. I dropped to my knees on the grass that was still morning damp. The sun had not penetrated the shade of the trees which bordered the cemetery. Sitting there, I shivered involuntarily.

"Grandma Lena," I said and sighed. The wind turned and a sailing leaf caught in my hair. I pulled it out and felt the trifling pull at my scalp, as if Grandma Lena's fingers were braiding my hair one last time. So I pulled at my breeze-tangled hair and coiled of few of my locks over and under, weaving and plaiting.

As I was braiding my hair, I heard footsteps on the path behind me and turned to see Travis standing there.

"You weren't at home, and you didn't come to the lake . . ."

He was alone.

"Is Sam with you?" I asked.

"I took him home to Bryce."

"Oh."

"Bryce's car was packed, and he told me you'd gone out for a walk. Actually, he was very civil. I am not sure I would have been if I were in his shoes. Anyway, he said he would stay with Sam and wait to leave until you returned. I told him I'd try to find you."

"What made you come here? I haven't been here all summer."

"Dumb luck, I guess. I saw you walking on the path as I drove by."

Shyness washed over me. *What should I say to him?* I started tidying, pulling on the long clumps of grass that were obscuring Lena's marker.

Travis squatted beside me and began to help, picking up the stones and twigs lying on the ground. He was so near to me that I could feel the cool of his body, still wet from the lake.

"Lena was my mother's mother," I blurted before I lost my nerve. "Those notebooks Nonna left me were to tell me that it was Lena all along."

Travis stopped what he was doing and looked at me. "What exactly are you trying to say, BJ?"

"I am trying to tell you that you really are my cousin, Travis. I am Lena's granddaughter."

Travis sucked in a breath, but remained silent.

I knew he was having a hard time making the connection, so I continued my explanation. "Back when your grandfather died, Nonna and Lena knew that you and I were developing feelings for one another. Rather than telling everyone the truth, they orchestrated a fight with your mom over your granddad's funeral. That fight was designed to keep us apart and keep our mothers from ever finding out the truth."

Travis sat down, his back to the stone. He set the pile of twigs and rocks beside him on the grass.

"But if that's the case, why would Anja write it all down in a letter to your mother?" Travis asked.

"My mom had cancer, and Nonna felt guilty, I guess, keeping everything from her. I think she somehow felt responsible for my mother's condition. Though I suppose it doesn't really matter. She never gave the letter to my mother."

"How long have you known about this?"

"I've known since the day Sam came back from Michigan."

Travis raised his eyebrows. "This has been quite a week for you, hasn't it?"

"You could say that." My heart was beating faster. I still couldn't ask Travis what I wanted to ask him.

"Who else knows about this?"

"Nobody."

Travis leaned on one arm and turned to face me.

"Nobody has to know, BJ. This doesn't change anything for me. Does it change anything for you?"

I almost laughed with relief. I was so afraid that Travis would never be able to overcome this knowledge that I never considered how I felt.

"No, Travis, I don't care. Anja's name is on my mother's birth certificate. Nobody would have to ever know, and it wouldn't keep us from ever—" I stopped suddenly.

"From ever what? Getting married? Is that what you were going to say?"

"I was going to say, 'continuing our relationship.'"

As soon as I said it, I saw Travis's look of rejection. I amended my own words. "I'm not saying that marriage isn't part of that continuation. If this thing with Lena doesn't bother you, then anything is possible."

"Lena brought us together," he said.

"And, if you remember correctly, she had a hand in keeping us apart."

"We're not apart now, are we?"

"No."

"Is it really over with you and Bryce?" This is the question he'd wanted to ask me all along.

"Yes," I said and saw Travis's relief, as it transformed his features. "I talked to him this morning. We are both moving on with our lives."

"And moving on . . . that is something we'll do together?"

"Yes, Travis."

"Good," he said.

I had hoped he would kiss me, but he didn't. Instead, Travis fumbled at his side. "We should mark this occasion. Hold out your hand."

Travis placed an object in my cupped hand, and I pulled it to me to discover a rock he had collected from Lena's grave. It was ordinary sandstone, a splinter of the kind of rock used to build the farmhouse. This particular stone was about the size of my palm, rough and tan—quite unremarkable. I laughed at Travis's gesture, but I understood. The piece of sandstone wasn't something I could wear like a diamond, but rather it was something tangible I could grip, to hold on to this place of endings and beginnings.

This is my inheritance.

"Do you like it?" Travis asked, smiling

"I'll keep it forever."

I shivered again, either from the cold or the anticipation, I didn't know.

"I think we're finished here," I said, rubbing my arms.

Travis stood and offered me his hands. I put the rock in the breast pocket of my shirt and grabbed Travis's wrists. As he pulled me up and into his embrace, I couldn't help thinking: if Nonna had written her letter in order to bring about a healing, she had, in that moment, realized her purpose.

BROCHURE